On The Way Home

We The People

A Novel

John C. Morgan

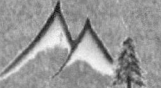

Selkirk Publishing LLC
Coeur d' Alene, Idaho

For my loving family,
Kim, Tim & Kyle
And to all Americans
May we always remember
Our Forefathers' Dreams
For America and family.

Chapter 1

MOUNT RUSHMORE
May 25ᵗʰ 2015, 8 p.m.

Former Congressman Harold Robertson had pushed himself beyond the point of exhaustion driving to Rapid City, South Dakota, to attend a special Naturalization ceremony at Mount Rushmore that evening. It was Memorial Day. The Department of Immigration and Naturalization in Chicago had sent out invitations to past and present members of the United States Congress, and all Illinois State Senators and Representatives, to attend this one of a kind ceremony for ninety-three immigrants, eleven of whom were Iraqis who had lost their families to Islamic State terrorists. It spoke worlds about the pain and suffering on their part and Harold knew firsthand what it was like. He'd lost his older brother Alex during the Tet Offensive of '68 in Vietnam, and it was something he'd never quite shaken off, always remaining in the back of his mind through the years.

It was a clear, cool spring evening when he pulled into the parking lot at Mount Rushmore at 8 p.m. He got the last handicap spot in front of the main building, something the war had afforded him. He still carried small pieces of a rocket's shrapnel in his lower back, a condition the surgeons usually took the wait and see attitude with, because they didn't want to do further harm. He'd been fortunate for more than thirty years, in that he wasn't crippled by their presence. The past decade had taken its toll though, leaving him dependent on a cane to steady himself on bad days, which were becoming more frequent.

He was late arriving and made his way down the steps on the right side of the outdoor amphitheater, leaning heavily on the railing after the fourteen-hour drive. The floodlights illuminated the stage filled with the soon-to-be American citizens. A speaker was talking about their journeys to America and the hardships and courage it took to leave everything behind. Harold was proud of these ninety-three people because they, and millions like them, are the people who built, fought for, and sustained America. Yes, he was proud of them, just as he was of his ancestors, who had fought in the Revolutionary War. He'd attended many of these ceremonies during his eight years as a member of the US House of Representatives, and no matter how many, it always brought a flood of emotion to his face. He was glad he'd come so far for the brief, yet life-changing ceremony.

As he made his way down the right aisle, a dark-haired man got up from his third-row seat and brushed past him, speaking in a hushed tone on his cell phone. His face was young and worried and he walked in a stiff manner like he had an injury. A black trench coat hung from his sharp, narrow shoulders. Harold stopped and turned, his gaze following the man up the stairs to the top of the amphitheater. Something about the man spoke of danger. He glanced back several more times, trying to rectify the uneasy feeling in the pit of his stomach, a feeling that Harold had not felt since the war.

He stopped at the second row where a partial aisle seat was vacant. Harold smiled at the father of a family of four, and they slid over a few inches to make a little extra room for him.

He surveyed the participants on stage and the news crew in the center aisle several rows back. A young man shouldered a large camera and a woman reporter was speaking, from what he guessed was a local news station. He got settled in his seat as best he could. His back hurt from the long drive and the hard bench didn't help it much. Just as he'd always done, he began to study each hopeful face on the stage, trying to imagine their story and what it meant to them to be here this night, a night unlike any other in their life. This evening they would join the American people in all of their diversity, each adding their special talents and humanity, and continuing the American culture of, "We the People."

His eye caught a young, beautiful woman in the front row, not more than twenty feet from him. She was dabbing a tear while she held the hand the man next to her, their eyes locking in a gaze, which spoke of an enduring love and hopeful future. Was it her brother? Or was this her husband? She wore a gold hijab and was clothed in a dark gown. The man wore a suit, like so many of the others on the stage. Perhaps they were two of the Iraqis who'd escaped from their war-torn country. There were more than twenty women wearing hijabs in the group and most were seated next to men of similar age.

The speaker concluded his remarks, and the official oath was being administered when it was interrupted by loud voices on the far left side of the amphitheater. A woman screamed as the first shots tore through the amphitheater, snapping Harold's head towards the sound he'd not heard in forty years. The savage roar of automatic rifle fire and screams of terror ground time to a standstill in him, ripping open old wounds amid all the sounds of death. His hands automatically gripped his M-16, even pulling up his arms into a firing position, but it was only a memory of a weapon. He was knocked out of his seat, slamming his head into the concrete steps, by the man fleeing with his family. His eyes never left the far side of the stage, where the gunman stood emptying his first thirty-round banana clip and fumbled to load another. While he did, a woman in a headscarf charged screaming: "Allahu Ackbar." She struck him as his weapon discharged, nearly cutting her in half as she crumpled on top of him, and they both fell to the concrete.

More gunfire erupted in front of him from a man dressed like the one who'd brushed past him. He fired into the fleeing people on stage, dropping them in droves, as they rushed towards the back of the stage, and the only cover there was. What Harold's eyes took in, his brain had no words for, nothing to compare it to, except his time in a war zone. It drove him to his feet and the six short steps to the madman in front of him. Harold launched himself at the gunman's shoulder, feeling the impact of their heads as they collided, knocking them both to the concrete. Everything he'd learned about hand-to-hand combat simply spilled out of him without a thought. He felt the man's neck snap in his vicious assault, a sickening, unmistakable sound.

Harold's heart pounded in his chest, filled with the rage, which had propelled him into action. His arms were still locked in a tight embrace of the man's head when he began to realize what he'd done. He'd never killed, never fired a shot in the war. And now, he lay beside the man whose neck he'd just snapped. More gunfire erupted, only this was different, mere pop, pop, pop coming from across the stage. He tried to push himself up to see, and that's when he knew he'd been hit. His left arm and shoulder buckled underneath him. All the screaming and gunfire ceased as suddenly as it had begun, replaced with cries of the wounded. He groaned rolling away from the man and stared up at the night sky. His ringing ears drowned out the cries of those on stage as his eyes blurred, and the steady throb in his shoulder carried him slowly into darkness. The last thought in his mind was of his wife, Ruth, and her death smothering him in pain.

Chapter 2

DAMAS, SYRIA

May 26ᵗʰ, 7 a.m.

Amul Al Atrash rose early and made tea. He was visiting his wife's family for the week. He needed some relief from keeping a low profile in his cramped Damascus apartment these past few months. He was alone in his war-ravaged country, having lost his parents and wife in a US air strike in Al Bab five months ago. Unspeakable violence and terror had visited him every night in his dreams, visions of warplanes roaring above and raining death on those below, in the relentless strife within his homeland. Some nights he lay awake till dawn, the hatred seething until he finally fell asleep from exhaustion, often sleeping through morning prayers, and deep into the afternoon hours. At least he had his wife's family to visit, although they blamed him for their daughter's death. The only reason their daughter was in Al Bab was to help her husband's parents in their day-to-day existence. Her death laid like a pall over them all, suffocating and heavy.

Al Atrash had forsaken his family name, an old and proud Syrian family, to pursue a life of violence against his enemy, the people of the Western world. He'd devoted the past sixteen years to amassing a large network of cells and contacts in the world, which he used to terrorize those who lived in opposition to his faith. And yet now, he was all-the-more driven by the same proud heritage, the death of his parents, and his wife's death, to strike back in vengeance. He'd trained his son Amir from a young age and was now using him as an extension of his own hatred. Eighteen-year-old Amir Al Atrash was somewhere in America making connections with a sleeper-cell in Houston, Texas. His son was on an important mission in America, which made him immensely proud.

He turned on the TV to the wwiTV – RTV News and closed his eyes to listen to what was happening in the world. He dozed on and off to the soft drone of the newscaster's voice. The household wouldn't be awake for a while; Sayid and Lina Badri liked to sleep in when they could.

In the far distance of his half-awake state, he heard a familiar sound. The sounds of an automatic assault rifle jolted him awake. His heart raced and his eyes searched the scene playing out on the flat screen. He had no idea where this was taking place until the newscaster said it was Mt. Rushmore, an important National Park to Americans. The station played the scene over three times, each time filling in the details as reported on American TV. The third time it played, he moved in close to see who the shooters were, and that was when he realized that one of them might be his son, Amir. The newscasters paused the recording three times: first for the Iraqi woman charging the gunman, then for the man who flung his body at the other gunman and broke his neck, and the final scene of a man shooting the other gunman with his semiautomatic handgun as he fell to the concrete.

Al Atrash stood rigid in front of the TV, too stunned to breathe or blink. There on the screen was his son's face buried in the American's arms, both their faces appearing clearly, one lifeless, the other contorted in rage, both captured in the still-shot that would forever be burned into his heart and mind. His son was dead.

Chapter 3

RAPID CITY HOSPITAL

9 p.m.

Harold had woken in the ambulance seated next to one of two male paramedics who were monitoring an Asian man on the gurney. He was strapped into a seat beside the gurney and wore a neck brace. He was facing an unconscious man covered in blood. Harold's left arm was in a sling and bound to his chest with a strap, and ached more than before. The brown-eyed youthful paramedic had patted him on the knee and told him he'd be fine. The siren screamed in his head all the way to the hospital.

Now, he was lying on a bed encircled by a curtain and began to realize what had happened. Images from Vietnam flashed across his mind along with the woman lunging at the gunman, all playing to the muted sounds of war forever locked inside his head. The scarfed woman repeatedly came into view, just as clearly as if it were happening all over again, only this time in the well-lit room of an ER, miles away from the amphitheater. Her face in all of its pain and anguish, with the full knowledge of what she was doing, brought him a degree of comfort. She was a warrior, giving her life to save those around her, on this her first day as an American citizen. He began to weep for her bravery, her utter abandonment to quelling this strife and silencing the maniac in front of her. Never had he witnessed such devotion, ever. He wept silently for her and for his brother, but most of all for the loss of his Ruth. The pain spilled out from deep within him and carried him to a place of fear, fear for his sanity.

He'd killed a man with his bare hands and not even thought twice about it. Harold Robertson reeked of death, and it frightened him more than death itself.

"Sir. Mr. Robertson. Can you hear me?"

Someone was calling from afar. His name sounded hollow and empty inside his mind. The voice ruptured the silence again, only this time it gained a foothold in his mind, and pried his eyes open to the bright lights in the ER.

"There you are. Do you know where you are?"

He coughed and cleared his throat. "I think so. I'm in a hospital in Rapid City?"

"Yes. Very good. And do you remember what happened?"

"I was shot, I think." His mind was clearing now. He wasn't sure if that was a good thing, with gunshots and muzzle flashes from the attack invading his waking mind in the background.

"You're safe now. The doctor sewed you up about an hour ago. We've been pretty busy here with six of the wounded. The others are at hospitals across the region. You're one of the lucky ones. You only had a broken clavicle and flesh wounds. We'll get you into a room for the night shortly. Do you think you could drink some water?"

He nodded. She raised his head using the controls for the bed. The ice water felt good in his dry mouth. "How many?" His voice cracked with emotion.

"I don't know. Sorry. I've been too busy," she frowned.

Her sad brown eyes carried him right back into the middle of the horror and everything he'd not felt while it all was happening. She wiped a tear with her sleeve. "I'm sorry. . . "

He couldn't stop himself from falling back into the pit of terror, with all its sounds of death, the loud reports of automatic fire, the horrific rage on the young woman's face as she attacked the gunman, the awful cracking sounds from a neck being broken, all more real to him now than at the amphitheater. When would it end? Her hand was covering her mouth and hiding a face contorted in pain from all the horror she'd seen. He raised his free hand with the IV tube and found hers, pulling gently, needing to be close to someone. She caressed his face with her hand.

"You don't remember, do you? You don't know what you did. Your surgeon told me he saw it on a live-feed from the amphitheater. Oh God, I watched too."

Her breast was heaving in short, halting spasms. He stroked her hand feeling sorry for one so young and innocent having to witness such an atrocity.

"I remember," he whispered. "I remember everything." She pulled away, wiping her face and smearing her eye makeup. She looked beautiful to him, puffy eyes, and all. "Thank you for caring for me," he looked at her nametag, "Thank you, Suzie, I won't forget you." She left without another word, having to attend to other more needy patients.

He thought of Ruth lying in a hospital bed ten months ago, already brain dead from an aneurysm the day before. They had taken her off life support and she'd died in his arms, her warm, fragile body finally succumbing to what was inevitable. "I'll never forget you, Ruth," he murmured and fell asleep.

The clock on the wall said it was after three o'clock in the morning. It had been six hours since the incident and he'd survived. He dozed on and off until the vampire squad arrived an hour later to draw blood, but he was only half-conscious of anyone in the room. His surgeon woke him at six o'clock on his way home after a harrowing shift of twelve hours and three surgeries, two of which ended badly. Dr. Bennett patted him on the knee, just like the paramedic, saying what a lucky guy he was, and thanked him for his heroism. Harold listened, but it all sounded so surreal as if he wasn't really there at all. He fell asleep right after the conversation and didn't wake until breakfast arrived at eight o'clock. There were several notes on the tray, along with a bowl of thick oatmeal and wheat toast, all of which he ate greedily.

He opened the first note halfway through his cup of coffee. His eyes roamed to the bottom of the plain, white copy paper. It was from Suzie Walker, his nurse in the ER.

"Mr. Harold Robertson,
I am sorry I forgot to thank you last night.
I guess I was caught up in the frantic pace of
having to deal with so many at once. Please
forgive my behavior. I need to thank you.
You touched my heart in a way no one else
ever has. You helped me to see how
very fragile and precious life really is. Thank you.
I'll never forget you."
Suzie

He folded the note and tucked it into the sling, which held his arm immobile. He dried his eyes with the sheet and opened the other piece of paper.

"To one so brave, who saved countless others.
The ER staff. THANK YOU."

The sheet contained personal signatures, little hearts drawn here and there, and other gestures of appreciation. He tucked it away with Suzie's note. These two pieces of paper were more meaningful to him than all the legislation which had passed through his hands during his eight years in office. They were real words. Words from the heart. He'd barely removed his hand from under the covers when there was a knock on his door. As it swung open, it revealed a familiar face.

"Congressman Robertson, I'm Abbey Nelson, with the local news station, KIRK. May I come in?"

Harold stiffened, recognizing the woman from the amphitheater – the reporter with the microphone. He grimaced in pain, his body rigid, every muscle taut and ready for flight. He nodded for her to enter against his better judgment. She was a reporter looking for a story. She said something to her cameraman, who was partly visible in the doorway. She walked to the foot of his bed and stood a little slumped over, her face and eyes reflecting the horror she'd seen. Yes, she'd been there. One of the lucky ones who got to walk away. He frowned at her, not wanting to answer any questions. "Can't this wait? I don't think I can right now." He shifted his position trying to get comfortable, willing himself to relax. His taut muscles pulled on his injuries and caused him more pain.

"Of course," Abbey spoke in a hushed tone. "I understand. I just wanted to thank you for your bravery. You probably saved my life and I wanted to tell you in person before the whole country descends on this small town. You and the Iraqi woman saved us from certain death. Thank you. We can't thank her because she didn't survive."

"I know. I watched it all happen." Harold fought back the images. He didn't want to talk any more. He wanted to rest in the oblivion of a mindless sleep and she was interfering, but there was something about her which seemed familiar like they'd met. "Do I know you?"

"Yes, we've met a number of times in Illinois and DC. I covered you during your years in Congress, and your campaign for governor, always at a distance though. I spoke with your wife on one occasion. I'm so sorry for your loss. Well, I should let you rest, but I would like to interview you today before the national reporters arrive. If you don't mind."

Abbey was fidgeting with clipboards on the end of the bed. She was nervous and probably still in a bit of shock from the night before. "Come back in an hour, but bring everything you know about those two maniacs and the woman who charged one of them. Also, you'll have to tell me what you and Ruth talked about."

He stared blankly at her, wondering why she seemed at ease and tried to remember having met her like she'd described. And then he actually smiled at her, which he thought strange. She was pretty, a black-haired gal like his Ruth, except Abbey had brown eyes, and Ruth's were green. She marched off with a smile on her face like she had some secret she wasn't telling.

Chapter 4

THE INTERVIEW
May 26th, 9:45 a.m.

Harold tried to fall asleep, but couldn't stop thinking about how he knew this woman; that and her face kept popping up. Abbey Nelson was just one of the many reporters who covered national politics. And then he remembered that she often asked the hardest questions, ones which usually had no simple answer. She behaved like a hometown girl in her early approach to reporting: always friendly, helpful, and the least likely to trip-up a Representative. But that's not how she acted during his run for governor. He remembered her having graduated into the ranks of veteran TV reporters: persistent, direct to a fault, and one who could easily lead her prey down a slippery slope, and into saying things they hadn't intended. In other words, she dug for and generally found the facts and sometimes the truth in her interviews, effortlessly extracting the needed items, and then casually thanking the befuddled politician. That's what he remembered about her. And now, he was about to submit himself for a full-on interview, which would change both him and the nation: Terrorist attack at our national treasure – Mount Rushmore – at a Special Naturalization Ceremony.

Twenty minutes before the interview, he pushed the call button for a nurse to help him get dressed in his clothes from yesterday, clothes which had dried blood, bullet holes, and the stench of death about them. Nurse Nancy refused and called Trevor, a nurse's aide. Harold and Trevor got along just fine, chitchatting mostly about all the girls Trevor had dated in the program at Black-Hills State University. It helped to put Harold at ease, hearing about the normal exploits of a young man attending college. But on the way out, Trevor had asked him if he was scared at any time during the attack. He'd smiled and nodded. "You bet."

Abbey knocked and entered a few minutes early with her cameraman in tow, giving Harold a disapproving look when she saw him dressed in the bloody, torn clothes.

"It's all I have Abbey," he shrugged his shoulders, forgetting how much it would hurt, and then laughed at his mistake, making it hurt all the more. Her eyes darted away like she didn't want to see any more pain.

"Where would you be comfortable for ten minutes? Bed? Chair?" She asked.

"I will stand for part of it, at least until I have to sit down?" Harold surely wasn't going to have anything to do with the bed. He'd rather stand in pain than lay in bed for the interview, especially since he'd dressed in yesterday's clothes. Abbey nodded to the cameraman to move the chair wherever he thought the light from the window would best enhance the picture. The sun was bright coming through the east facing window and filled the room with a warm glow. Harold sat on the edge of the bed while they prepared the room.

"I don't know your name," he said to the cameraman. The man didn't appear to be any worse for wear with the goings-on yesterday, but looks could be deceiving.

"Chet Givens," he replied. "I'm very pleased you're alright Mr. Robertson."

"Me too," he smiled weakly. When they shook hands,

Harold knew how Chet really felt. His hand trembled. Chet moved the chair into the sunlight, drawing the drapes partially closed to mute the brightness. He removed a cable from the wall-mounted TV and plugged it into his camera, motioning to Abbey that he was ready.

"Mr. Robertson," Abbey said. "I need to inform you of two national news crews outside, waiting to gain access to a conference room for an interview with any willing survivors. The hospital administrator is currently dealing with their pushy attitude and said you don't have to talk to them if you don't feel up to it. Douglas Morton is a friend of mine and is very good at handling people, so you needn't worry."

"I appreciate both of your concerns, but dodging a bullet is easier than keeping the press at bay. I'll be fine. But you will be the one who calls the shots with them." He knew how important the interview could be for her, having captured a savage terrorist attack on video. "You two were there after all. You deserve an interview on national news as much as I do."

The interview began like any of the other countless ones he'd done over the past eight years while in office. He stood opposite Abbey next to the chair, her hand casually extending the mic towards him. She asked him how he happened to attend yesterday and why he'd sat in that particular place in the amphitheater. Then she asked him what he thought was happening when he heard the first shot. He willed himself to keep his face relaxed, blinking back the pain his tight muscles were causing in his shoulder and lower back and answered with a quiet voice.

"I got an invitation to attend the ceremony at Mount Rushmore and decided to come. I've always enjoyed these special moments, which our new citizens have longed for, with some having suffered greatly to get to this point in their lives. It represents what America is all about; the freedom to live a life of their own choosing, and the ability to worship in their own way without persecution. Eleven of these new citizens had lost most of their family to terrorists with extremist religious views. Yesterday I watched as one woman brought the fight to American soil for her right live free. She is a true American hero. I will always see her face when I think about what it means to live free in America." He took a deep breath, fighting to keep control, and rubbed his eyes. "She gave her life on her first day as an American. I will always remember her bravery in the face of certain death." He wiped his eyes with his bloody sleeve and chuckled. "Old habit I guess."

"If you don't mind Mr. Robertson, I would like to show the footage Chet got at the ceremony, at considerable risk to his life. I must warn the viewing public, the images could be deeply disturbing, as they are the untouched footage of the attack."

Harold stared at the TV monitor horrified by what he saw: the muzzle flashes bright and hypnotic, the deafening reports of automatic weapons fire, the screams of people running for their lives, and the deafening silence of those cut down in the mayhem; the woman's cry of, "God is Greater," and then the gunman right in front of him emptying his thirty-round clip into the fleeing crowd, and this older man who he barely recognized as himself, tackling the gunman and wrenching his neck in one fluid motion. What Harold saw on the screen was something he'd not been able to at the amphitheater; the other gunman across the way firing at him on full automatic. How he hadn't been killed was beyond his comprehension. At least fifteen shots were fired at him, with some ricocheting off the concrete in a trail of sparks. It was at this very moment he remembered the "CRACK" of a supersonic bullet passing by his head. He leaned heavily on the chair back, his face locked in a blank stare. Abbey helped him to sit down.

"Should I call the nurse, Mr. Robertson?"

He gazed up at her dazed and momentarily forgetting he was in a hospital room. "I should be dead," he said after a long pause. "He shot right at me and only grazed my side and nicked my shoulder." He stared blankly at the mic in front of him and the camera lens to one side of Abbey's face. He was confused by the images in his head and the ones on the TV. How could he have escaped with so little injury?

"Ah, I remember the sound. A bullet passed by my head. It was very loud." He blinked in disbelief, not knowing how someone less than twenty-five feet away could have missed his target. His eyes fell on Abbey's gaze, her face showing genuine concern for the man she was interviewing.

"Do you remember now since you've seen it from a different vantage point?"

"Yes," he mumbled, shaking his head in disbelief. "How long was the video? It seemed forever as it was happening."

"Nineteen seconds," Chet answered.

"And how many died?" his sullen voice asked.

"Fourteen dead, twenty-seven injured," Chet said.

Harold hoisted himself out of the chair. "I'm done," he mumbled. "I need to rest after seeing that." He staggered past Abbey and Chet, and stumbled onto his bed, looking down at his blood-stained shirt. Why had he worn this for the interview? He felt ashamed of himself for doing such a stupid thing. He swung his legs up and pulled the blanket over himself, shivering in the coolness of his sweat-soaked shirt. He closed his eyes and willed the intruders to leave, falling into a kind of stupor, and then moments later, sleep.

Chapter 5

EXPOSURE

1:15 p.m.

Harold woke two hours later to the humming of a nurse, who checked his IV drip, took his vital signs, and refilled his water pitcher. Margaret Whitcomb was indeed a happy person by all appearances. She never stopped her whisper of a tune, tagging the first four measures of six songs he recognized, and several more he didn't know. It was so very soft and pleasant to the ear, he doubted if anyone had ever asked her to stop.

"Mr. Robertson, you're looking very well. How do you feel?"

He started to speak, but all that came out was a gravely, croaking sound. "Sorry," he said after clearing his throat several times. She handed him a water mug and raised his head. He sucked too hard on the large straw and choked, dribbling water onto the blood-stained shirt he'd forgotten he had on. Her humming never skipped a beat as she wiped his flushed face.

"Happens all the time. Nothing to worry about. We might want to do something about the shirt though. A friend of yours dropped off a clean one. If you want, I'll help you with it."

"Okay." He guessed it was Abbey who'd brought it for him, seeing as how she'd frowned at him for wearing the blood-stained one for the interview. Margaret very carefully slipped his sling off and threaded his arm into the sleeve. He felt much better once she got him dressed in the extra-large, blue dress shirt.

"I want to thank you for your bravery before my shift ends," Margaret said when she'd finished. "Forgive me, but I have to say this. Everyone I've talked to wants to thank you for your courage. Our little news station has had nonstop coverage and a lot of history about your years as a US Congressman, your run for governor, and the death of your wife. I'm so sorry for your loss. Anyway, I want you to know how much you are loved and how highly we all think of you. I'm quite sure there are plenty more people across the nation who feel the same way."

"Ah," he cleared his throat again. "Thank you." Harold wasn't prepared for what he knew was coming. It was inevitable. A landslide of media coverage would begin soon. He smiled at Margaret, who wasn't humming at the moment. Her keen eye was surveying him inside out, probably as to his mental and physical well-being.

"I'm going to bring you a couple of cold packs for your lower back and a hot pack to alternate with the cold ones. You've been nothing but uncomfortable since you arrived. I assume it's been like this for some time."

"Now and then," he said. He thanked Margaret as she walked out, leaving him to wonder if his war wounds were really that obvious to someone who didn't even know his medical history from forty years ago. The doctors in Vietnam had made the right call not to risk paralyzing him for life for such small pieces of shrapnel. They'd said it was better to live with a little pain than to risk losing the use of his legs for life. There was a quiet knock on his door, which abruptly swung open, revealing an older man leaning on a walker. "Don't mean to interrupt or anything. Wanted to meet the man who kicked the butts of those sorry-assed terrorists. Bob Clark here."

The grizzled face with two day's growth was attached to a short, narrow-shouldered body, and was halfway into the room when Margaret came back. She didn't seem at all surprised to see Bob Clark in Harold's room.

"Now Mr. Clark, you've come a long way down the hall from your room, so I won't tell you that you have to leave just yet. So speak your peace and then I'll have an aid walk you back."

"Hell, woman. I don't need no a-sis-tance," he said with a Texas draw and then set his eyes back on Harold. "Hell son, you're all over the news, and they're calling you a hero. And they're damn-well right."

Bob Clark stopped three feet from the bed and snapped his hand up in a crisp military salute while gripping his walker with his other hand to keep from tipping over. Harold returned the salute with his left hand, minus the snappiness.

"Thank you, Bob. I do appreciate you coming all this way to say that to me." Harold grinned at the man, knowing he'd been in Vietnam by the looks of him and his words of thanks. But he didn't want to engage any further, so he turned on his side so that Margaret could place the cold packs where they were most needed.

"I best be goin' before that a-sis-tance arrives." Bob winked at him. "Come on, Margaret, help me to the door."

Bob turned his head halfway around and grinned at Harold. He was clearly enjoying his time in the hospital with all the attention he was getting, probably way more than usual. Bob was no sooner out the door than there was another knock, and a tall man dressed in a dark brown business suit entered.

"Mr. Robertson, I am Douglas Morton, the hospital administrator. May I have a moment of your time?"

"Okay," Harold pricked up his ears. "What brings you to

my room?" Harold shifted the cold packs a little and grabbed the hot pack, twisting it to activate, and put it on the back of his neck, where the muscles were radiating pain up from his lower back. Margaret had read him like a book.

"Are you comfortable, Mr. Robertson?"

He nodded and managed a weak smile. He knew what was coming – the Media.

"I'm guessing you know why I'm here, so I'll get right to the point. All the major national networks have their mobile teams assembled downstairs, along with a host of cable, and newspaper reporters. They are pressing me to arrange a press conference. They know that Abbey Nelson has already interviewed you because it was carried nationwide this morning. They want more, Mr. Robertson, which I'm quite sure you already know."

He nodded again. Douglas was soft spoken and had a reassuring voice. Harold liked the man. He could be a powerful asset when it came time for the press conference, giving him an option to end it all abruptly if needed. "Yes, I was expecting this. I trust you'll be there?"

"And your surgeon, Dr. Bennett. We'll put a halt to it if we think it's getting out of hand. So, you needn't worry. I told them that it wouldn't happen until three o'clock this afternoon. Does that sound alright to you?"

Harold's reluctance was acknowledged by the man's thoughtful gaze, but they both knew it had to be. At least he had a couple of hours to get used to the idea and prep himself. "Thank you, Douglas. I'm sure it will be fine. Will Abbey Nelson be there?"

"I don't know. She went home a while ago. The hospital's resident Social Worker, Dr. Walton, spoke with her and her cameraman before they left, wanting to be sure they had someone to help process the events of yesterday. You all acted with such courage. I'd like to have him visit you and help you deal with the stress."

"Not yet. Tomorrow if you don't mind." Harold's jaw set, hardening his face. He'd dealt with a similar situation after his brother's death in Vietnam. He absolutely hated talking to a 'shrink' as he called them, but the family doctor had insisted since his brother's death was so violent. The Army had shipped back a coffin filled with body parts, at least the ones they could find after the Tet Offensive of '68'.

The death of Alex had ripped apart his mother's heart, leaving her barely able to function. Later that year, she had to be admitted to a mental institution to be cared for, since the family could not care for her. Harold was a sophomore in high school, and like his mother, was left feeling empty, only he'd managed to bury his grief and continue with his everyday life, unlike his mother. After the funeral, his father, Ben, had never spoken of Alex again, leaving Harold to fend for himself. It was a dark time, one he rarely thought about.

It left him with a lingering anger towards his father, for not being able to help his family cope with the loss. Harold was quite literally left on his own and was deeply troubled the rest of that year, all of which he held in, never letting anyone see his pain. His father died at fifty-nine of a broken heart. He'd never recovered from the loss of his wife and son.

So, no, he wouldn't be talking to a shrink, not today or tomorrow, not ever. His eyes darted from the floor to Douglas and back again. He was being observed by the trained eye of a professional, who knew when someone was hiding their pain just beneath the surface. He cleared his throat and locked eyes with him. "I'll be okay. Been here before." Douglas nodded and left him alone with his demons.

Harold woke an hour later to Margaret's humming of the Battle Hymn of the Republic. She was hovering above him with a smile on her face. He blinked several times, thinking that he was dreaming. "You," he finally said.

"Yes," she said interrupting her humming. "Your lunch has been sitting here for over an hour. Shall I sit you up?"

Margaret pressed the bed control and raised him into a sitting position. She swung the bedside tray table with his lunch and water mug in front of him and unwrapped his ham and cheese sandwich, all with a smile.

"You'll need the energy to face the multitudes downstairs, but I'm sure you know that."

"Okay," his soft, submissive voice made Margaret laugh. He bit into the dry sandwich, stuffing his face with half of it. "Mm," he nodded his approval. Margaret laughed and shook her head. She opened the mayo packet and squeezed its contents onto his plate for him to dip the sandwich into.

"There's someone here to see you."

Margaret moved out of his line of sight to the doorway, where Abbey was leaning against the frame. She said something to Margaret on her way out, and then came in and sat in the chair at the foot of the bed.

"How long were you standing in the doorway?" Harold asked.

"Long enough to watch Margaret in action. She's good with you."

"She does have a knack for reading my health issues. I thought you went home."

"Bad dreams woke me after an hour. So, I came back to see you, and . . ." She hesitated.

Harold had seen a lot of things in his life, but he'd never once seen a look like there was on Abbey's face. In one fleeting moment, he was drawn in by this woman's eyes that were suffering in silence. Her arms, now tightly folded across her chest, were squeezing the breath from her.

"Are you all right?" he asked in an urgent voice. His eyes glanced at the man in the doorway, with camera in hand. He didn't flinch, staring straight at her.

"Maybe you should sit down," he said swinging his legs off the bed. She retreated a step, her eyes now flitting from floor to him, to bed, and back to him. A pained frown took hold of her face, revealing the stress she carried with her from the night before. Abbey might as well have been shot because she sure looked like she had.

"You don't remember do you?" she said, the words barely making it past her tightly folded arms.

"How could I forget?" he said a bit confused. What did she mean? She closed her eyes and began to cry softly. He stood and pushed the tray table out of the way, and reached his hand out to her. She had no way to deal with what she'd seen at the amphitheater.

"Would you hold me?" she said softly, wiping her eyes.

He touched her folded arms gently and they slowly began to release their knot. Their hands found each other's and locked tightly. Her eyes rose up to his. He gently pulled her forward into his arms.

"I'm so sorry you had to see . . ." He couldn't find the right words. She'd seen death in all of its rage and ugliness last night, and it was all coming to bear on her emotionally. Their embrace made him uncomfortable after a moment. He was comforting her, but she was stirring up feelings in him, he'd locked away after his wife had died. He didn't know what to do. He was confused by his feelings.

"Douglas came to see me," he said finally, trying to break free of his confusion. "We both agreed I have to meet with the media this afternoon at three o'clock." She released him and stepped back.

"I know," she said.

Her soft brown eyes met his, sending a shiver through him. "What did you mean, 'I don't remember?'" he said, his eyes searching for answers

"Maybe later, we'll talk. I'll go with you to the news conference. If that's okay with you?"

He was relieved and confused at the same time. He didn't understand what she meant but was glad she would be there with him to face the media.

"Thank you. It makes me feel better that the three of us who were there . . . will face the media together." He glanced to the side at Chet Givens, who looked exhausted and ready to collapse.

The three of them were like deer caught in bright headlights at night, standing stock-still and frozen in time.

"I have some things I need to do before the interview. I won't be long," Abbey said, moving away towards the doorway.

He sat down on the bed, a bit dazed, and very confused about the feelings roaming around in places which hadn't stirred to life in some time.

"I'll be here," he said patting the bed. She paused in the doorway and turned to face him.

"I didn't mean to confuse you. I'm glad we . . ." she hesitated. "I'll see you at three o'clock."

She left, leaving him to wonder what she'd meant to say. He didn't really know Abbey very well at all, other than she was a courageous woman, who'd stood her ground yesterday. That was all he needed at the moment. A friend of like-mind and determination.

He lay back on the bed and slid his legs under the covers, closing his eyes to try and get a handle on his feelings. Abbey had stirred something up inside of him. He fell asleep wondering what she'd left unsaid.

A voice dragged him from a dream about Ruth and their young daughter Gracie.

"Harold, it's time to get ready," Abbey said.

He was slow to wake from the memory of a summer trip to a Wisconsin dairy farm, which boarded vacationers, giving them the chance to learn the art of cheese making. He woke up thinking it was time to milk the cows at four o'clock in the morning.

"I'm awake," he mumbled rolling over and pulling the covers up around his shoulders. It was the pain which actually woke him up. The intense, immediate pain in his bandaged shoulder.

"Ruth?" he murmured and moved his arm to relieve some of the pain. He blinked disconcertingly at this woman standing over him, who didn't belong in the dream.

"You need to get ready and be downstairs in ten minutes." Abbey jostled his good shoulder.

"Okay," he said, his mind slowly registering who Abbey was. He planted his feet on the floor and rubbed his face, yawning. Where was he? The thought went round and round.

"The Nation is waiting, Harold. Are you there?"

"Oh, yeah, getting there." He rubbed the sleep from his eyes, remembering where he was, and what had happened to him. "I'll be a minute," he held his hand up. He hadn't been so deep into a dream since he was in high school and sometimes woke up to a body half paralyzed.

"Did you want to change back into the bloody shirt for this interview?"

Abbey's sarcasm finished the job of waking him up, bringing him all the way back from Wisconsin, and back into the Rapid City hospital.

"No thanks. Are you always this . . ." he couldn't think of the word he wanted to say. "Argh," he growled.

"Getting my game-face on," she laughed.

He got up to splash some water on his face. He ran his fingers through his thinning, shortcut gray-brown hair, and was ready. He started towards the door, but stopped, looking at his bare feet. He turned around to see Abbey dangling his shoes from her fingers with a smile plastered on her face.

"Shirt and shoes required," she said.

About the time the elevator doors closed to take them to the ground floor, he started to laugh at his antics in the room, and Abbey's smart remarks. "You really are in good form, aren't you?"

"Years of on the job training. Pays off every time." She patted his shoulder.

"Thanks for coming with me. I'm quite sure it's going to cost me." He raised an eyebrow. He was beginning to feel like he was ready for the blitz of questions which awaited him. Abbey led him to the open doors of a large conference room. Inside was the window to the world. Everything said, every gesture, and every unanswered question was important in delivering a message. They paused in the doorway for one last check-in with each other. He was basically a mess, appearance-wise: unshaven, slightly disheveled hair, arm in a sling, pants with scuffed knees, and a broken tooth, which he'd just discovered with his tongue in the elevator– chipped really – but right up front.

"How do I look?"

"Ready," Abbey replied. "You look ready. Now, go get 'em," Mr. Robertson.

From the moment he stepped through the doorway, there were cameras and lights in his face, and above the din, there was the voice of Douglas Morton calling for an orderly interview. Harold smiled of all things, feeling right at home with the throngs of reporters, and from the look on Abbey's face so was she. They walked the thirty feet or so to the front of the room. All of his pain fell away in those thirty feet, and his head had cleared, knowing full well the implications of what had happened at Mount Rushmore.

He stepped up onto the raised podium with Abbey and

took his place beside the hospital administrator and Dr. Bennett, his surgeon. The room quieted and Douglas introduced Dr. Bennett, and explained the ground rules for the interview, making sure everyone understood that he or Dr. Bennett could end the news conference if they thought it necessary for their patient.

Harold stepped to the lectern and adjusted the mic, nodding he was ready. Several familiar voices sounded at once and he pointed towards a well-known TV newscaster. "Go ahead Bob, you get the first question."

"I know I speak for everyone here in saying we are glad you are alright. Can you tell us what went through your mind when you attacked the gunman?"

"Instinct, I guess. When I watched the woman charge the other gunman across the stage, that act of courage on her part put me in a fight mode, instead of flight. I reacted the way I was trained when I was in the Air Force at Da Nang, Vietnam. Actually, the Air Force didn't train me, an Army friend of mine did . . ." he fumbled trying to remember the man's name when his face appeared. "Garrett Yost, an Army Ranger, trained me in hand-to-hand combat. I reacted to a threat just like he'd taught me to when I didn't have a weapon. I didn't really think about it at all. I did forget part of my training though, the part to know when to duck." Harold watched as everyone in the room laughed at his allusion to what a US President had said when he was shot.

"Next question." He pointed at another national TV newscaster, Jodi Wright.

"Mr. Robertson, we know that fourteen were killed and twenty-seven wounded. Do you know if this was an act of terror planned by ISIS? And if so, was it carried out by a home-grown cell?"

"You tell me. I've been busy sleeping in my hospital bed and trying to dodge the vampire squad at four o'clock in the morning." Again, there was laughter. "Seriously though, I've not had the chance to talk to anyone about it. The question is better suited for the White House. Have they said anything yet?" He'd asked the question, knowing they'd have a response for him.

"There's a press conference scheduled as we speak," Jodi responded. "We're monitoring it in the back of the room."

"Thank you, Jodi. In all seriousness, one of America's basic values was attacked, the right of a citizen to live free. For those on the stage, their journey to become an American citizen was met with an act of terror, and for some of them, it was the reason they'd fled their homelands. Make no mistake about the real American hero. The Iraqi woman displayed more courage than I've ever seen, and she was just sworn in as an American citizen. In the first minute of her citizenship, she fought for her freedom and died right before our eyes, all captured on video thanks to two brave souls, Abbey Nelson of KIRK, and her cameraman, Chet Givens. They stood strong so all could see firsthand what went down. They are heroes as well. They showed the world what happened yesterday and they gave us the key as to how to respond as Americans. Can you tell me what that is?" He winced inside, having asked them to answer a question like he would have in his high school history classes. There was a deafening silence in the room as he stood his ground and waited for an answer. There was a little commotion in the rear of the room as a loud voice rang out.

"Cause Freedom ain't Free. Ya gotta fight for it."

Harold knew who that voice belonged to; it was Bob Clark from down the hall. Bob's head popped up momentarily. "Thank you, Bob Clark," he yelled. "Members of the press, meet Bob Clark from down the hall. Bob, you a Vet?"

"You bet. Army, 1st Cavalry Division at LZ Betty, Vietnam 1968. And I knew your brother, Alex Robertson, God rest his soul."

Harold felt his legs give out at the mention of his brother. Abbey caught him by his injured arm, sending a wave of pain through his shoulders, neck, and back. The pain made him dizzy and blackened the room as he pulled the lectern over trying to remain upright. Another hand caught him from the other side and steadied him. After a moment, the dizziness left him and he got himself straightened up.

"Thank you, Douglas. I'm okay. I want to continue." He took a deep breath. "I'm good." He turned back around as Douglas picked up the lectern and straightened the mic.

"Sorry about that. Old war wounds flare-up from time to time." He took another deep breath, burying the image of his brother. "Now, where were we? Bob, we'll talk later. Next question." He leaned on the lectern with his free hand. He motioned to a Washington DC newspaper reporter, who was as old as he was.

"Jake Normans, Washington Free Press. "Your brother was killed in Vietnam in '68'?"

Harold nodded. "Yes. Could we keep the questions focused on the incident at hand?"

"Of course," Jake said. "You've seen the video I take it; and the Park Ranger who died taking out the other shooter? Can you tell us your thoughts when you viewed it?"

Harold stared blankly at the man. He had no idea that a Park Ranger had died. "What was his name?" he stammered.

"John McFadden," Jake said.

Harold's silence caused a stirring among the members of the media. *Why had he forgotten those few seconds of the video?* His mind raced through all the images of that night. "I'm sorry," he cleared his throat and continued.

"Like I said earlier, the courage that woman displayed moved me deeply. I reacted and I killed a man, just like John Mc Fad. . ." He covered his mouth and fought to control his emotions. Abbey hooked arms with him, squeezing his hand.

He looked down into her strong brown eyes, then up at Jake Normans and the room full of cameras and reporters, taking a long deep breath. "In those nineteen seconds of chaos and courage, I think you will find all the answers as to what it means to be an American. Those ninety-three people seeking citizenship were attacked for their courage to start their lives over in a new country. They are no different than our ancestors who fought, shed their blood, and built this country into what it is today. They are free-thinking humans. They are a part of this great experiment called America, "We the People," as written in our Constitution. There is no America without her people; you and me and those ninety-three new Americans, some of whom gave their lives in their first moments as Americans. Those people, who lost their lives yesterday, did so giving something to all of us. Our freedom. Those nineteen seconds speak worlds to our precious freedom, which we all take for granted every day. That's what I feel about those nineteen seconds. Thank you all for coming. If I ever get out this place," he looked at Douglas and smiled, "then, I'd be honored to meet with all of you out at Mount Rushmore, and go over my point of view. I'll only do this once though . . ." his voice trailed off . . ."

Abbey caught him by the arm as he tripped backing away from the lectern. "What say you and I get some dinner, my place, or yours?" He chuckled. Abbey laughed at him, nodding and steadying him by his hand. He stood motionless and stared at her for a long time, searching, trying to understand what was rattling around inside his head. She'd arrived in the middle of a terror attack, as the one who could understand him, because she was there too. But his feelings, he didn't understand; where they were coming from, and why this was happening was a mystery swimming in his head

"Shall we?" Abbey said in a quiet voice, taking him by the hand.

As they stepped off the podium, he had the strangest feeling, one he could only attribute to the after-effects of shock from the attack. He was outside of himself in a calm that only comes on rare occasions. He was seeing his life beginning anew. He was no longer sixty-four years old, he was waxing a shiny new coat on his life, and it felt good, the freeing kind of feeling he remembered having with Ruth when they decided to marry and start a family. Floating, that was the word. Floating on air.

Chapter 6

ABBEY'S PLAN

5:30 p.m.

Harold walked towards the rear of the room, arm-in-arm with Abbey, never once feeling his feet touch the carpet, nor did he hear the numerous thank-yous from those lining the aisle. His anticipation grew with every step of what would happen next. Strangely euphoric was the feeling he had walking with Abbey Nelson. He was like a high school kid on his first date, at least until his legs wobbled, sending him sideways into the door jam. He recovered and looked into Abbey's eyes. His heart was suddenly ripped apart by the presence of this woman beside him, clashing with the memory of his wife, who he still loved dearly.

"Why now?" he mumbled.

He'd felt the same way about Ruth when they met after a football game at a Clayton High School Sock Hop. He was a giddy schoolboy at the first dance and that's when he knew beyond a doubt, he was in love. He was fourteen years old and he was in love for the first time in his life. Abbey's eyes caught his again, sending tremors throughout his body. He needed to get away from all these people.

They weren't three strides out the conference room door when Abbey stopped him in his tracks.

"What is it? Something tripped you up as we walked through those doors."

"I, uh . . .don't know," he stammered, taking back his hand from her. "I'm feeling really light-headed." He rubbed his face.

"Maybe I should eat something."

"Okay, I am a little hungry," Abbey said.

People were staring at them, but he didn't seem to care. He was still feeling the effects of his walk on air. They found a map of the hospital in the lobby and followed those directions and their noses. Tonight's fare was chicken fried steak, which turned out to be pretty darn good. Even the broccoli was crisp, hot, and had a tasty cheese sauce.

He began to feel more relaxed as he ate, looking up from his plate from time to time at Abbey. It still felt surreal to be with her, but it was okay for reasons that eluded him. It was like a dream, of sorts.

"I think I have room for pie," he said, setting his fork down. "Can I bring you a piece?" She nodded. He brought back two slices of apple pie alamode and coffee. And for some reason, the door opened for a conversation with the first bite of pie, and it was one he'd not soon forget, like everything else in the past twenty-four hours. The euphoria was returning.

"I think I'd like to go home and rest after they release me, but I don't know if I can do that . . . I feel like I need to be alone, but if I go home, I don't think it would work . . . I mean . . . What do I mean?"

Harold looked up from the piece of pie and into Abbey's eyes. "I don't want to leave you." He mumbled wiping his mouth with his napkin. *God, why did I say that?* He hid behind the napkin, having no idea what was happening to him.

"I'm sorry. I'm very confused at the moment," he said as their eyes met. Abbey tentatively reached for his hand, further intensifying the feelings of uninhibited wildness inside of him. *This is nuts, his rational mind screamed and scrambled to gather itself together.*

"I, uh, don't know what I meant by that. What are you doing . . .?" his voice trailed off. He pulled his hand back and dropped his napkin on his plate, clearing his throat loudly. Their eyes met again, only this time it was softer, and not as intense. Her eyes were filling with tears.

"I need to say this," he began again, "even if I don't understand why I am. I don't want to be away from you and at the same time, I don't think I could be with you at home. Ruth is everywhere. It's still her home. Do you know what I mean? So, I don't know what I'm going to do. I'm really not making much sense, am I?" Harold's face was so hot it almost was painful.

"I understand your dilemma," Abbey said taking his hand back, "really I do. Why don't you think about . . .?" she paused.

"Why don't I what?" he said softly, looking into her brown expressive eyes.

"Why don't you, not go home. Why not go the opposite direction and go find yourself? I don't know where your daughter lives, but you could use this time away from home to visit her. Right? But, that's not really my plan. When you were running for governor of Illinois, I noticed something about you I'd not seen when you were a US Congressman. I sensed you were looking for more than what you were familiar with, hence the run for governor. But I think it goes beyond even that. The reporter in me knows you're capable of so much more, and I think you know that too. You have a dream, a very old dream I think. A dream which will land you in Washington, DC. Tell me if I'm wrong, but I don't think I am."

Harold was mesmerized by what Abbey was telling him. It didn't explain the wild and crazy feelings he had, but she had just opened a door to something he'd not thought about in so long, he'd forgotten how important it was to him when he started teaching a Western Civilization class at Clayton High School in his hometown. He wanted to see America, but more importantly, he wanted to meet Americans from all walks of life. It was always in the back of his mind, an odd and distant knowing, but he really felt as if he had something to give to the American People. He didn't have a clue what it was, but he always thought if he could just meet them face to face, he'd discover what it was.

"How did you know?" he said excitedly. He squeezed her hand between his. Abbey shrugged her shoulders.

"I mean really. Is it that obvious?" he exclaimed. Abbey nodded. Harold was remembering the intensity of his dream quest, and it was being fueled by Abbey's bright and shining face from across the table.

"Well, then there must be something to it. Please continue." Harold was excited now, just as he'd been in the classroom, teaching young minds about the true nature of their country.

She raised an eyebrow. "I think if you do this, it will land you in DC. I don't know how I just know it will. Maybe as a Senator?"

He took a deep breath to try and calm the turmoil inside for the moment because there was a storm brewing, a big one.

"You know, when I got the invitation to attend the ceremony, I almost convinced myself it was too far to drive for such a short ceremony, one which I'd seen many times before. But it kept nagging at me like it had a life of its own. It was only last week that I finally decided to come. And look at me now. I got shot! I killed a man, landed up in the hospital, and just had the best interview of my life. When we were walking out of there I felt . . . well, my feet never touched the floor. I was floating on air. Go figure."

"Yeah, go figure," she said wiping her eyes with her napkin.

"What's wrong," he asked. "Why are you . . ."

"Because . . ." she said dropping her hands into her lap.

"I don't understand," he said. Harold was taken back by the fire in her eyes, and it was directed at him.

"Well then, let me explain," Abbey said wiping her face.

Abbey's words drilled right through him, sitting him up straight, and clearing his mind.

"I've known you all my life, and as a journalist, I see a man who has a deep and unbridled love for his country. It's who you are. When you ran for governor, that's when I knew it for certain. It's why I love you, Harold Robertson. It's why I've always loved you. You have a heart as big as the sky."

His face was hot again and a smile was spreading across it, a smile with a life of its own. It was all because he was talking with Abbey Nelson, a news reporter from. . . He didn't even know where she was from. "Where did you grow up?"

Abbey's face flushed hard. He'd hit a soft spot.

"Clayton," she whispered.

"When. When did you graduate high school? I don't remember ever seeing you." He was excited. Had he known Abbey and forgotten her?

"Class of '78'."

"And where did you live? In town?" She shook her head, smiling like a Cheshire cat.

"On a farm north of town."

His mind was racing to remember anything. He was in the class of '69', so she was eight or nine years younger. The word farm rang a bell, and then it hit him, he'd played with her older brother during the summers. They had pick-up baseball games at the field in town and then ride their bikes back to the farm to practice some more. He was several years older than her brother, but her brother played shortstop with such speed and agility that Harold always picked him first when they chose-up teams.

"Jimmy! Little Jimmy! Now I remember. He was a good ball player." His grin was so big, like a cartoon character.

"He talked about you after every game," Abbey smiled,

"like you were some baseball god. You have no idea the effect you had on him. He lives in Springfield now; married, three girls, and still plays baseball – coaches actually. He's a physical education teacher at one of the high schools. But you and I never really knew each other growing up."

"You're blushing again. You had a crush on me? How old were you?"

"Seven, but it didn't get bad until you were a senior in high school and I was ten."

He laughed. "Wow. This is too strange. Did Jimmy know?"

"My whole family knew, but never said a word. I guess they didn't want to spoil it for me. It's not funny Harold Robertson. It was really hard on me. I couldn't think straight for months on end. I used to dream about you too, like the dream you woke up from today. And then you went away to college and got married, and so did I. We both got busy with life, but I never forgot about you. We met up again when you were a Congressman and I was a journalist."

"Wow." Harold's head was swimming with emotions. He shot his hand across the table and grabbed hers. "This is nuts. I'm right back in all the wild and crazy feelings of high school, and it's making me dizzy." He took back his hand and held his head. This was all too much at once.

"I think you better take me to bed . . . I mean to my room to go to bed, not that I'm going to be able to sleep." His face was hot and he was totally embarrassed at sixty-four years of age, but oh so alive.

Chapter 7

DEAR ABBEY

By the time they got to his room, he was exhausted and ready to fall into bed, and forget about everything. There were just too many layers of emotions, everything from the terror and murderous rage at Rushmore, to a kind of love he'd not felt since . . . Abbey was staring at him with gentle, knowing eyes.

"What? Am I doing something wrong with my face again? I'm tired – dog tired." She smiled and nodded, then helped him take off his shirt, and put on the hospital gown, leaving him to undo his trousers and wiggle them to the floor. She pulled back the covers and stepped back, cupping her hands around her nose and mouth. She looked so vulnerable, so lovely. Their eyes met.

"Where will you stay tonight?" The words seemed so lame as they fell from his lips. Why had he said that?

"Here," she pointed to the chair by the window.

Harold lay down and slid to one side of the bed, his eyes glancing down at the place beside him. "For a few minutes?" She lay next to him without a word, gathering his free hand in hers. With her eyes as deep as oceans, she turned her head and gently kissed him on the lips, their eyes closing slowly around the moment.

When he woke sometime later, Abbey was in the chair and curled into a ball under a blanket. The light coming through the partially open door came with a quietude of the early morning hours in the small, regional hospital. His shoulder ached and was throbbing, probably because he'd slept on his side, putting pressure on the wound – not his fault, as he always slept on that side. He turned his head to look at Abbey, who was facing away from him. So many feelings. Too many feelings for him to deal with. He turned away and fell back asleep.

The vampire squad woke him precisely at 4 a.m., drifting silently into the room and setting up at the foot of the bed. They were done in less than two minutes and moved on to the next victim. He'd probably sleep through it tomorrow night if they didn't have to wake him. He glanced over at the lump in the chair, wondering how she could sleep like that all night. The few nights he'd slept on his couch in his Representative's office, he had always regretted it the next morning, wondering why he'd done it more than once. "My dear Abbey, how do you do it?"

He drifted in and out of a restless sleep, dreaming of Ruth's final day at home when she collapsed right in front of him, while they were in their backyard planting snapdragons in July. There were no goodbyes, no last kiss, no crinkled smiling eyes, just a limp body on the grass, bathed by a warm summer day. Nothing could ever take away the horror, the unrelenting loneliness of those final moments in the backyard; they haunted his every waking and sleeping hour for weeks on end, and this early morning's relapse was no exception. Abbey's voice woke him. She was talking in her sleep; something about her report on the terrorist attack – the shots heard around the world. The reports of automatic weapons fire echoed in his head, as he lapsed in and out of sleep awhile longer, finally rousing himself enough to shut off the madness of that night.

He rolled onto his side to stare at Abbey's form in the chair, carefully supporting his arm as best he could. "My dear Abbey. What are we going to do?" He murmured, half-asleep. Abbey had shattered the illusion of his prison, where he'd held himself after Ruth died, freeing him to live again. But what to do with all of his memories of family and all the days of loving Ruth. What do I do with those? That feeling rolled around in his thoughts until he fell asleep again, surrounded by an air of renewed life and a love he still didn't understand.

He dozed on and off until the morning shift woke both him and Abbey at 6 a.m. The nurse did the usual blood pressure, temperature, and pulse checks, and was gone in less than three minutes. Abbey was stretching in the chair, her first signs of movement all night.

"Sleep okay?" His voice crackled. She yawned and her head nodded yes, as she got up and wandered into the bathroom. His last dream popped back into his head as the door clicked shut. The three of them, Ruth, Abbey, and himself were talking in his backyard, something about keeping up the flowerbeds, and planting a new apple tree to replace the one an ice storm had split in half two winters ago. He remembered Ruth smiling and talking comfortably hand in hand with Abbey, which only added more complexity to his already overwrought and confused mind. Ruth was holding a four-pack of snapdragons, just like she had that awful July afternoon. But what did it mean? Harold opened his eyes, trying to shake off the memory of that day. He tried to focus his mind, anything to keep from reentering Ruth's three-day death march before they pulled the breathing tubes out. He was there for all of it, every spasm and quiver in her body desperately trying to hang on to life. As she died, so did he; his reason to live seemed to ebb right out of him. A shiver ran down his spine at the thought of abandoning Ruth's memory for this person he'd only known for twenty-four hours. He turned away from the sounds of running water in the bathroom and the person in there who was disturbing his universe.

"I'm sorry, what did you say?" Abbey's muffled voice asked.

His mind froze. Had she heard him? The only person ever to hear his thoughts was Ruth. They'd always done that at odd moments. *God no, that's not possible.* His overwrought mind yelled. *We don't even know each other. Or do we?* He reached to the bedside tray to get his water mug – his mouth was suddenly very dry. In the middle of his distraught thinking, he inhaled the first sip of water, sending him into a choking spree. It brought Abbey racing out of the bathroom.

"You okay?"

By the time he finished coughing up most of the water a minute later, he had a nurse, two aides, and Abbey standing over him, making him all the more angry with himself.

"Sorry," he said on the final cough. Abbey sat at the foot of the bed after the audience had departed, and observed him like a reporter studying her interviewee for signs of unspoken and hidden thoughts to address. It made him so uncomfortable, he swung his legs out of bed and stood, wobbling, but able to walk to the bathroom to escape her probing eyes. He closed the door and peed, venting at himself about everything that happened during the past day, but most of all, about what was happening between them. *He couldn't do this. He didn't want to do this. He was in no shape to do this, not now or in the near future.* The thoughts swirled round and round until they escaped his lips.

"I can't do this Abbey," his gravelly voice heaved the words out and reverberated off the tiled walls and floor. He was sorry he'd said it, but he needed to say it aloud if only to hear himself say it. He was muttering about his shortcomings when the answer came back.

"I know. We'll figure it out if you give us a chance."

Abbey's soft voice delivered the exact message he needed. He used the same words with his history students when they were having difficulty understanding why things had happened the way they did in the adult world. He knew their young minds couldn't possibly grasp the complexity and utter chaos of human history. So, "we'll figure it out," gave them the freedom to understand it at a later time.

Again, he was asking himself how she knew to say the very words he needed to hear? It didn't hit him over the head like some epiphany, but it did make him realize that there was a connection between the two of them, which he couldn't explain, and that maybe the dream of the three of them in his backyard was him trying to explain to himself his feelings.

As he stepped through the doorway, the anger and confusion were gone, just as quickly as it had set upon him. "I'm sorry. I'm having a hard time with all of this." His eyes never left hers, as he shuffled back to bed, letting out a long sigh when he sat down on opposite side of the bed. "I'm confused and need some time to think, anywhere but here would probably be good."

"Okay, after you leave . . . we'll talk."

His breakfast arrived, giving them both a chance to break away from the loggerhead of confusion and emotions. He knew the outcome of such things from his time in Congress, locked in disputes of passionate ideals trying to find a home in a committee with him, the young freshman Congressman from a rural area, usually on the short end of the stick. Harold laughed at the memory, the kind of laugh that could get everyone's attention because of its volume. The nurse's aide smiled at him setting the tray down and exited quickly.

"What was that about?" Abbey said looking out the window.

"From my days in the House – leveling mountains with words – what we were headed into, well me anyway. What's for breakfast?" he said, uncovering a plate of scrambled eggs with a strip of bacon and whole-wheat toast on the side. "Come on over, we'll share." He looked more closely at her half-turned stance. She was crying softly, trying to hide it with her hand.

"This is my fault," he offered. She shook her head. He set the lid back on the eggs and started to walk around the bed, meeting her halfway in an untamed embrace, both of them needing to be close. "I'm sorry. I'm just an old poop, you know. Ruth always said that when I got this way." Abbey nodded her head against his chest.

"I know. She told me when you were running for governor."

Abbey's fingers gripped his shoulders, sending pain and shivers of need throughout his body. She let go and stepped back, looking deep into his eyes.

"There's no need to apologize. I know how much you loved your wife. We talked about that too, and the schoolgirl crush I had for you. We laughed a lot about it while you were on the campaign trail. She confided in me Harold, and I didn't understand why at the time, but maybe she knew something wasn't right with her, that something was going to happen to her. She never said she was ill or anything though."

They sat quietly together for a while, which he was glad for because she'd stirred the pot again, bringing up a trove of feelings locked away. Sometimes, he knew he was better off not saying a word, just letting a silence speak its peace instead. Ruth had taught him that because they could butt heads pretty good sometimes, and the outcome was never what either of them wanted.

"Abbey," he said with their eyes meeting, "thank you for telling me what Ruth said to you. It means more to me than . . ."

His hand shaded his brow and eyes, and the powerful hurt that was erupting inside. "God, I miss her so," he said turning away. Abbey rubbed his shoulder, trying to help him. He turned back towards her, needing someone to hear his awful truth.

"I was so afraid when I heard that man's neck snap . . . I felt myself slipping away . . . like I wasn't a human . . ."

Abbey sat next to him on the bed and waited quietly for him to collect his thoughts and feelings, which he knew might take a while. She stroked his head and shoulders, humming softly. Harold knew himself well enough to know he was losing a battle, which didn't really need to be fought. He'd done the right thing killing that man. But this other thing with Abbey? He loved this woman and the harder he fought against it, the more ground he lost. It was a hopeless cause, this need of his to hang onto his memory of Ruth, thinking that he could make her real again – if only he could . . . It took a few minutes, but eventually, the huge block of sadness slid off his shoulders, and as it did their eyes met again, in full sight of what lay before them.

"I'm sorry," his hopeful face shined with relief. "I'm a little slow on the uptake when it comes to expressing myself, always have been. I don't understand it, but somehow I know that whatever we decide to do, you know, with all this," he waved his hand in the air, "this connection we . . ." He ran out of words – Harold Robertson, the great orator of the US House, was speechless.

"Shh," Abbey took his hand from the air. "We don't have to understand it right now. It'll come to us." She said quietly.

You know Harold, she's right.
It'll come to us. So, quit trying to
understand something that will
always defy explanation.

Harold smiled and nodded in agreement with himself. He'd never understood the way he loved Ruth, so why should he feel he needed to with Abbey. His little talk with himself – crazy talk if you asked him – simply said to shut up and go with it. Abbey was looking at him oddly.

"We better be seein' about eatin' those eggs before they get cold." He patted her hand.

They laughed in the small, quiet way that only two people who had known each other for years could. He didn't understand it, but he couldn't deny what he felt for this woman beside him. Second chances are elusive events in life, and they didn't wait around if they weren't claimed in the moment. He'd learned that much in life.

Chapter 8

MARCHING ORDERS
May 27th, 8 a.m.

It wasn't long after breakfast was cleared that Dr. Bennett walked into the room, joking with a nurse, all smiles, and carrying a clipboard under his arm.

"Good morning, Mr. Robertson. Did you sleep well?"

"Okay, I guess. You're cheerful this morning. Care to elaborate?" His surgeon raised an eyebrow while he wrote something on Harold's chart at the end of the bed.

"I was informed this morning that two of the critically wounded in another hospital are out of the woods and going to make it. And, you'll be going home today. I'll leave instructions for your follow-up visits with your primary care physician. You should get the paperwork before noon, and a packet of bandages. Nancy," he motioned towards the nurse who'd come in with him, "will answer all your questions. Mr. Robertson, everyone I know wants to meet you and say thank you for what you did. You're a very courageous man."

Harold shook Dr. Bennett's outstretched hand. "Thank you for everything. Oh, tell the 4 a.m. vampire squad, they're good. I could have slept through it if they didn't have to wake me." Nancy laughed.

"I'll pass that along to my sister Vicki."

He laughed with her. "I'm sorry. Do you all know Abbey Nelson?" He'd forgotten to acknowledge her presence.

"Yes. Abbey is well loved around town," Dr. Bennett said. They were alone again and he was glad he was being discharged today. "Were you going to shower?" he asked Abbey.

"With you?" She laughed. "No. I'm going home to clean up. I'll be back to pick you up. I need to stop by the station for a minute and find out about that interview at Mt. Rushmore you promised. I better get going . . . in case it's busy."

He took her hand to keep her from rushing out. "Are we good? I mean . . . I don't know what I mean." His brow furrowed, worried that somehow she'd slip away from him. Her fingers rubbed his worry lines and caressed his cheek.

"Yes, Harold Robertson, we're good. Way more than good. I'll be back before noon."

Her hand gently slipped from his and she was gone. The room felt cold and empty almost immediately. He sat on the edge of the bed and tried to think about everything that had happened to him, finding it difficult to focus on anything at all. It was all run together in some formless mass in his thoughts, and even after a long hot shower, it still wasn't any better. A nurse helped him dress, into the shirt Abbey had brought and his scuffed trousers. He sat in the chair that Abbey had slept in and gazed out the window at the blue sky and swaying trees; inside, he was stewing about something, which he couldn't quite pin down. He dozed off for a while until the smell of freshly brewed coffee woke him.

"Coffee, black," Bob Clark said.

A tall paper cup with a plastic lid on it was thrust in front of him. He glanced up at Bob and smiled. "Just what I needed. Thank you, Bob. You know what I like." He took the cup, popped the lid off, and breathed in the aroma of strong black coffee, sipping several times with deep satisfaction. "This is pretty good stuff. Where'd you get it?"

"Downstairs at the real coffee stand in the cafeteria. Got

you one of these too."

Bob gave him a small white paper bag that smelled like donuts. "Oh, man. Now you've gone and really done it. A chocolate covered cake donut with sprinkles." Harold grinned, stuffing half of it into his mouth. "Mm," he chomped away, washing it down with a swallow of coffee. "You're the best . . ." Bob held up his hand to stop him.

"Wanted to tell you about Alex – nothing you'll find in the reports either. We weren't all that buddy-buddy, but he told me a story about a little girl he found wandering alone a couple klicks outside of camp six months before he . . . Anyway, he made sure she got medical attention for her burns and got the locals to track down her family. He took her home a couple weeks later to a family with nothing left after the VC had punished them for something he never found out. Alex snitched rice and meat from the mess as often as he could. After he got blowed-to-shit, the little girl showed up with this."

Bob laid a dirty, torn six-inch-tall, homemade doll in his hands. Harold's eyes flooded. He didn't know why either.

"You keep this. After the war, I never got up the courage to give it to your family. When that little girl gave it to me, I knew it was one of her only possessions and was meant as a thank-you gift."

Bob rubbed at an old hurt etched into his eyes. Harold looked deep into his sunken, but grace-filled eyes. "Thank you, Bob Clark, for the story and the little girl's gift." He wiped his eyes and stared at the crudest toy doll he'd ever seen. Bob shook his hand and left, shuffling along with his walker. Harold wept for the brother he loved, who died in a war which wasn't supposed to be.

Nancy came back sometime later and caught him in a daze, staring out the window at nothing in particular. He was back in Vietnam, as the observer of a 140mm rocket exploding twenty yards away, something he'd done countless times. It was never pretty either, with the gruesome details taking front and center stage and magnified threefold. The blunt-force trauma of an explosion was not something the brain cared to recall if it even could, but it never stopped him from cooking-up some version of the event, which defined his experience of the war. Always, it was the same, never changing, with the same cast of characters and events playing out with precise accuracy. Currently, he was semi-conscious and staring at a medic's serious face, framed by the lush greenery of the jungle.

"Mr. Robertson. Mr. Robertson, wake up."

Nancy's soft voice brought him back into the hospital room. He blinked with surprise when he found that he was not looking at the medic. She stood over him smiling.

"Sorry, I was dreaming." He made several attempts to sit up, finally succeeding with her help.

"You're drenched in sweat, Mr. Robertson," Nancy said, taking his vitals. "Are you alright?"

He nodded. It was nothing new to him.

"I brought you a packet to take home, bandages, tape, and waterproof patches so you can shower."

She got his bandage changed and helped him back into the damp shirt. She gave him a few pointers on how to do it for himself. When she was done, Nancy sat next to him and told him what her sister Vicki had shared with her. Apparently, this morning at 4 a.m., he was talking in his sleep when Vicki came in to draw blood, and it wasn't pleasantries either.

"You were cussing up a blue streak and very agitated," she said.

"Tell her I'm sorry, will ya." Heat filled his face. "Guess I'm angry at those terrorists, huh?" Nancy stood and faced him.

"Do you have someone to talk to about it?"

"Well, not really. But the boss man said I should talk with his shrink. I said no thank you. I'll be okay. Been here before." Nancy nodded that she understood, or at least accepted that he could deal with the traumatic events bouncing around his noggin. He stretched out and promptly fell asleep again after she left. The next thing he remembered was Abbey waking him, saying it was time to go. He signed the release forms and was wheeled out the front door to Abbey's Ford Escape, wondering what was in store for him.

"Where are we goin?"

"Station for a briefing and then my place. You'll see."

The KIRK station was only three and half minutes away but felt like a world away to him. She led him to a conference room and brought him a bottle of water. When she returned with a tray filled with coffee carafe, cups, and a half dozen cookies, two men followed her into the room. She introduced him to Travis London, the station manager, and Brett Carson, the National/Regional Director of News. They explained what they had planned for an hour-long special report on the Terrorist Attack at Mt. Rushmore. They'd already set up and done the background shoots and history of the two terrorists, and when he was ready, they'd do the live segment on site. Harold shuddered at the thought of a live-feed, but he knew what was at stake for the national affiliate, because of Abbey and her cameraman's footage. They wanted to shoot tonight, if possible because it was close to forty-eight hours since the shooting.

"I can manage," he said making a face when he shrugged his shoulders. "Better to do it now before I forget any more details." Brett stood and shook his hand, saying that he was needed on site, something to do with the Department of Homeland Security and the news crew. He handed Harold a large manila envelope with the scripted outline for his segment. Travis sent Abbey after something and then sat next to Harold, opening his laptop.

"There's been a lot of trouble at the crime scene between the Feds and our national news affiliate. You'll be walking into some bad blood tonight. Let me show you what our cameramen shot yesterday."

Harold's eyes widened as he watched an in-your-face, angry confrontation. "Looks like an interesting evening. Who authorized the filming at an active crime scene?"

"The President leaned on the Secretary of Homeland Security to document this in a timely fashion for the American people. At least, that's the unofficial story. We don't have carte blanche access at the crime scene, but we have enough to be a thorn in the Fed's side. I'll assign you an aide for whatever you deem necessary while on site. Abbey will be one of the main interviewers along with a National News Anchor. They'll take good care of you, so you don't have anything to do, except tell your story. Abbey said she was going to take you home so you can rest, or we can get you a motel room – your choice."

"Abbey's place will be fine." She breezed in with an armload of folders and spread them in front of him.

"This is what we have on the two terrorists, their country of origins, education, family background, everything we could find that wasn't classified, and everything that the government has released."

He pulled out the picture of the man he'd killed, a faraway shot of him in a crowd. Harold laid the picture on the table and turned away. "Guess I'd better get used to seeing him, but not right now."

He got up and left the conference room and walked down the hallway to a drinking fountain. He splashed some cold water on his face and inhaled a snoot full. "Great. Just great." He sputtered between coughing bouts. He returned and sat down to examine all the folders' contents, discovering a young man who'd been recruited by his father at the tender age of nine years old. "What kind of a father would do this to his own son?" he growled into the empty room.

"The kind who hates without logic and sees no harm is too great for those who don't share his devout beliefs," Abbey said returning. "His son is in paradise now, according to their belief. Come on, let's go home – to my place – so you can rest. Bring all this if you want."

Harold got up and walked away, unable to deal with the information about the man he'd killed. He didn't want to know any more at the moment – maybe tonight – when he had no other choice, but to know the person in the pictures. How anyone could justify beliefs such as this man's, was unknowable to him at the moment. The pit of his stomach ached even more than when he'd killed the man.

Abbey's house was a new rancher, cozy and well-lit by a large picture window on the east end of the living room, and a sliding glass door on the west end. He went straight to the overstuffed sofa and flopped down, hurting his shoulder again. "Do you have any beer? I could use one right about now." Abbey went straight to the fridge and brought two clear glass bottles of a classic American beer. She sat beside him and clanked his bottle with hers, both of them taking long draughts in silence.

"I hate that man," he cursed in an angry voice. "He ruined my whole life in a matter of seconds. I hope he rots in his fetid paradise. Shit." Harold sank back into the cushions holding the cold beer bottle to his forehead. "I'm a mess inside, Abbey. I don't know if I can do this. I mean, all I'm going to do is lose-it and make an idiot out of myself." He tipped the bottle up to his lips and sucked it dry. "Do you know what I want to say about that terrorist?"

"Yes, I have a pretty good idea. You lost a brother to war. You nearly lost yourself to it too. All that anger has to go somewhere, and when you killed that man, it all went into one act of rage. A rage against evil and to those who would commit their lives to such atrocities."

Abbey set her bottle down and lay her head on his chest. The closeness and smell of her helped his anger to subside. He kissed her head, caressing her hair and breathing in the scent of her, knowing that he wanted her with a fierceness he'd not felt in a long time. She lifted her head and pressed her lips to his, speaking of the hunger within her. He wanted to hold her in his arms . . . he winced in pain and pulled back. His eyes never left hers. He wanted her more than anything. He lay his head back against the cushion and sighed deeply. "What are we going to do now?" he whispered, almost to himself. "I'm here in your home, on your sofa, looking in your eyes – and we both know . . .

"Shh. Let this be enough for now."

Her gentle voice calmed him but did not change the intensity of feeling within him. He nodded and shifted positions, letting out a long belch. They both laughed. He stood and pulled her up into his one good arm, both of them belching nearly into each other's face, bringing more laughter into the moment. She ducked out of the embrace and held up her index finger to him.

"I'll be right back. Don't go away."

She ran off down the hallway and he followed her to her study. Bookshelves lined three walls and were filled with knickknacks, pictures, some very old looking books, and a lot of journalism-related books, papers, and folders stuffed with newspapers on the bottom shelves. She was bent over next to a desk with a laptop and vase of fine silk flowers, cattails, and dried baby's breath flowers, next to a brass desk lamp. He stood behind her so that when she rose, she did so into him. He grabbed her quick and kissed her, then let her go, smiling.

"Harold Robertson, just exactly what are your intentions?"

He laughed. "What did you get?" She opened a file folder, the kind with the string that winds around a disk to close the flap.

"This." She held up a newspaper clipping.

It was a picture of him and her brother Jimmy dressed in Little League uniforms. They were posed together with him leaning on a bat, and Jimmy looking up at him. He was the team's assistant coach the summer after he graduated high school. Paper-clipped to the folder was a small square photo taken through a chain link fence of him by the dugout, airborne, wild-eyed, and mouth wide open. The colors were faded and turning bluish, but it was unmistakably him. "Wow. You took this picture?" He watched as the blood rushed into her face and her eyes betrayed her decades-old secret love affair. "You really did have it bad, didn't you?"

"Yes Harold, I told you already. A month after I took this picture you were gone and I was miserable for months on end. Nothing my parents could say or do helped in the least. Finally, I just got over it, mostly."

"I'm sorry. I had no idea. If I'd known, I would have said something, you know, about puppy-love, not that I would have known what I was talking about." He kissed her on the cheek.

"Got any more photos?" She emptied the contents of the

folder on her desk. They spent the next thirty minutes reminiscing about their youths, and how lucky they were growing up in the small town of Clayton. Her phone rang as she gathered up the bits and pieces of her past and returned them to the bookcase. He wandered through her house, while she talked, and wound up in the kitchen with his head in her fridge, looking for something to nibble on. He cut up some apples and sliced some cheese, and went looking for crackers in the cupboards when she walked into the kitchen.

"Crackers," she pointed above the fridge. "That was Travis about tonight. You need to know something about this special newscast. While you were recovering in the hospital, the whole country was erupting in a dialogue tainted on the violent side towards the recent arrivals of Muslims from the Middle East, and their sympathizers in this country. Nothing's happened yet, but there are signs indicating it's only a matter of time before it does happen. Lots of hate talk on the internet and some cable shows. It's going to get out of hand, and soon. Travis and I want you to know that everything was scripted by the National News Director's team. We had no input whatsoever, so don't be too surprised tonight when they broach this subject and ask for your support to help quell the masses. They think you'll carry a lot of sway with the American people through this one special report. Travis and I think they'll approach you about doing several follow-ups. Harold, I have to tell you that I talked with Travis about what I see in store for you, you know, about your dream of meeting the people. I pitched my plan to him on it yesterday, and he's all for it if you agree."

"Agree to what?" Harold frowned. "Sounds like you all want to plan my life after what happened. I think you know better Abbey. I'm pretty bull-headed when it comes to my ideas and their execution."

"I know, I know. I told him you'd resist, but here's my plan, if you want to hear it. We started to talk about it in the cafeteria yesterday – about your dream. Why don't we sit down in the living room and eat the snack you fixed? I'll make a pot of coffee."

"Okay. But I'm already resisting the whole thing if Brett pushes the idea at me like I belong to him and will perform whatever he asks of me." Harold exhaled with a degree of anger. He'd been here before with the media moguls, albeit on a much lesser scale. He snatched the box of crackers from the top of the fridge and took the plate of apples and cheese into the living room, flopping down on the sofa and losing three slices of apple in the process. He brushed off a piece of lint from one and shoved it in his mouth, chomping on it while shoveling in the next. Abbey came in and sat down in the chair on the other side of the coffee table. She eyed him like she had in the hospital when she was playing journalist. "What!" he said a little too abruptly, startling her. "Sorry. I didn't mean to sound . . ."

"No, I understand completely. You're angry, and rightfully so. I didn't want you going into tonight's interview and run headlong into the demands of National. But I meant what I said in the cafeteria and would like to talk further about it. And I think you would too. I'll get the coffee."

She leaped out of the chair and was gone before he could say anything. He smiled at the whole scene, knowing he'd been abrupt with her. "Sorry," he yelled towards the kitchen doorway.

"You should be," she said entering.

She walked into the room carrying a tray of cups and a carafe, setting it down on the coffee table. She poured and sat next to him, smacking his thigh. "Thanks. I guess I deserved that." She pulled out her phone and leaned into him, swiping the screen until a page appeared.

"I wrote down some ideas. Some of them are from when you

campaigned for governor a few years back. I titled it, Marching Orders, back then."

She handed him the phone and leaned back on the sofa, giving him some space. He reached out for his coffee, nearly spilling it, and took several sips. "You make a strong cup." He scrolled through several pages of notes. It was a rough outline of a typical campaign trail for any candidate running for office.

"You did all this yesterday?" he said, duly impressed. Her shy smile told him she'd worked on this long before the Mt. Rushmore attack. "It's good, you know. You're good at this. And you talked with Travis about all this?"

"Some, not all. Nothing about the part where I go on the road with you." She smiled.

His head turned in slow motion like he couldn't move any faster until he came face to face her hopeful eyes. "You're a sneak, you know, but a good one. Is there more than what's on your phone?"

"Not really. The rest is in my head and yours. You had plans on your run for governor. You had it written all over you, in the way you presented yourself to the public. I never could figure why you weren't elected, other than the incumbent was entrenched, and had more money than you."

"Yeah. So I see you ended with a list of names. What's their part in your plan?"

"People I know across the country who work in the media and public broadcast stations. Travis kicked-in a few. Here, you missed a page."

She took him to a different page with a map, names and addresses, venue locations and dates. His mouth hung agape, seeing what she'd planned for them. She laughed and grabbed his arm. "Oh, you're way past being a sneak," he said staring at her phone screen.

"This is what I spent most of my time on yesterday. See," she pointed. "You could be in Seattle by next week, and we'd never have to stay in a motel. All these names are people who offered to put us up for the night on your way home . . . to here."

She was pointing to Washington DC on the list, three pages forward. "You couldn't have done all this yesterday. Could you?" he asked.

"It's not complete, but it's a good start. We can fill in the rest along the way."

"Whoa girl," he sank back into the cushion. "How could you possibly know I'd be interested in this wild proposal? I mean, we don't even know each other." As soon as he'd said it, he knew that he'd hurt her feelings . . .

Of course, you hurt her feelings.
It's what you do.

He frowned at the all-to-familiar thought, which had occupied his mind ever since Ruth died. He didn't like it much, but he knew he had to own it because he'd said hurtful things to many of his friends after her death. He set his cup back on the coffee table and got up, walking to the picture window to get some space between himself and Abbey. "I'm sorry," he mumbled to her front yard. He turned to face her, rubbing his face with his only free hand. "Before I say anything else to upset you – and me – I think I should lie down and rest before tonight's melee backs me into a corner, more than I am right now. Can I lay down on the couch in your office?" She nodded, wiping her eyes. He walked away down the hall to her study and lay down, falling asleep in short order.

Chapter 9

THE RUSHMORE PROCLAMATION

8 p.m.

Never fall asleep after hurting the one you love, those were his waking thoughts in Abbey's study. It is not enough to say you're sorry and then walk away, thinking all will be well. You must fight for what you love and those who live within your heart. Those were his words to Ruth on such occasions and they were in his heart now for Abbey.

Harold stretched and kicked off the comforter, his waking mind recalling those thoughts, ones which needed to be heard by him so that he might speak them to the one who occupied his heart. "I do love you Abbey, and I don't know why I said those mean words," he whispered into her study. His shoulder throbbed from being cramped. He rolled off the couch and onto his knees and sat on his heels.

"Crap," he grunted into the gray leather cushion. There was blood seeping through the bandage and staining his shirt. He got to his feet, wobbling a bit, and slowly walked down the hall and into the living room, where the packet of bandages was on top of a small table by the front door. The sound of clattering dishes was coming through the kitchen doorway. He took the bandages to the bathroom across the hall from the study and followed Nancy's instructions. He put the blood-stained shirt back on and went to apologize to Abbey, again, only he'd try to do it right this time. Ruth had always told him . . . he plugged the memory leak as he stepped into the kitchen.

"There you are. Did you fall asleep?"

"Yes, thank you. Abbey, I'm not very good at this, but I do know when I have hurt someone," he said from across the kitchen. She stopped what she was doing and turned towards him.

"You don't need to say anything more. I got over it."

Her eyes said otherwise. "Yes, I do need to say more, if not for you, I need to do it for me." She was staring at his bloody shirt, perhaps trying to distract herself from how she really felt. "You see, I care a lot for you, but I don't know how to feel about . . . feel about loving someone else, you know, besides my wife." His gaze fell to the floor as if he'd find the right words there. "I love you," he mumbled. She was standing right in front of him when he looked up, her eyes searching his with crystal clarity. He reached out with both arms to draw her close, ignoring the ache from his unslung arm. She tucked her head under his arm and pulled him in close.

"It's okay. I understand. I said too much, too soon. But, I meant every word," she said softly.

They held each other until he had to let go because of the growing ache in his shoulder. He stepped back and cradled his aching arm with his other hand to allow his muscles to relax. "I had to change the bandage and couldn't get back into the sling – don't want to either."

"Maybe I have something that would fit you. A couple of years ago, my dad had an operation at a hospital in Chicago, and I wound up bringing one of his shirts back with me to Rapid City. I never washed it, because I liked to smell his aftershave. It brought back strong memories of my childhood. Come try it on."

She took his hand and led him to her bedroom and sat him down on the end of her bed, while she rifled through the closet and extracted it quickly.

"You allergic to wool?" she asked.

She pulled out a Pendleton western-style dark blue plaid shirt and held it up, twisting it side to side, inspecting it for moth holes, finding one small one under the armpit. She shrugged her shoulders and thrust it at him to try on.

"I'll need a tee shirt to ward off the scratchy fibers," he said. She opened her bottom dresser drawer and got a race tee shirt from the 1996 Chicago Marathon, which was big enough for two of her. "Let me guess, not yours?" She shook her head.

"Dad and I attended a few times. We liked to watch, but never entered any."

Abbey helped him slip out of the bloody shirt and threaded his hurt arm into the tee shirt, and then stretched it up and over his head, and into his other arm. The Pendleton had a whiff of aftershave and body odor "It's all I have. Seems to fit okay. But, we can go to the store if you like."

"No. This is fine. In fact, it's way better. Let me guess – Old Spice?" He sniffed the inside of the shirt collar. She rubbed his arm smiling. "I'm hungry," he said, grabbing her arm before she could retract it, and kissed her on the lips – hard. "Feed me." He laughed and started back towards the kitchen. He helped her scramble some eggs, with cheese, and toasted four slices of whole wheat bread. It was getting close to when they'd have to leave for Mt. Rushmore, so they ate quickly while the coffee brewed. She went to change into a pantsuit, leaving him to ponder the outcome of tonight's live feed. He'd thought very little of the implications of what had happened, being too caught up in his own stuff.

"Would you bring me a cup please?"

Her words carried down the hall and faded rounding the kitchen door, but just the sound of her voice reminded him that he'd promised to bring her a cup of coffee when it was done – five minutes ago. He got up and did that, pausing to look at family photos in the hallway on the way back. One photo showed her standing with her older brother Jimmy on the front porch of the farmhouse, looking out over endless rows of corn. It must have been the middle of summer because the corn was quite tall where it met up with the lawn. The corner of the barn showed in the picture, with a covered stack of hay – probably the first cutting. Abbey walked in as he was swimming in memories of his youth. She was ready for work, all spiffed-up, suitable for an on-air broadcast. He, on the other hand, smelled of aftershave, body odor, and wore a rough-and-ready Pendleton – still, better than his blood-soaked shirt.

"We should get going," she said.

"Right." He swished some water in his mouth to get the egg out of his teeth, swallowed and headed for the door, grabbing his cane by the front hall table, and followed Abbey to her white Ford Escape in the driveway. She filled him in on the logistics of the shoot during the thirty-minute drive. Mostly, he stared out the window, not thinking of much of anything, knowing he'd be cast down into a dark hole in a short while. He was not looking forward to reliving these particular nineteen seconds of his life.

Abbey pulled in behind her station's transmission truck, which was parked in the bus area in front of the main entrance. She poked her head into the KIRK van on their way to the entrance, and the seven hundred foot walk to amphitheater overview area. Looking past the empty seats to the stage area, which was busy with FBI, Homeland Security, and filming crew, sent Harold reeling back in time forty-eight hours. He held onto Abbey's arm and leaned on his cane as they descended the amphitheater steps to the crime scene.

Every step led him closer to the sights and sounds of that night: the speaker's voice echoed in his thoughts; the reports of automatic weapons fire; the screams of terror; the crack of bullets passing by his head; the grinding of bone and cartilage; the acrid smell of gunpowder. He stopped at his row and leaned against the hand railing, his eyes surveying and his ears pricked hard against every voice. The hair on his neck bristled with fear and death, and his spine tingled with electricity. "This is bad," he murmured, just as Brett Carson spotted them from where the camera crew was set up. Behind all of them, lurked death, and the chalked outlines of bodies on the concrete stage. Travis waved them over to the far side of the stage. He was standing with Abbey's cameraman, Chet. They gave Brett as wide a berth as possible, not wanting to engage with him just yet.

"Welcome to the Rushmore Circus," Chet said.

Harold didn't laugh, seeing that Travis wasn't in the best of moods. "You look stressed."

"Oh, yeah. But it doesn't have anything to do with you, but here's something that does. Abbey accidentally printed the pages she created about your cross-country trip. They were found by Brett's assistant, Jeanette, when she was copying notes for her boss. I only know because I saw the look on his face when she gave them to him. So, it'll probably come up in the interview. Also, they have a clip on your run for governor in Illinois to tie into the proposed trip. Tony Franks, the national news anchor, will no doubt put you on the spot with surprise questions about a possible run for the Senate or the Presidency. Are you?" Travis took a step back.

Harold swallowed his irritation. "Don't think so." His sharp words ending the conversation.

"Hey, here you are," Brett Carson from the National News Division said, interrupting them. "We have a couple of things to go over and questions you'll be asked by our anchor."

Tony and Jeanette followed Brett over, lending their bright and shiny faces to the circus performers, and Harold's headache. He put on his public face, the one he kept safely tucked away for such occasions. Pleasantries were exchanged and he was stolen away by Brett to walk him through his part in the special report on terror in America. God, he wanted to be anywhere but here. Brett never said a word about the papers Jeanette found, but he did say they'd be showing short clips from his past run for governor and his eight years as a Congressman. He barely spent five minutes with Brett, leaving him feeling a bit helpless and at the mercy of the media. It shouldn't be like this, but he knew the man was busy and had been harassed all day by the Feds.

He was walking back towards Abbey and Chet when Jeanette caught him by the arm – the injured side. "Crap," he said between gritted teeth as he wheeled around to find himself face to face with Brett's assistant – who was as tall as he was. The pain on his face must have been obvious because she looked horrified.

"Oh God, I'm sorry. I didn't mean to hurt you. I'm so sorry."

She probably would have gone on apologizing if he didn't interrupt her. "Think of it as a wakeup call to get me ready for the interview, Jeanette. Since you know where everything is here, how do I find a cup of coffee?" He smiled and she looked relieved. She seemed pleasant enough and had an honest face, but could she be trusted? *Well Jeanette, who stole the walking papers from the printer room, what say ye?* He was amusing himself at her expense. At least he wasn't showing the anger which lurked just beneath the surface. Her sharp brown eyes seemed to take it all in because she swished her long auburn hair out of her face, changed her stance, composed herself, and let out a little sigh. Her quick and acute eyes landed back on his, fully recovered from her gaffe.

"I'll be right back. Cream and sugar?" she smiled.

He shook his head and she disappeared to the far side of the stage where several tables were set up with water bottles, coffee, sandwiches, and pastries, all compliments of the Feds he guessed. He'd passed the media's paltry coffee setup before descending into the seating area – there was no one at the table when he'd passed. The Fed's table was bustling. She came back with his coffee and a pastry. "Thanks, Jeanette. Tell me, is Brett a good man to work for?" She eyed him, looking for signs of where the question was headed.

"Yes. He's an intelligent and detail-oriented Director of National News for the network. He always gets his story right. You'll see firsthand tonight."

"How is it that you came to work for him? If you don't mind my asking."

"I was hired right out of college as an intern. Brett saw me on set one day, and the next day I was working with him."

Harold nodded. "Lucky you. Would you mind filling me in on my segments, so I know what to expect and not fumble for words? And one other thing, Abbey and I would like those papers returned." Harold watched as Jeanette's composed face erupted in confusion and guilt. It was obvious that she'd taken them.

"I gave them to Brett," she said, with downcast eyes.

"Very well. I'll speak to him about it then. Can we go over

my segment now?" Harold asked in a quiet voice. He smiled and gestured with his hand for her to lead the way.

"Certainly. Let's walk through it." Jeanette said.

She never flinched once and didn't mention the papers again, while she helped him prepare. When they were done, he found Travis and relayed the information, and then sat down in the same place he'd sat for the ceremony, to wait for the show to start.

He quieted his mind, closed his eyes, and thought of Abbey. So much had happened between them in less than forty-eight hours, it made his head spin, but in a good way. She had helped him avoid a looming and certain bout of depression. He knew himself well enough to expect it – no guesswork there. In the ten months since Ruth's death, he'd fought hard not to succumb to depression. His doctor had given him several different medications, none of which he took.

Instead, he used the same technique he'd employed while a Congressman: outlining the problem, practiced quiet time, and visualization of probable outcomes, all with a sense of detachment. It carried him through those eight years of scuffles in the House, and it served him well with the death of Ruth. It kept him sane through insane moments.

Tonight was shaping up to be one of those moments, so he quickly ran through the worst and the best he could muster about everything. He knew above all that this special report would be replayed countless times in people's homes, in an effort to bring some semblance of order back into their minds, after the senseless killings and rape of life. Nothing could please him more than to defeat the terrorists' intent to visit their brand of insanity on the American people, by replacing the fear with understanding and unity. He felt Abbey sit beside him. He knew it was her because . . . just because he knew. He slid his hand off his lap and into her welcome grasp. "Is it time?" he said quietly.

"Yes. But we can sit here for a while during the background clips on everything. I wanted you to know I'll be asking about your thoughts after you killed one of the terrorists. I'll be asking about Ruth, so the viewers can see you for who you are. Take your time and don't worry, no matter what comes up. Harold, I want you to know how much I love you, and even though the emotions will be difficult, these few moments will connect you with all the American people. It's who you are, Harold Robertson. It's the beginning of your dream to meet with the people of this nation. It belongs to you."

He opened his eyes and caressed Abbey's cheek. "I love you more than even I know." Their eyes met as the cameras and lights were turned on and the amphitheater floodlights were turned off. A peace enveloped him, knowing Abbey was right, about this being the beginning of his dream, and where it would lead them was anyone's guess. They sat together for ten minutes before Jeanette came over to take him to the place where he'd passed the terrorists on the amphitheater's stairs. He would begin his journey there.

When she handed him some notes they'd written for him, he got the sense that she was the one who was nervous, which he thought ironic. A cameraman was two steps below him and the anchorman, Tony, stepped around him and stood between them. Harold held up his hand to block the camera light at first until his eyes adjusted. Another camera came up behind him in the seating area. Tony introduced himself and gave him a quick rundown before Brett's ten-second warning, when he turned sideways to be able to address the camera.

Harold had been here before doing interviews. He was

reasonably comfortable, except for his shoulder, which hurt because of the weight of his arm pulling on the wound – better than wearing a sling. Tony ran through his introductions before extending the mic towards Harold, and the first of many questions, which only he could answer.

"Did you sense danger when the man passed you on the steps?"

"Two things: first, he was very young and appeared worried as he spoke on his cell phone; the other was the manner in which he walked, quite stiffly like he had something impeding him under his long coat; it struck me as odd, so I followed his movement all the way up the stairs before finding my seat."

"His name was Amir Al Atrash, son of Amul Al Atrash, from Syrian. Both are on the Terror Watchlist. Let's walk down to your seat. What was the mood of the ceremony?"

Harold's firm grip on the railing kept him from stumbling twice because he didn't want to be seen on TV using a cane. The pain in his back was sharp and radiated out from where the shrapnel was lodged, and he knew why. He was nervous and every muscle was taut, just the same as when the first shot was fired. Tony was waiting for him in the second row.

"Are you in pain?" Tony asked.

Harold frowned at the little man and had to stop himself from saying what he wanted to. "Leftovers from the war." He said in matter-of-fact tone.

He described the scene as he remembered, with all the hopeful faces of ones about to receive the greatest gift of their lives, especially the refugees from Iraq, who had lost everything, including family members to the terrorists. Tony offered his arm– he declined. Harold was confused for a moment when it came time to enter into the infamous nineteen seconds. He was distracted by the five FBI men and women on the far side of the stage. One of them was approaching.

"The FBI and Department of Homeland Security have shared with the American people some of their ballistics findings. Based on the video recordings, they've reconstructed part of those nineteen seconds." Tony said.

Tony motioned to the FBI agent to proceed. He stepped up on a ten-inch platform with a bar extending from it towards the back of the stage. He stretched out nearly horizontal and leaned heavily on the bar in a flying leap position. A dozen or so ruby laser beams lit up in the fog that another FBI woman was dispensing with a portable unit. The other cameraman stood back by the array of lasers to show the trajectories of the bullets as they appeared all around the man assuming Harold's position just before he struck the terrorist.

"As you can see, you were surrounded by bullets and only two hit you."

Harold was especially interested in the three laser traces next to the man's head. He walked up behind the man and started to count the laser tracts, twenty-three in all. He turned towards Tony and the cameraman with emotions flooding his face. "He missed me twenty-one times, in what, a second and a half?" He slid two of his fingers between the man's head and the closest red track. "I should be dead," he mumbled.

"Probably, but you're not," Tony said.

The laser beams were turned off and the fog thinned out. The pain in his back subsided when Abbey joined them. He didn't even notice the dull ache coming from his shoulder. He smiled at her.

"We're joined by the local affiliate's Abbey Nelson, who

was here for the ceremony. She has some questions which will help the viewers understand why you took the course of action you did."

The stage lights were on now and both cameramen were positioned as Abbey stepped alongside Tony. As happy as he was to see her, he knew what was coming, just as surely as if it were all scripted for a movie. Their eyes met for a brief moment, helping him to relax. The glare from the bright camera lights hit him from two directions as she began.

"Thank you, Tony. Congressman Robertson, the American people, including myself, are in debt to you for saving so many lives. All of us would like to know what drove you to this act of heroism. Can you tell us what was going through your mind at the moment you took action?" Abbey asked.

Abbey extended her mic to him with a faint smile on her lips. "Yes, of course, I'd be happy to share my moment of insanity. I did what I was trained to do forty years ago – to remove the threat if at all possible. There was no conscious decision on my part. I did what any trained combatant would have done, which includes our local police forces. Our job is to serve our country. I look back on the scene you've presented and I am struck by the single-mindedness of that training – to focus on the threat. I don't mind saying, that after having seen the twenty-three laser tracks around that gentleman's body, that if I'd stopped to think about it . . . well, who knows what I would have done. No one wants to die, but it certainly looked as if I had a death wish. Ms. Nelson, I did what I was trained to do – eliminate the threat . . . I'm repeating myself, aren't I?"

"We are most grateful for your heroism," Tony said.

"Could you tell us then, what was in your mind after you killed the terrorist?" Abbey asked.

"It's a funny feeling . . ." His vision quickly blackened, all except for Abbey's face, which was down a long tunnel. A hand grabbed his arm and steadied him. His eyes never left her distant face. She steadied him with both hands, jamming the mic into his armpit. She was straining to hold him up. He lowered his head and waited for the blackness to clear. *Hero faints on national television, breaks nose on concrete stage.* This thought drifted by his slowly awakening mind. Abbey was standing practically nose-to-nose with him when he fully returned. "Hi, there," he whispered with a smile. He knew she was blushing even though he couldn't see it through the bright lights. As flustered as she must have been, she had the years of training to take a step back and continue with the interview. He admired her strength.

"Perhaps we should move on to . . ."

"No," he interrupted. "I'd like to answer your question. It wasn't a funny feeling. I killed a man with my bare hands and I felt like I was lost to the human race. I blacked out with that thought on my mind – I would never again find myself acceptable as a human being. And I thought of my wife, Ruth. I wouldn't wish for anyone to have those thoughts. They're empty of life, like a dark void. But it doesn't change anything. I would do it all over again because of what I saw in that woman's face who charged the other terrorist, she gave her life for her country in the first few moments of becoming an American citizen. That's heroism. Maybe it's why I did what I did. She gave me the courage. My heart goes out to her family." He rubbed his face, trying to halt the impending march of emotions. "What's going to happen with the survivors? Will they finish taking the oath soon?"

"I don't know. They certainly deserve better than what they got," Abbey said quietly.

"Let's move on, shall we. You probably haven't seen the

man who killed the other terrorist, John McFadden, a Park Ranger who just happened to be entering the amphitheater when the shooting started. We have a monitor over here," Tony said.

Harold walked next to Abbey with their shoulders touching to the other side of the stage. They stopped in front of a large flat screen and he got to see what happened while he was lying on the concrete floor, semi-conscious. Six, pop-pop-pops could be heard, but the picture on the screen was of benches, concrete, and flashes of the terrorist's automatic rifle fire in the distance. Chet had finally dropped to the concrete after several bullets ricocheted in front of them. It was lucky he and Abbey weren't hit. When the reports of the automatic weapons fire ceased, the stage came back into view as Chet stood to continue recording. Bodies were strewn everywhere, including the terrorist lying beside his weapon, and a Park Ranger, slumped over the first-row bench.

"This is Ranger McFadden's wife," Tony said and introduced them.

A wave of heat rushed through Harold when Melissa McFadden stepped beside Tony. The wife of the man who had saved his life. Harold was heartbroken – she looked so young. "I am so very sorry for your loss. Your husband saved my life and the lives of many more in attendance." He gently took her hand and squeezed it between both of his, her eyes flooded with pain. Harold's gaze fell to the concrete, completely unable to grasp the kind of loss she must be enduring. He let her hand slip from his and stepped back, mumbling to himself how wrong it felt that he should live and the young married couple's lives should be ripped apart in a senseless act of terror. Anger flashed through his mind and body, an anger which ran much deeper than only this incident. Melissa reached out to him and took his hand back, gripping it tightly.

"Thank you for your courage. I pray you tell others about what happened here." Melissa said.

Their eyes met again, only this time there was hope in her eyes. She must be a very strong person, he thought, when Tony's voice interrupted the moment.

"Two heroes whose country owes them a deep debt of gratitude," Tony said.

The special report went on for another ten minutes, showing the chaos and quick actions by those present. The first ambulances took twenty minutes to cover the twenty-three miles from Rapid City. Chet did an outstanding job of covering the carnage with Abbey, stopping to help some, where they could, but mostly documenting the scene for the nation and world to see. Harold retreated to the front row of benches and waited for Abbey to finish her assignment.

Chapter 10

THE INSTALLMENT PLAN

10 p.m.

Abbey was somewhere between giddy and two sheets to the wind, having downed one too many beers at her dining room table several hours after they'd left Mt. Rushmore. For one thing, she was talking much faster than he could understand, bouncing from town to city, union hall to city hall, bowling alley to major league ballpark. She was mapping out her plan, scribbling notes, shuffling maps, and lining up places to stay, each with multiple names written beside them on what she called her installment plan. Truth was, he was the one doling out his dream to meet and greet the American people in installments – odd sort of name. They'd stopped for pizza on the way home, picking up two six-packs of beer. They were working on the second pack, and he was sure that at any moment, she would do a face plant on the dining room table – she was going that fast – so she had to run out of gas at some point. But he was more than happy just to be alone with her.

"You're not listening anymore," she accused him.

"My brain can only take in so many words before it all starts sounding like gibberish."

"Ha, ha. Now, if you look at our schedule . . ."

He covered her mouth with his hand. "Let's go sit in the living room." They settled in on the sofa, leaning against each other, their feet stretched out on top of the coffee table – shoes off of course.

"I thought that went well, don't you? I mean everything floowerred . . ."

He covered her mouth again before she took off like a rocket. "Yes, it went just fine. You're very good at your job. Pretty good at catching me too." He laughed and kissed her hand. "We should think about sleep. It's getting late and you're a bit tipsy. I'll need some sheets and a light cover. I'll sleep here," he patted the sofa. Her eyes were searching his again, darting from one to the other.

"You got an off button?" he asked. She pouted at him and tried to stand, falling back onto the sofa. He gave her a little push on the back the second time. She went to the linen closet in the hallway and got him what he needed, dumping it beside him as she passed behind the sofa. "Hey, installment plans, right?"

She didn't say a word while she cleared the table and turned out lights, passing back the way she'd gone. "Good night," he said with his head laid back, looking up at her. She managed a quick smile and went to her bedroom. He made his bed on the sofa and turned off the floor lamp beside the end table. He stared at the shadows on the ceiling for a while, nodding off several times, until he lapsed into a deep sleep.

Sometime in the early hours he got up to pee and stopped at her door to listen on the way back. She was muttering on about something.

He woke to the yellow rays of the sunrise coming through the living room window, bathing the light tan walls with a pleasing glow. He loved the early morning hours, a time when he could think clearly and not be distracted by all the busyness the day would bring soon enough. He wandered into the kitchen to make coffee. It was 5:25 a.m. on the coffee brewer clock. Abbey had readied the pot the night before when she was putting away pizza and beer, leaving him only to push the brew button.

As the coffee pot began to gurgle, he was transported back into his kitchen with his coffee pot, and his Ruth, carrying with it a sense of betrayal, from where he stood in Abbey's kitchen. He leaned against the countertop and stopped himself from taking it any further. Ruth was gone, and there wasn't anything he could do to bring her back; his feeling guilty certainly wouldn't do her any good. Would she always be with him, haunting his every thought when it came time to love again?

He was mumbling to himself when the last gurgle sounded from the pot. He filled a large mug he found hanging on a mug-tree by the pot and opened the sliding door to the backyard to sit in one of the thick-cushioned chairs. He got chilled in a hurry, only wearing the tee shirt Abbey had given him. He hadn't even pulled on his pants.

He went in for a refill and dressed, feeling much warmer with the Pendleton shirt holding in all his body heat. He finished his second cup and slid down in the chair, propping his feet on up the small table, and closed his eyes to enjoy the crisp morning air. The coffee and morning chill cleared his head of last night's ordeal with the media. He sat thinking about his dream and the road trip that Abbey called the installment plan. He liked the idea more than he cared to admit to her, mostly because she was in it with him. Last night, Abbey had raised all the flags, called up the reserves, and declared the adventure was off and running. She'd left him in the dust. He laughed at the images of them on the road together, her just over the next rise waving him on, and him chugging along behind, trying his best not to slow her down too much. The sound of the sliding glass door interrupted his daydream. "Morning," he said as she sat in the chair next to him.

"You're up early."

"Hard not to be when the sun's up at 5 a.m. Thanks for fixing the coffee pot."

"Always do. About last night, I was a little wound-up, wasn't I? I get that way sometimes when I'm on a story that's going to rock the world."

"Yeah. I could tell. Listen, I didn't want to rush into anything. Besides, you were pretty wired last night. I'm sorry if I was off-putting by sleeping on the sofa." There was a long silence. He told himself to let it go. Now was not the time.

"I'm cold. I'm going in."

He followed her in and poured a dab more in his cup. She sat on a stool at the kitchen counter, drained her cup, and poured what was left in the pot. "You have to work today?" he asked, leaning on the counter.

"Yes, for a couple hours. Afterwards, perhaps you and I ought to talk about us."

Abbey's face was half-hidden behind the large mug. "Everything okay?" He was fishing and she was hiding.

"Okay enough. Just a beer headache. We can pick up your truck today if you like."

He felt really awkward at the moment. She was being elusive. "Sure. I better get cleaned up." He rinsed his cup and put it in the sink, letting his hand gently slide over the top of her shoulders as he walked by her.

They met up out front half an hour later. She looked nice. "I appreciate everything you've done for me and I am looking forward to spending some time alone with you on the road if it works out," he said buckling his seatbelt.

"I think you'll understand better when Travis fills you in on what's happening after the special aired last night. He left me a message at 5 a.m. this morning."

While he waited for Abbey at the station, he watched the local morning show, which was linked with the New York affiliate. He had a hard time grasping the scope of the story they were telling. Both of the terrorists killed at Mt. Rushmore had entered the country on an unknown date and location The young man he had killed was the son of a known Syrian terrorist, but his whereabouts had been in question for more than a year.

The country was now on a heightened terror watch with extra armed military and police stationed at all transportation hubs. President Warren would address the nation later in the day. The report went on to say that since this was the year before a Presidential election, the extra security patrols could last until next November's election.

Harold was worried now, not so much about terrorists entering from outside the country, but those sympathetic to the cause who could be reached through social media and the internet. He was well aware of the encrypted smart phone's capabilities in the coordination of terrorist's activities. He needed some air after hearing all the threat reports. He got directions to Abbey's cubical and stopped by to say he was going outside.

"Hey, don't be long. Travis wants to meet in a little bit. There's a bench on the eastside."

He breathed a little easier outside in the sunshine. He'd been preoccupied with his own problems, so much so that he never thought about the possibility of the attack being planned outside the country where tracking terrorists was difficult, having to rely on foreign service intelligence where sharing wasn't always up to date. He managed to calm down before the meeting with Travis and Abbey.

Walking into the station manager's conference room was an eye opener, even more so than the morning news shows.

There were three suits around the table, one of whom he recognized as the Deputy Secretary of Homeland Security, who had been watching the night before at the amphitheater.

"Good morning, Harold," Travis said. "As you can see, we have some visitors this morning. This is Gene Drake, Deputy Secretary of Homeland Security; Paul Scots, Regional FBI Director; Carl Rosser, Personal Assistant to the White House Chief of Staff. Please have a seat. Mr. Rosser has a personal message from the President."

"First of all, a grateful nation extends a heartfelt thank you for your heroism and devotion to this country. It is good to see you up and about so soon. The White House was contacted by Travis London shortly after the attack at Mt. Rushmore. He simply asked how he and staff could help, having been the onsite news crew for the Immigration and Naturalization Ceremony. The President asked me to come and talk with you, Congressman Robertson because Travis made us aware of your tentative plans to travel the country and meet with the American people. It seems that Abbey Nelson is the driving force behind it, according to Travis. So, we are asking how we can be of service to you during your travels. I believe we are all well aware of the gravity of what happened three days ago, and the effects it could have on our country. You and Ms. Nelson seem to have an excellent plan in place, and the President instructed the three of us to see how we could help you fulfill your plan."

Harold's head was swimming and his back was hurting more now than it ever had. "Please excuse me if I get up and walk around. My back is on the fritz again." He stood, carefully stretching while holding on to the back of the chair. He glanced towards Abbey with a chagrinned face. He was embarrassed to be a cripple sometimes, and now was one of them. "Please, continue." Gene stood and thanked him for his service in Vietnam, and conveyed his sympathies about his brother's death.

"I am here because the strength of our country lies with its people. That you want to address the American public after what happened at Mt. Rushmore, is one of the greatest displays of patriotism I have ever seen. The DHS relies on the local level to furnish intelligence, which would be impossible to gather in any other fashion. Your connection to the people of this nation will strengthen it immeasurably. I've been asked to assist you at the local level. Mr. Robertson, I don't know if you are aware of the power for unity you hold as you meet the people of our nation. Your part in the news report last night has set into action a ground-swell of support all across the country. The President personally conveyed to the Secretary of the DHS the importance of the newscast. Travis said he butted heads with a few Federal employees, but overall, it came together nicely."

Paul chuckled and nodded. Harold figured that he was the source of the "bad blood" that Travis had mentioned the other day.

"Do I have you to thank for the ballistics demo?" Harold raised an eyebrow.

"Yup. It was pretty amazing how many bullets flew around you. How are those flesh wounds anyway?"

"Better. Only hurts when I laugh." Harold drew more chuckles from everyone. "Abbey's been a great help to me, and they both deserve a medal for making themselves a target while documenting the attack. I welcome all of your help. The only thing I want to know is who brought the donuts and coffee today?" Harold had always known how to elicit laughter, even when he was young it had come naturally to him. It proved most useful in politics, because of the often heated debates in Congress.

Even though he welcomed their willingness to assist Abbey and himself, he couldn't help but be wary of the government's subtle agenda to manipulate everything, and everyone it touched – it's just the nature of the beast. Of the three suits present, he thought he could trust the FBI Regional Director the most because he'd risen through the ranks of agents, so he was battle-hardened and knowledgeable. Paul Scots would always tell the truth, or at least as much as he could, given his position.

They exchanged phone numbers and the meeting ended, with Harold left sitting alone to contemplate what he wanted to do and what the powers-that-be wanted from him. Funny how life delivers the required bells and whistles when they're needed, but these in particular – he used Bob's word – a-sis-tance providers – were quietly manipulating their agenda behind the scenes, and that was unacceptable.

He went outside to sit in the sunshine and think about his immediate future, at least the one which Abbey had planned for them, definitely not the one hinted at by the suits. It was all happening too fast and too soon after the shooting. His head was still swimming in the mess left behind from the incident, and he kept flashing back and forth to his time at Danang. Abbey sat silently beside him and wrapped her arm around his shoulders.

"You okay? You seem far away after the meeting and unhappy."

"Yeah, you could say that. You're not telling me everything you have in mind. You're doling it out in installments and what I need is the whole picture." He turned his head to look her in the eyes.

"Okay, Harold Robertson. It's really quite simple. I want to see you campaigning for the Presidency. Seven people have already declared their intentions to run in the GOP. I want to see your name in the hat along with theirs. That simple enough?"

Harold's eyes widened at the intensity in her voice. She had every intention of leaning on him just as hard as she could to convince him to run. It was written all over her beautiful face and charged with bolts of energy in her every word.

"You're serious, aren't you?" She nodded, smiling. He stroked his chin as if it were some Aladdin's Lamp he could call out the genie to fix his spinning head. "You know, I'm not qualified. If I'd been elected governor of Illinois, then I might be."

"Harold Robertson, you know perfectly well what it takes to be President. You know that every new President has a learning curve to complete. Let's leave today. We could be in Gillette in a matter of hours. We'll take it one day at a time. Besides, you know you want to try and do this – meet the people. It's your dream. So do it."

Abbey folded her arms across her chest like she knew she needed to protect herself from what was surely coming from him. He smiled at her, stroking his chin again and pointed at her. "You're good and you know it." He started to laugh; not the kind of laugh he was used to, but the kind when someone you love invades your space with their thoughts and feelings, and you know that what they are saying is right. Because it's making you laugh at how right you know it really is.

"Dinner in Gillette, you say? Okay. Why not." He unfolded her arms and hugged her. More like squeezed the breath out of her. And then he kissed her equally as hard.

Chapter 11

THE REPUBLIC OF CYPRUS
May 28th, 5 a.m.

Amul Al Atrash came ashore between the Mori power station and the Le Meridien Limassol Spa and Resort on the island of Cyprus before dawn. He'd drawn upon his contacts in Beirut to arrange for a fast boat with no questions asked. The two-and-a-half-hour ride at night had almost ended with them being sighted by a Port of Cyprus Marine patrol boat ten miles from shore. It would have all ended there if their captain hadn't killed the engines and running lights. Al Atrash had no passport or visa to enter Cyprus, and the patrol boats were always on the lookout for illegal immigrants, drug smugglers, and illegal fishing boats.

He jumped off the bow with his sandals and shoulder slung bag in hand into two feet of water, walked along the beach for half a mile, and then by the San Rafael Resort to sit at a bus stop. He would ride the bus into the port city of Limassol and meet a dock worker at a prearranged time, who would drive him to the Mediterranean Star, the cargo ship which would take him to the Port of Houston, USA.

He was shown to his quarters where he would spend the next eighteen or so days, plenty of time to think ahead about how he would avenge his son's death. He would make no calls and stay off the internet, hopefully, his entry into America would go undetected. He knew he was under surveillance by all the Western Powers' Intelligence Agencies. What he didn't know was how up to date they were.

Chapter 12

LIMASSOL, CYPRUS

Police Station, 8:12a.m.

Miriam Reynolds was growing impatient with the Sergeant behind the desk. She'd been there for forty-five minutes, and they still hadn't taken her seriously about seeing a man come ashore at 5 a.m. She was on holiday with a good friend from her home in Scotland. This was one of three stops in the Mediterranean, and she'd been out for her usual walk along the shore at dawn. She was staying at the Le Meridien Limassol Spa and Resort, situated right on the beachfront.

"Sergeant, when are you going to take my information? I've been waiting almost an hour." She stood and started to walk out.

"Ms. Reynolds, I'd be happy to take your information now." Sergeant Bashare said.

"About time." Miriam plunked down in the uncomfortable wooden chair. "As I've said, I was walking next to the Le Meridien Resort on the beach at dawn. That's when I heard the power boat. I walked a little closer to the water and saw a man jump off the bow of the boat. There was enough light to see him. The boat backed away from the beach and left quietly. The man walked towards the hotel where I'm staying. He was carrying a large shoulder bag. That's what I saw at 5:10 a.m. this morning. Did you get all that?" She leaned forward trying to see his report.

"May I see your passport?"

She handed it to him and turned to look around the police station. No one was paying any attention to them, except for a man behind a glassed-in office. He kept eyeing her.

"Thank you, Ms. Reynolds," he said handing her passport back. "That will be all."

Miriam Reynolds left the police station feeling slighted. She thought that seeing a man jump off a boat before dawn was important. Who knows where he was from, an illegal maybe?

Chapter 13

DAY ONE

May 28th, 3 p.m.

Halfway to Gillette Harold sprang the question on Abbey. "Hey, you want to sleep in the camper tonight?" He offered a hopeful look, almost boyish grin like they were on a first date. He felt foolish. She didn't respond at first, only glancing at him sideways.

"No thank you. A motel would be better."

"Just kidding. But, maybe down the road, we could work in a couple of nights at a National Park or something. It'd be fun." Her downturned mouth said – no way. "Well then, maybe when the inspiration strikes. So, in the meantime, tell me all the details of the plan. You do have one, right?" he chuckled. Abbey laughed at his haughty tone.

"We're going to have fun, you and I. You're on a quest and I'm on a mission to present you to the American people – pretty much the same thing I think. And yes, I do have a well thought out plan. Travis and I have contacted all the local affiliates from Wyoming to Oregon, and I can tell you that everyone is excited to host your dream of Meet the People. There's a string of six affiliate stations from here to Seattle, which are working on providing a venue in their towns and cities. They're doing their best on such short notice to include: mayors, city council member, state representatives and senators, local businesses, you name it – they're getting them. So you see, Harold Robertson, I do have a plan, and it's unfolding as we speak. Something this exciting hasn't happened since the 60's peace rallies, Equal Rights marches, sit-in's, Woodstock, and lots more. You're the man of the hour and can help unite our country again in a common cause steeped in American Values. Those three governmental officials we met with today will do everything in their power to assist you in your cause."

"Yeah, so long as it serves their agenda." His cynical tone surprised even him. "I'm sorry. Those weren't the words I wanted to say."

"Maybe not. But they needed saying. It was obvious to me by your tone and the look on your face. We'll deal with the baggage as we go, myself included." She smiled. "You have to realize that Travis and I represent a very small affiliate, and have little or no influence with the Network, so we're trying really hard to pull this off, and not be run over by National. You have no idea how hard Travis had to fight to keep our station involved in the Special Report at Mt. Rushmore. I've never seen him so worked up about anything. So, give us the benefit of doubt, because we're going to do this one the right way – not some news hype to gain viewers and national sponsors."

"I know you will, Abbey. Hey, what say you and I find a bar with a live band and kick-up our heels? It'll be fun. And I could use some fun right about now." She gave him an odd glance, but one with mischievous eyes, and curled-up crow's feet at their edges. "I'll take that as a yes." She turned away with her hand stifling a laugh.

They checked into the Marriott in Gillette and asked the young woman minding the front desk where they could find a live band on a Thursday night. She told them of one just south of town, but their rehearsal ended at 5:30 p.m., and they would not be playing tonight. It was customary to sit-in on rehearsal, but they didn't take requests. He thanked her and went to his room to shower and change. Abbey had insisted on separate rooms – something about public perception.

Curt's Saloon was five miles south of town and was unremarkable from the outside, with weathered board and bat siding, and a flashing neon sign on the roof. There were hitching posts by the entrance and the usual barroom smells wafting through the open door. The inside was simple and clean with a heavy wood bar and two dozen or so tables, and a small stage with a dance floor in front of it. There were twenty or so people sitting at the bar and tables, including two families with children. The five band members were talking amongst themselves, one of whom was a petite brunette, dressed in boots, tight jeans, an oversized white shirt with tails hanging out, and a well-worn straw cowgirl hat. The other members wore tee shirts, jeans, and boots. As they sat down in the middle of the room, a waitress dressed in boots and jeans, with a white blouse, came over immediately.

"Hi. What can I get you?"

"Could we see a menu please?" He could tell right away they didn't have any such thing.

"We got pretty much any kind of sandwich you could want, and the cook made beef stew for tonight."

"Perfect," Abbey said. "I'll have stew with whatever beer you have on tap.

"Make that two please." He was feeling a bit uncomfortable as the waitress walked away, seeing that everyone had turned to see who the strangers were. Neither one of them was dressed anything like what was normal in the room. He smiled at the family two tables away at the same time the band began playing, which brought him some relief because everyone turned their attention to the stage. "Abbey," he half yelled. She shushed him and thrust her hand across the table, fishing around for his. He was happy to oblige. They listened to the country western song, enjoying the young woman's voice.

When the song ended, the drummer got up and said something to the lead guitarist, and walked to the bar where he got a glass of beer.

What happened next made him anxious for some reason. The tall well-built drummer approached their table with the look and intention of speaking to them. For the life of him, he couldn't figure out why he was so bloody nervous.

"Howdy. I'm Jake and I couldn't help but notice that you all are from out of town. Wanted to welcome you to our little corner of the state. Hope you enjoy your stay with us."

Jake turned around and headed back for the stage like it was a perfectly normal day – like any other Thursday. Harold's heart was still racing when the waitress brought their food and drinks. He thanked her, but the band drowned-out his words, leaving her with a smile on her lips. He was hungry, so he dove-in, finding the stew to be hearty, flavorful, and with a distinct afterburn, which led to two more beers. People gradually filtered in as 5:30 p.m. approached. He was enjoying the music, a full belly, and a greater degree of comfort with his surroundings. Just before quitting time, the sheriff came in and sat down at the bar, ordering a beer. Jake left the stage and sat on the stool next to the sheriff, patting him on the back, and said something which turned the sheriff's head towards them. That sinking feeling was returning to Harold's stomach, when the sheriff slid off his stool and walked right up to his side of the table and stuck his hand out to shake, to which Harold obliged, watching his puny hand disappear into the sheriff's beefy paw.

"Mr. Robertson, would both of you come with me, please? Mame," he tipped his Stetson.

Harold's heart had flown the coop as this rather large man in uniform led him and Abbey up to the stage. Sheriff Larson stepped up to the mic and introduced them to the

Thursday night crowd.

"I don't know if you got a chance to see all the details of what happened at Mt Rushmore a few days ago, but I want to introduce the man who thwarted the terrorist attack. This is Harold Robertson, an American hero. Some of you might know Abbey Nelson from channel 5 news."

Sheriff Larson slapped him on the back as everyone in the room stood and cheered. It got very loud for a very long time. He was a lot embarrassed. The sheriff walked them back to their table to nods and little waves of thank-you from those seated at every table. They'd just gotten seated when the little girl from the family two tables away came over and hugged them both. She was all of five or six. She ran back to her table, sitting and covering up her shy smile with her hands. Harold was moved deeply by the genuineness of everyone, especially the little girl. So there he sat, embarrassment flashing on his face like a neon sign, meeting his first group of people who were fulfilling his dream.

"I'd just like to thank you both," Jake said quietly into the mic, "for being so brave. I didn't want to say anything when I came over to say hi, 'cause you were eating dinner."

Everyone laughed with Jake, while their eyes fell on Harold and Abbey, thankful eyes, proud eyes, from one American to another. They didn't leave Curt's Saloon until eleven o'clock, and Abbey had to drive him back to town because he'd had his glass filled at least once by everyone there.

Chapter 14

MEDITERRANEAN STAR

May 29th, 7a.m.

Amul Al Atrash lay in his bunk, thinking about his wife and parents, blown into pieces at the hands of the Americans. A still, silent rage swirled in his head, tightening his muscles into rigid knots. He rolled out of his bunk and looked out through the small rectangular window above it at the calm waters of the Mediterranean Sea. It had been three days since he'd seen the news report at his sister-in-law's house, having spent the last twenty-seven hours sitting in his cabin, waiting to leave Cyprus.

He'd have eighteen days to think about a plan and how it would all play out. He was sure of one thing through all the unknowns that lay ahead, retribution was coming soon. Nothing could speak to his unrelenting sorrow, except revenge, fueled by the slow-burning rage that lived within him.

He lay back down and fell into a fitful sleep, one filled with violence, fed by all the acts of terror he'd committed through the years, the worst of which was training his son Amir to be just like him. He'd never forgiven himself for ruining his only son's life, even if it had ended with glory and a secured place in paradise. Al Atrash slept with a war raging within himself, a war he'd lived with all his life, but never once had he looked back and wished to change anything about it – of that he was certain. Soon enough, he'd connect with the cells in America, and gain the means to carry out his mission of revenge. He'd do it for his son and for his family with the knowledge he'd soon be in paradise with his wife, son, and parents.

Chapter 15

DEMONS

May 29th, 3 a.m.

"For the Love of God!" Harold sat straight-up, alert, pensive and drenched in a cold sweat. He was breathing hard and fast and frightened to his very core. The room was dimly lit around the edges of the blackout curtain, making the unfamiliar surroundings seem ominous and foreboding. He swung his legs off the bed and rubbed his face and head. The dream was coming back, and the words he'd yelled were hauntingly close beside him. "For the love of God," he whispered. And then it hit him what they meant. He'd killed another human being and had yet to reconcile his deed. Everything that had raced through his mind, every emotion, especially the fear for his sanity, had erupted in his dream. The crack of the man's neck still echoed in his head, a sickening reminder of his rage. He walked to the bathroom and splashed water on his face, leaving the lights turned off, so as to not see himself in the mirror. "Crazy," he mumbled, returning to bed. "Maybe I should have seen that shrink in the hospital." The words so loud in his head, he thought he'd actually said them. He lay back down to wait for dawn.

He drifted in and out of a fitful sleep, aware yet not, but enough so that he felt his demons circling the bed. He got up at 5 a.m., showered and made the small two cup pot of coffee, glad that the sun would soon be up. There was a tapping on the wall between their rooms – Abbey was in the adjoining room. He tapped the wall in response and then dressed to go knock on her door.

"You're up early," she said opening the door. "Breakfast doesn't start for twenty minutes."

"Yeah, I know." She headed for the bathroom to shower, leaving him sitting on her bed, wondering what he'd hoped to accomplish by invading her room at 5:40 a.m. He turned on the local morning show out of Sheridan and only half-listened to the news from the surrounding counties, and the weather forecast, which was typical for late May; cool, overcast, and highs in the sixties. He was about to turn it off when the host said she had an interesting local item from Gillette. *Probably some hungry coyote prancing down the main street,"* he thought to himself. Abbey was humming in the adjoining dressing area, just around a partition, some song they'd heard the night before. She came around the wall the same time as the picture of them with the sheriff in Curt's Saloon popped onto the screen. His eyeballs retreated into the back of his head and he groaned.

"That's a good picture of you, Harold, before you drank yourself under the table." Abbey laughed. "I guess someone's phone captured the moment."

He shook his eyeballs back into place. "Yeah, good shot." He turned the TV off and proceeded to mumble something about his morning. Mostly it was incoherent, but some of it must have been intelligible because Abbey came and sat next to him, wrapping her arm around his back. He paused his gibberish long enough to look her in the eyes. "Did you hear me through the wall?" She shook her head. "That's good," he mumbled. "Maybe I'd feel better after eating."

"Give me a minute."

He felt like he was rehearsing a dirge, for himself. Those few mumbled words had resurrected his early morning nightmare. He paced around the room like some caged animal, all the

100

while telling himself that he wasn't crazy – well, maybe a little.

"You okay?"

He stopped mid-stride and headed for the door, opening it and waited for her to follow. He was dizzy when they stepped out of the elevator and maybe a little hungover. His first steps were awkward at best. He made it into the breakfast area adjoining the front desk area and sat down at a small two-person table. She brought him a mug of coffee and added a lot of sugar and cream, not the way he liked it, but anything would probably help at the moment. He downed the sugary mix and breathed easier, leaning back in his chair. "Guess it was worse than I thought." She nodded and left to get some breakfast for them.

Later in the morning, with fifty or so miles gone by, Abbey pulled into a rest stop, and parked away from the restrooms – he didn't think it wise if he drove just yet.

"Okay, let's talk about it."

They got out into the cool morning air, walked to a picnic table, and sat down to discuss his delusional behavior. "Maybe I'm more like my mother than I thought. She couldn't survive the loss of her oldest son and had a psychotic break, from which she never fully recovered. When I woke from my nightmare this morning, my sanity was getting sucked out of me at an alarming rate. Why should it bother me so much to take the life of such an evil man? I mean . . . What do I mean?" He stopped to ponder, but what happened next scared him beyond anything he'd experienced in a war zone. He remembered what he'd felt just before blacking out at Mt. Rushmore. He had slipped into unconsciousness, feeling his humanity being drained from him, becoming a walking dead man.

"What Harold? What did you just see? The look on your face was scaring me."

He looked across the table at Abbey's frightened eyes. "I saw myself dead. Alive, but dead. It's what I felt at the amphitheater after I . . ." His mind fell silent and empty of feeling. It woke me at 3 a.m., all the carnage, and the awful sound of his neck snapping. I think I'm losing it, Abbey. My mind slips in and out of this dark void, and I can't seem to reconcile any of it with my logical mind. It scares me because I watched my mother slip into the same dark void. They wanted me to talk with a shrink at the hospital, and I'm thinking now that I should have."

"Do you trust me? I mean, really trust me?"

Abbey's piercing eyes lay hold of him, digging deep into his mind. They were almost hypnotic in their power to connect with him. He nodded.

"Good. Then it's time to get on the road, Harold Robertson. You have a dream to fulfill, a mission to accomplish, and you owe it to the people of our country to do just that. It's your turn to drive. It will help you focus on the mundane. Will you do that for yourself?"

Abbey stood and extended her hand to him, luring him away from his dark hole, and back into the cool gray Wyoming morning.

Chapter 16

RNC

9 a.m.

James Picford entered the Republican National Committees' building in Washington, DC, anxious to dig into the latest news reports, which he never did at home. Interacting with his wife and two daughters was more important than anything the Party or world had to offer. But when he walked through the front door, it was all about the business at hand for the next nine or ten hours. He was a compartmentalized kind of thinker and always stuck to his schedule. Being the elected President of the RNC was an honor, which he'd worked hard for over the last nine years. He excelled at rising to the needs of his Party, especially during the lead-up time to a Presidential election, just a short seventeen months away. He breezed down the hall to the conference room where he would be briefed on all the latest Party news by the department heads. Eight candidates had declared their intentions to run so far, but it was the one who he knew almost nothing about that he was the most interested in. Harold Robertson was a person of interest. A man of the hour. American hero and patriot.

"Where is he now?" James asked from the head of the long solid oak conference table.

"He's in Wyoming. Gillette to be exact," Sally Sturgeon said briskly and clicked a TV remote.

James watched the scene play out in Curt's Saloon with Sheriff Larson introducing Harold and Abbey last night to the cheers of the patrons. The clip was thirty seconds of pandemonium following the announcement, and then there was handshaking, backslapping, and a big hug by a little girl. The final seconds of video were of Harold and Abbey dancing. "That's great. I want this guy to know that we need him running for President. The Party could use someone like him – a patriot. Get me everything on him right away, so I can get up to speed with his history."

"Here's what we have at the moment," Sally thrust a wad of papers into his hands. "He was a four-term Congressman from Illinois and a retired high school history teacher. His wife died last year, of a brain aneurysm if I remember correctly. He lost an older brother in Vietnam, where he also served and was awarded a Purple Heart. That's about it."

"Well, dig deep, and go to his hometown if you have to, but find any skeletons so we know who were dealing with. This guy, far and away, outstrips anyone else running, or anyone in the wings not registered as yet. Let's get to it."

Chapter 17

SHERIDAN, WYOMING

11:56 a.m.

Two things happened on this fine Wyoming morning: he faced his demons with the help of Abbey at a rest stop, and the good people of Sheridan, Wyoming were waiting for them to pull into town, a TV news crew and hundreds of at the ready, smartphones, tablets, and good old-fashioned cameras. He waved to the gathering crowd out front of the TV affiliate station, KYIP. He wondered who thought up these Yippee-ki-yay call letters. Abbey led them into the lobby where much to his surprise, there was a camerawoman and male reporter waiting.

"You guys been waitin' for us?" His smart-ass remark fell flat on the stone floor. Great, now he was embarrassed, and about to be broadcast. "Sorry," he said passing by the woman with the camera on her shoulder on his way to a drinking fountain a few steps behind her.

"Thanks for waiting Sheryl, Bob," Abbey said, greeting them with a hug. "We had to stop for twenty minutes at the rest stop."

His face was wet from splashing water on his face and neck when he rejoined them. "Hi, I'm Harold. Sorry 'bout that inappropriate comment."

"Mr. Robertson, you're fine with whatever you say, after what happened to you." Bob stuck his hand out to shake.

Harold pumped it a couple times, relieved to be off the hook. "So, I'm all yours for as long as the boss here," he pointed to Abbey, "says we have." Abbey made a face at him, which he returned.

The next thing he knew, they were outside after a two-minute interview in the lobby and immersed in what must have been two hundred people or so. It was hard to tell because they were still gathering from all directions. The street was shut down with police cruisers blocking both lanes, light flashing and whooping sirens chiming in at intervals. For a moment, he thought they were going to be part of a parade, and march down to the nearest saloon for a midday dog and a beer. The thought made him laugh aloud – all of which was caught on camera. "I'm a one-man circus," he thought.

"Mr. Robertson, I'm mayor Rawlings. You can call me Shep. We don't want to take up much of your time. We just wanted to thank you for your true American Spirit, and for dodging all those bullets."

The crowd erupted in cheers. Harold's eyes panned the happy mob's infectious cheering faces, drawing him into the midst of it all. Everything he'd thought was wrong with him was now made right – the demons fled the scene. He waved, not knowing how to thank them for lifting him out of his dark hole. He felt a tug on his shirt and looked down to find the same little girl from Curt's Saloon the night before. She had an arm full of wildflowers and sprigs of sage, with a huge smile on her face. He knelt down and hugged her, thanking her for the gift, and then lifted her up for the crowd to see – more applause and whoops. He set her down and she disappeared among the people. Sheriff Larson snuck-up behind them and thrust a bullhorn into his hands, and motioned to the crowd with a sweep of his hand. Harold pulled the trigger and the thing squawked and screeched, quieting the crowd.

"I want to thank you all for this very warm welcome, and for Sheriff Larson's," he reached behind him and tugged on his large uniformed arm, to bring him forward, "kind intervention last night in Gillette. I want you to know that the reason I'm starting this odyssey is that it's always been a dream of mine to meet and greet Americans from all around our great country. Thank you so much." He handed the bullhorn back to the sheriff and turned to Abbey, looking for what was next.

"Let's give Harold a warm Wyoming sendoff for his journey." "Yeeha!" Sheriff Larson bellowed into the bullhorn.

The crowd echoed back twice as loud, making Harold laugh so hard his breath left him. When he recovered he raised both arms in triumph. He couldn't remember the last time he was this taken by a crowd. Abbey grabbed one of his arms and kept it up high with hers. He would never forget this moment.

The sheriff escorted them out of town, lights flashing, siren whooping, and waved as they got on the ramp for Interstate 90. "Unbelievable," he said getting up to speed. "You didn't have anything to do with that, did you?"

"Only the part about informing the TV station when we'd be in town. The rest was all the residents of Sheridan reacting to your coming to town. It was pretty amazing, wasn't it? Oh, and that little girl, her name is Carly Simmons from Casper. I spoke with her parents who were standing behind you and they told me their daughter insisted on driving up to see you. It seems that her Grandpa Ryan had his life saved by your brother, Alex. She wanted to say thank you for him. Long story short, the sheriff in Casper contacted sheriff Larson for a little help finding us. Small world, isn't it?"

The road blurred at the thought of the little girl and her grandfather's story about Alex. Maybe he didn't know his brother as well as he thought he did. He wiped his eyes on his shirt. "Yeah. It is sometimes."

Chapter 18

DAY FOUR

May 31ˢᵗ, 6 p.m.

Harold was outside the Performing Arts Center in Spokane, WA sitting on the steps which led down to the Spokane River, thinking about the past four days. So much had happened both planned and not that he was finding it increasingly difficult to keep track of it all. Travis and Chet had joined them in Helena, MT. Chet would be tagging along in his KIRK van with his technician, Vance until they made it to Los Angeles. He was to document this leg of Harold's odyssey, submitting material for National to work into Special Reports on Monday evenings in June. Chet had to return to Rapid City then, and wouldn't rejoin them until they got to Chicago. National would rely on the local affiliates along the way for coverage. Travis didn't like it much, but those were his instructions from the home office because Chet was needed for the 4ᵗʰ of July celebration at Mr. Rushmore, and a follow-up report on the Terrorists' Attack at Mt. Rushmore – more of a history/documentary on possible Terror Cells in America.

"Hey, you coming in?" Abbey said from behind Harold.

She sat next to him on the steps and slid her arm around his back, laying her head against his arm. "Just getting my bearings and watching the ducks. It's peaceful here." He sighed, long and slow. "How many days do we have before we're done?"

"A hundred and two, I think. But, we'll take days off along the way. Both of us will need to recharge. Harold, we'll be fine, you'll see. We should go in now. You don't want to be late like we were in Missoula."

"Okay," he grunted getting up. They walked around to the front doors, where a military escort accompanied him in and down the aisle to the stage. The sound of twenty-seven hundred people whispering can be quite loud because that's what he heard all the way down the aisle to the steps on the left side of the stage. When he reached the top step, a tall, brunette in a navy blue evening gown came from the side as the main curtain was raised, revealing a full-color guard and drummer entering from the wing. The snap of the drum cleared his head and brought back the memory of his brother's homecoming with a full military escort at O'Hare airport. The middle-aged woman offered her hand to him and led them a few steps to the side of the color guard, which was now center stage. The Air Force National Guardsmen stopped their cadence stepping and the snare drum rolled loudly.

"Ladies and gentlemen, please rise for our National Anthem." The voice pierced the hall.

Harold placed his right hand over his heart and the music began. His heart rose into his throat right away, just like it always did when he sang the National Anthem. The voices in the hall rose steadily until the final note. He was keenly aware of the audience's patriotic mood, with his senses heightened by the bristling energy present. The color guard planted the American Flag and the State of Washington's flag at stage right next to where he was standing.

"Mr. Robertson, let's turn to face the audience." The woman said softly. "My name is Shirley Harwick and I am the mayor of Spokane."

"Pleased to meet you, Shirley," he said with a crackling voice, which he cleared.

"Good evening, ladies and gentlemen. It is my pleasure to introduce you to a true American Patriot. He comes to us from the great state of Illinois, Land of Lincoln, and is no stranger to the ways of government, having served eight years in the United States Congress. He also served four years in the Air Force as a first lieutenant, receiving a Purple Heart during his second tour in Vietnam. He is a man who understands what it takes to survive and succeed, having taught history at the high school level for twenty years."

The audience understood her humor and interrupted her introduction with laughter, himself included. He patted her on the shoulder as a gesture of thanks.

"I won't tell you what you already know, but I'll say it anyway. Harold Robertson is a fearless patriot in the face of death, having saved countless lives one week ago at Mt. Rushmore. He was there to honor our country's newest citizens in their first moments as American citizens. Please join me in welcoming Harold Robertson."

Shirley extended her hand, which he took, pumped once, and drew her into a soft bear hug, which brought cheers amongst the raucous applause. He turned to face the audience and promptly bumped into the microphone feeling immediately embarrassed, but there was no place to hide on stage. He grinned at the few people he could see down in front, because of the bright spotlights. He thumped the mic with his finger. "Well, I'm in trouble now. It works." The audience laughed.

He fumbled in his jacket pocket for his two pages of notes, unfolding them ceremoniously next to the mic. For some reason, they seemed foreign to him at this moment, like he'd never seen them. He frowned, alone on the stage. "You know, I made these notes on the road from Helena today, and I don't think I can read my handwriting." Again, more laughter. He stuffed them back into his pocket and gripped the mic pole with one hand.

"Allow me to share one of the briefest of moments in my whole entire life. The two seconds it took one of our newest citizens to throw herself at her attacker, knock him down and be cut nearly in half by twenty rounds from his automatic weapon. In that one terrifying and horrific moment, from my place across the amphitheater's front row, I witnessed the sum of a person's worth. She gave her life for her spouse, family members, friends, and everyone on that stage, myself included. What I felt was not a tragic loss, but the indelible strength of the human spirit come to bear. I have not witnessed such courage firsthand since I left the war zone in 1972.

While tragic by all standards, I choose to see her as a true patriot to the cause of freedom. She came from a country torn apart by war, had lost countless family members and friends, escaped and found her freedom in America. And even though it only lasted for a couple of heartbeats, she was the freest person I've ever laid eyes on. All that in two seconds, and yet a lifetime spent striving for those two precious seconds of valor, of immeasurable courage, of boundless love for others . . ." His eyes flooded as he fought to keep control.

"Her name was Badra Safar and I shall never forget her." He stopped again and wiped his cheeks with his hand. "You should see me when I'm happy – I look the same." He smiled into the laughter and put away the handkerchief.

The rest of the hour was something of a blur, talking about those nineteen seconds, and what really happened that night, the night America came together in unity of cause and spirit, but most importantly he spoke about his dreams and his plan for America.

His plan. What was his plan? He taught it in the classroom for twenty years, hoping to instill in the young minds, the importance of every American taking a more active role in their country's leadership. Get involved, he'd said. And make government work for the good of the country. It's the only way America can work to fulfill her dream – the Founding Fathers' Dream.

Where once again the middle class could be proud and make a decent living. That is what he really wanted to talk about, what it takes to be a unified country, working together shoulder to shoulder for the good of all as well as yourself. That way, the concept of entitlements would be swept away by everyday Americans fulfilling their dreams through co-operation with a government, which worked for the people, not against them. Apathy is a disease which can destroy nations and civilizations in the still of the night.

When he was done, before the applause began, he walked down the stairs and into the audience, hugging and laughing together with those whom he dreamt about all his life. It took a long time before he reached the front doors and the cool spring air outside. He would remember this night in bits and pieces in the coming days, stopping to revel in what had happened at the Performing Arts Center in Spokane, WA.

Chapter 19

DHS, DC
June 1st, 9:56 a.m.

"Sir, I think you'll want to hear this," Janis Kopeck said, special assistant to the Deputy Secretary of Homeland Security, said. "It's from our Embassy in Cyprus and was passed through the Directorate of Analysis, DA, at the CIA two days ago. They think there's a thirty percent chance that Amul Al Atrash has left Syria for an unknown destination."

"Thank you, Janis," Gene Drake said sitting down at his desk to view the brief video and documents sent from the Embassy to the CIA. He read the police report taken in Limassol, Cyprus on the 28th of May, from a Scottish tourist.

The Capitan of that substation was concerned about the circumstances, so he'd called his friend at the Embassy the same day to pass it along. The Regional Security Office at the Embassy didn't think all that much of it, so they sat on it for a day and a half before passing it along in a weekly report to the State Department, which immediately sent it to the DHS and CIA. But it wasn't until the CIA analysts examined the nighttime satellite imagery from the date in question, that they considered the possibility of Amul Al Atrash risking a venture outside of his country, his motive being that his son had been killed by an American. They were well aware of his parents and wife's death in a bombing mission carried out by the US Navy five months ago.

Since that mission, Amul Al Atrash had been targeted by the Intelligence Community in an effort to locate his residence.

The only connection that had arisen was the intercept by the NSA of cell phone and internet activity from two of his known collaborators and suppliers. It presented a higher probability for his departure from Syria, thereby generating the thirty percent probability that the speedboat departing Beirut for Cyprus at night was carrying Al Atrash. Since it was the only information connected to Al Atrash, it necessitated following through because he was a known terrorist.

Gene knew that Al Atrash was a high profile terrorist, a professional, who'd been active over the past twenty years and never been cornered or even had a good photo taken of him. Amul Al Atrash was a mystery man in the terrorists' networks, even to his associates. The death of his son would affect his judgment to an extent, so Gene took the CIA's assessment seriously, considering Harold Robertson was the person who had killed Amir Atrash. The President had instructed him to watch out for Harold, given his stature with the American people, and that he might wind up to be a Presidential candidate. And that's exactly what Gene had done from day one.

"Janis, get me Harold's cell number." He continued reading the background information on Amul Al Atrash and his son. Both were high up on the watch list, but now, the son's father was number one. Janis knocked and entered, handing him the slip of paper with Harold's number, which he called immediately. It went to voice mail after six rings. Gene redialed and again got voice mail. He left a number, but no message; Harold's phone would identify him as the caller, and that alone meant it was important. Gene filled out the paperwork involved with assigning Harold a Secret Service Agent, even though he wasn't a candidate yet. He could get it approved as a temporary assignment, considering the threat assessment. He sent the order to the Seattle office, knowing that an agent would be dispatched immediately since it was coming directly from the Deputy Secretary's Office. He also sent a personal note to the National Security Advisor to advise the President of the situation, not wanting to wait for the next day's briefing. He tried Harold's number again – getting voice mail. He called Janis into his office.

"I'm going to need all the background we have on Harold Robertson. I want to know how he's going to react, once he learns that he's being actively hunted by a known terrorist, father of the man he took out at Rushmore. Thank you, Janis."

"Right away, sir."

Chapter 20

EPIPHANY

June 1ˢᵗ, 1:12 p.m.

Harold and Abbey were having lunch down on the water at The Catch of the Day, seated outside on the pier overlooking the Puget Sound, with a huge umbrella shading them. What more could a guy want from life? Abbey had ordered the seafood mixed buffet served in small courses with fresh, hot rolls, which had a thick, buttery crust. He'd never had a better lunch, and the Cabernet wine was perfect. They both had dismissed Chet and his technician, Vance, for the afternoon, needing some alone time to sort through things. Abbey was managing him, and he was glad for it because Ruth was always the one to rescue him when his schedule surged past the limits of hours in the day. He'd never learned how to say no to those who made requests of his time.

After lunch, they rode the Ferris wheel next to the restaurant, getting a panoramic view of the Puget Sound. Car ferries connected the larger islands and the Olympic Peninsula, moving the people of the Sound from home to work and back. That's where they were staying, on Bainbridge Island, overlooking the water in a cottage by the sea – a very large cottage by his standards.

Mac Jenkins was an old friend of Travis's, having left Lincoln, NE the same time that Travis had moved to Rapid City, where he worked his way up to station manager. Mac was a successful venture capitalist and loved to take Travis fishing for king salmon ever three or four years out of Aberdeen on Grays Harbor. He and Abbey had the cottage to themselves, as Mac was in LA on business.

On their way up to the top of the one hundred seventy-five tall Ferris wheel the second time, he was envisioning his lifelong dream of meeting America. It had started off at Mt. Rushmore with a traumatic event, which was setting the tone of his journey. He wasn't sure if that was a good thing or not. It certainly wasn't what he'd thought it would be when he was a young freshman in Congress.

"You're far away," Abbey patted his knee.

"Yeah. Thinking about what I'm doing on this trip across America, or at least what I want to do. I liked what happened in Spokane. I just don't know if I can make that happen again. Looking out over the Sound, I don't feel . . .well, I just don't feel capable at the moment." He scooted closer to her and put his arm around her.

"It's only been six days since the attack. I'm sure you're feeling the effects – as am I. Give it some time and try not to think about it too much."

"You're probably right," he sighed.

"Is that your pocket buzzing?"

"Huh, oh yeah. I'm trying to ignore it."

"It might be important. At least look at who it's from."

He slid his legs forward to get in his front pants pocket and the annoying buzzing of his phone. On the screen, he saw the note of four missed calls from the same number.

"Whose number is that?" Abbey frowned.

"I'm trying to remember," he said. She got her phone out and scrolled through her contact list.

"I put Gene's number in my phone at the meeting we had at the TV station. Four calls in less than five minutes – it must be important."

"Right. Gene Drake's number." He tapped the return call symbol next to the number. His eyes scanned the Seattle waterfront. It was a beautiful, clear day and the morning mist was burning off rapidly in the midday sun. They were almost to the bottom and would be let out in a few moments when Gene answered.

"Harold. Glad you called back. Are you able to talk at the moment?"

"Just about to get off the giant Ferris wheel in Seattle," Harold said. "Why? Something come up?"

"Call me back when you're off the ride," Gene said.

The call ended abruptly, making Harold think something important was up. "He hung up on me. Said to call back when we're off the ride." He gave Abbey a quizzical look. Their car was moving into position at the bottom and the pretty young attendant unlocked the door, and they stepped out between the wooden posts. They walked back to the restaurant and were seated a few tables away from where they'd eaten lunch. He ordered them ice tea and called Gene. "Hey, what's up?" He said greeting Gene.

"Harold, I've assigned you a Secret Service agent because there is a threat assessment, which warrants placing you under our protection. You should be receiving a call from our Seattle office very soon."

"Why?" Harold interrupted him. "Why do I need protection? I'm not even running as a candidate . . . yet." His voice trailed off.

"Harold. Listen carefully to what I'm going to tell you. We've had probable cause to believe Amul Al Atrash, father of the man you killed, has left Syria and is en route to an unknown destination. We are erring on the side of caution because of his history. Normally, I would ask you not to say anything, but it seems someone at the Embassy in Cyprus has leaked the information about Al Atrash's movements. I just got a notification after I'd tried to reach you. I'm sorry to be the third wheel on your meet and greet travels, but it's necessary. I hope you'll understand."

"So, does this mean he's . . ." The line went dead. "He hung up on me again." He frowned.

"What? Harold, tell me what he said."

"He said the father of the man I killed has left Syria, but they don't know to where. Seems we're getting a Secret Service escort." The waitress delivered their ice tea and asked if there would be anything else. Harold's head was swirling at the moment, so he asked her to come back in a few minutes.

"Was Gene concerned that this terrorist will try to enter the US?" Abbey asked anxiously. "I mean, how could he after what's happened. They know what he looks like, right?"

He shrugged his shoulders. "I don't know. You would think they have a photo or at least a sketch." His phone vibrated on the table, showing an unknown caller. "Hello?"

"Harold Robertson?" The deep voice said.

"Yes. Who's this?"

"Sir, my name is Jerry Isaack, and I work for the Seattle division of the Department of Homeland Security. I am a Secret Service agent, and I've been assigned to protect you. In order for you to confirm this call, I'll need you to call our office after I hang up. You will be directed to our office to confirm the authenticity of this order. I'll meet you at that time. Please do this immediately following this conversation."

The line went dead and a number to call appeared on his screen. He touched the call icon and was connected with the DHS's office. They gave him their address and asked him to come as soon as possible. He passed the phone to Abbey.

"Here's where we're going." The address of the DHS in Seattle was displayed on the screen. "Said he wants me to come right over." He shrugged his shoulders.

He wasn't particularly looking forward to having a Secret Service agent monitoring his life, but if the threat was real, then he'd welcome the security of a well-trained agent. He called for a cab to pick them up in twenty minutes. Their waitress returned and handed him a note from the manager.

Many thanks for your patriotism and acts of valor. Come back anytime for a free dinner. Sorry I didn't recognize you before you paid for lunch today.
Jim Collier, Owner/Manager

"Thank you," he tried to read her nametag, which was obscured by a fuzzy critter hanging over it. She moved it to one side.

"Sherry," he smiled. "Would you thank him for us please?" She nodded and trotted off to another table on this busy Monday lunch hour. They enjoyed the complimentary wine Sherry brought back and the view, before going to collect their very own personal Secret Service agent. He left a note of thanks for the manager and Sherry.

After collecting Jerry, and riding with him to the Mariners game, they entered the stadium twenty minutes late. They waited just inside the gate as their escort was radioed to come walk them to their seats. The young man told them that the announcer would work them in sometime during the third inning, and not to worry about being a little late. He was supposed to have been introduced before the game, but things didn't work out that way.

Their seats were ten rows up from the Mariners' dugout

and Jerry stationed himself in the aisle two rows down from them. At the bottom of the 3rd inning after a double play by the Yankees as the players were jogging back to their dugouts, his introduction hit the big screen and loudspeaker.

"Ladies and gentlemen, if you'll direct your attention to the big screen, I am proud to introduce to you a true American hero, Mr. Harold Robertson, who along with Park Service Ranger, John McFadden, put a stop to the terrorists' attack at Mt. Rushmore on Memorial Day. Ranger McFadden was killed serving his country, and Harold Robertson is here with us today, along with Abbey Nelson, the journalist who was there documenting the naturalization ceremony. They're currently touring the country together. Please join me in welcoming them to Seattle."

Harold and Abbey stood and waved to the crowd, seeing that their image filled the big screen. America the Beautiful began to play over the loudspeaker system, and people began to cheer and sing, the half-full stadium coming to life with the realization of what was going on and who Harold Robertson was. The people behind him were slapping him on the back, while those in front of him were wanting to shake his hand, all while the singing got louder as everyone joined in. He waved in gratitude, feeling honored, and a lot embarrassed. The same young man who escorted them in handed him a microphone to say a few words. America the Beautiful finished after one verse and the stadium became silent. Abbey tapped him on the shoulder and whispered in his ear that he should thank them – and it made a fine picture on the big screen. There was some laughter and cheering, and then silence.

"Ah," he cleared his throat. "I want to thank you for your warm welcome. Sorry, we were late, we got held up at the

Secret Service office." He shrugged his shoulders. "Anyway, thank you. I know this terrorist attack has been difficult for us all to understand. It certainly has been for me. Abbey Nelson and I are traveling our great nation to help unify us and give us strength, by talking about the attack, and realizing that it can never tear apart the American Spirit which lives within us all. We are one nation under God and therein lies our strength. Thank you." He waved one last time and handed the mic back to the same young man The announcer said something else he didn't catch, and then the next inning began three minutes later.

It never occurred to him, until they were leaving during the top of the eighth inning, that he should have told them about why he had a Secret Service agent assigned to him. And that's when it hit him. He should enlist the American people to help locate the terrorist Amul Al Atrash because he was most assuredly coming to American to avenge his son's death by the hands of this man called Harold Robertson, and no one in the US Intelligence Community knew where or when. He thought this unifying task would be something to help people feel useful and not the victim of a crime, give them a reason to rally around the flag. Strength in numbers, when there is a common cause, is unbeatable, unstoppable, and could lift a nation's people out of anger and heartbreak and into victory on a grand scale. His epiphany, if you could call it that, was that the human spirit was indomitable.

Chapter 21

GULF OF MEXICO

June 16th, 3:38 a.m.

Al Atrash slipped over the port side near the stern, throwing his gear bag ahead of him. He rappelled down the side of the Mediterranean Star, stopping ten feet above the water, and pushed off as hard as he could, cutting the rope while gripping the other end of the same rope looped through a carabiner to pull it off the railing and into the water with him. He was a mile offshore and the ship was moving slowly as it approached the inlet to the Port of Houston. Going this slow, he wouldn't be drawn back into the stern of the ship. He inflated his life vest, and he untangled himself from the long rope, making sure that it all sunk into the choppy water. He unzipped the flap on his vest pocket and turned on the short-range two-way radio.

"Pickup," he said loudly, repeating it twice more. Then he turned it off and clutching his gear bag, he waited for his contact to arrive in a small inflatable boat. It would be dawn in an hour, after which the cover of darkness would fade quickly. He checked his watch – 4:06 a.m. The Gulf waters weren't cold, but seventy-two-degree water began to feel uncomfortably cool after twenty minutes of bobbing. He turned on his radio again and repeated: "Pickup," twice more.

"Five," his radio squawked with static.

His contact found him ten minutes later. He hauled himself into the eight-foot inflatable with a small electric trolling motor. He greeted Gary quietly and began to paddle with him, helping the silent electric motor get them back to shore before daylight exposed them. They used navigation buoy lights to guide them back to shore and the deserted beach where Gary's truck was parked. Twenty minutes later they were hauling ashore and dragging the inflatable a hundred feet to the truck. Gary strapped it in after covering it with a tarp and opened the stopcock to deflate it on the way to his house close to downtown Houston.

Gary handed Al Atrash a wallet with his new identity: a temporary Texas driver's license with no picture, Social Security card, library card, Bank of Houston VISA card, and sixty-three dollars in cash. He was now an American citizen from Texas. They drove through the little town of High Island on the Bolivar Peninsula and headed towards Interstate 10. No one else was on the county road and no one had seen them come ashore. Al Atrash was on US soil and unknown to the authorities. He was pleased that all was going as planned.

Chapter 22

DHS – DC

June 16th, 3 p.m.

E xcuse me, sir," Janis said knocking and entering. "This just came in."

She handed Gene a Houston Port Authority report dated 6/16/15, 10 a.m. "Thank you, Janis. Fax these to the number on the cover sheet." He handed her two folders marked Confidential. He scanned through the report she'd given him. It was taken from the First Mate, Nakos, onboard the Mediterranean Star, just in from Cyprus. His eyes flashed on the missing passenger reported by Christopher Nakos. The note said that only five of the six passengers got off the ship when they arrived in port and that he checked the man's cabin, finding it empty. Gene leaned back in his chair and weighed the possibilities. The timeframe was about right. It fit in with the report passed along by the Cyprus Embassy of a man wading ashore from a small boat. If it really was Amul Al Atrash who was the missing passenger from the Mediterranean Star, then he'd entered America and had disappeared.

"Janis," he said into the intercom. "Get me the Port Security Division of USCG in Houston, and then get me Bill Regis at the Houston office." He needed answers from the Capitan of the Mediterranean Star as to why he'd not said anything about the missing passenger. He would have both the Port Security Specialist of the Coast Guard and his Houston agent bring Capt. Raymos in for questioning and hopefully get some clarity one way or the other. He needed a quick response, otherwise, Al Atrash would vanish into America, and he would be left holding the bag.

Chapter 23

LOS ANGELES

June 16th, 1 p.m.

In the grand scheme of things, Harold had never considered himself to be a heroic man, merely an individual who was doing his job. He'd felt the same way when he was in the Air Force. Now his brother Alex, that was a different story. He was a hero in every sense of the word.

All the way down the Oregon and California coasts, he met with groups small and large and talked about his ideas for America in the coming years – his Plan. And in town after town, his image as an American hero had grown, so much so, that when he arrived in San Francisco five days ago, he was ambushed by hundreds of reporters, news crews, policemen, firemen, and thousands of everyday Americans, all calling him the "H" word.

It's not that he didn't appreciate the genuine words of thanks, but the constant attention was beginning to wear on him and make him uncomfortable. And now he was in the sprawling metropolis of LA about to encounter, not a sporting event where he waved and said ten or so words, but a stadium filled to capacity for a special event held in part in his honor. It was to be broadcast nationwide, and worldwide for that matter.

He was sweating as he stepped out of the stretch limo at the Rose Bowl in Pasadena, home of the UCLA Bruins, numerous Super Bowls and FIFA Soccer World Cups, stadium for the 1932 Olympic Games, not to mention the

Rose Bowl game played every year. What was he going to say that hadn't been said more than ten times already in the past two weeks? His meet and greet America was wearing him out. Abbey slipped his arm around his back and pulled him into a sidewinder hug.

"I know you're tired," Abbey said, "but let's try to have some fun. Everything is planned. Your speech will be on the teleprompter. The music will be stirring. And the people, well, they're going to be inspiring. Ninety-five thousand people in one place. It's gonna get loud."

"Loud is good," he smiled. Abbey slid her hand into his and squeezed, her gentle brown eyes reassuring him.

"I'm not sure if anyone ever told you that this is a benefit for the victims' families of the attack, and relief funds for refugee camps, and is hosted by three of the top international relief fund organizations, two Grammy pop stars, and several big-name movie stars."

Abbey's coy smile was telling him she was withholding something about the event. "Uh, huh. And where do I fit in, between the elephants and camels?" Abbey laughed at him as they entered through the main gate with Jerry. They were met by a guy wearing a headset and dressed in a tight-fitting black tracksuit. Jerry looked a bit anxious.

"Hi. I'm Charles. I'll be taking you to your seats."

There was nothing which could hold a candle to the feeling in his gut as they emerged onto the field, and he was met by the Governor of California and a Marine Color Guard. He followed behind the Marines, ascending the three steps to the large platform, where he stood while the National Anthem was sung by a Marine Tenor. He was suddenly at ease hearing the words which spoke of the heart and soul of the making of America. He stood beside Janet Sharp, the lovely Governor of California, as she introduced him to waves of applause and cheers, which can only be achieved in a sports stadium. She took his hand and raised it high as she could reach and he was instantly embarrassed from head to toe. *Am I glowing red in the bright lights?* he thought. He wasn't any different than any other man, other than he'd been crazy enough to tackle a terrorist and wrench his neck for all the world to see.

"They love you Harold," Janet yelled over the crowd. "Why don't you take that plan of yours and run for office. America needs someone like you."

Janet pumped his hand several times and abandoned him at the microphone. In all the boisterous cheering, he'd forgotten what he wanted to say, staring blankly at the slip of paper with notes he pulled from his pocket, totally ignoring the teleprompter in front of him. As the stadium fell silent, he felt himself sinking into the stage floor, disappearing, hiding, and otherwise wishing he were the invisible man. He cleared his throat, forgetting to turn his head away from the mic. It made a funny sound which echoed through the stadium, eliciting laughter from many. He shrugged his shoulders and laughed at himself, feeling the heat rise into his face. But he wasn't embarrassed, on the contrary, he was energized by the crowds' enthusiasm for why they were all here.

"Thank you all for being here to support the families of the victims of the terrorists' attack and the hundreds of thousands of refugees scattered around the world, who seek better lives. Through your compassion and generosity, and of all the millions of viewers throughout the free world, you are conquering heroes in humanity's war on injustice, and senseless terror that some chose to inflict on their fellow man. Here at home, America suffered a great loss at Mt. Rushmore, because the loss of any of its citizens to senseless acts of terror, is a loss to every person in our world who wishes to live free – free of oppression and free to think and live how they chose. In my travels to meet the good people of our nation, I've spoken about what's next for America. What do we want as a nation? I am proud of what I have heard in response from people like you all. Prayers of compassion and strength from the diversity of our heartland and heartfelt words coming from our children that ask us why. Why must we hate?"

Harold pulled his handkerchief from his back pocket and wiped his eyes. *So many emotions* he thought. He looked out over the stillness of the stadium, so thick with caring and compassion. He pocketed his hankie.

"When we were in Sheridan, Wyoming, a little girl from Casper came up and handed me a bunch of wildflowers and hugged me. She said that they were from her grandfather, who never got the chance to thank the person who saved his life in Vietnam because the soldier died that day. That little girl, Carly Simmons, will always carry with her the memory of her grandfather's grateful heart and pass it along to everyone she meets. We are the people of America and these are our stories.

I have a long way to go to complete my journey across America, just as American has a long road ahead. I want to thank you for your generous support by being here today to give back to those in need. It's who we are as Americans. God Bless you all."

He stepped back from the mic and waved, looking at his speech still scrolling on the teleprompter. He hadn't read one word from it. As he turned to leave before the first act was introduced, Janet caught him by the arm and turned him back around. She stepped up to the mic and quieted the crowd. *Now what?* he wondered.

"Harold Robertson is a quiet man, so I will ask this for

him. Is this not a man who possesses all the qualities we need in a leader? Does he not present himself in an honest and forthright manner? Could you trust your sons and daughters lives to his care? Would you be proud to call him the leader of the free world? Does anyone here want him to run for the Presidency? I mean, President Harold Robertson. Doesn't that just sound right?"

Harold was embarrassed beyond limits. He never thought of himself as qualified to run the country. The cheers and applause were deafening. Janet raised his arm again and then slid her arm around his back. They left the stage and walked across the field, all the while, the applause never diminishing. They both turned and waved before they stepped into the tunnel to leave. He was breathless.

"Harold, when your destiny kicks you in the butt, you can't ignore it," Janet said passionately.

He stopped dead in his tracks, wondering what on earth this woman knew that he didn't. He stared into her strong yet caring eyes as if he'd find an answer there.

"Abbey said you were thinking about it," Janet said, "and I've listened to your messages at every whistle stop from here back to Wyoming. Hell, Harold, you've got a plan. That's more than any of the other candidates have so far. Throw your hat in the ring – see what happens." Janet smiled.

"You're something, you know that? You should run, not me."

"Horse pucky!"

Janet turned and continued down the tunnel. He fell in behind her, not remembering that Abbey was still sitting in her seat, and he couldn't get to her this way. He turned around, bumping into his shadow, Jerry, and together they emerged back on the field. Walking back to his seat, a few people leaned over the railing to shake his hand as he passed by, to which he obliged, mostly by brushing fingertips as he passed. Everyone else was focused on the stage where a band was about to begin playing. He sat down next to Abbey and did his best to enjoy the next hour of loud music before they had to leave for San Diego to visit his daughter Gracie. He was looking forward to seeing her and his granddaughter.

FAMILY

June 25th, 6 a.m.

Gracie and her husband Ted lived in Pacific Beach in a little one-story bungalow, one block from the ocean. He had insisted that they stay at the house, even though it was already stuffed with his daughter's family. He and Abbey slept in the living room on the sofa with a queen size fold out bed, and Jerry, well, he got to camp out on the patio on a chaise lounge, which he said was exceedingly comfortable. Today was their second day there and Harold loved it that he could rise at 5:45 a.m., put on coffee, and take a cup to the beach to enjoy. It just didn't get any better. Jerry, of course, tagged along, on what he said was the easiest duty he'd had in several years. What with, home cooked meals, the company of a family of three, the fresh ocean air, and sunsets like he'd never seen, Jerry said he felt like he was on a paid vacation. Harold was enjoying his company in the mornings, talking about family, politics, the state of the world, most anything was fair game, and Harold was always game. Jerry was young looking for his forty years, married, smart as a whip, and something of a mountain of a man at 6'5" and 265lbs. Today, they took their coffee on the patio and then headed out for a walk on the beach to collect whatever seashells they could find. Harold liked the sand dollars, but they were usually broken. It was low tide this morning, so there would be more available on the flat stretch of Pacific Beach.

"So, tell me what you thought of the Governor's little announcement at the Rose Bowl. You never said a word about it in the nine days since." Harold bent low for a piece of frosted green glass. It could have been a broken 50's or 60's Coke bottle, but that was wishful thinking. He handed a piece to Jerry who was being slow to answer. Harold looked away from Jerry's cryptic gaze, out towards a few surfers a hundred yards out riding the smallish breakers.

"I think she said it for a good reason, Mr. Robertson. I don't know her at all, but I'd have to say she likes you as a person. It showed in her eyes and quick glances."

Harold knew he was skirting around the subject, what he always did until the person dug deeper. Harold caught his eye again. "You're not saying what's on your mind Jerry, but I understand. It's the way you're trained; to be observant of your surrounding while working. But I don't see any anybody else close to us at the moment, so tell me what you really think. I value your opinion." He gave him a slight nod with a raised eyebrow as a challenge.

"Just between you and me. I totally agree with the Governor. You are the right man for the job from what I can see. In my eleven years in the Service, I've not met anyone as knowledgeable as you. That includes a handful of Senators, Cabinet members, Congressmen, and two Governors campaigning for the Presidency. The kids you taught in high school probably couldn't appreciate your depth of understanding of what it means to be an American. And hey, you're a Vet, a hero, and the worst gin player I've ever met." Jerry grinned.

"Funny. Chess is more up my alley if you care to try your hand." He bent down to uncover a whole sand dollar. "Well, whaddayaknow. One that's not busted." He showed it to Jerry and then slipped it into the pocket of his sweatpants –

it was cool in the early mornings. "Since I'm on a roll, tell me about your family. We're going to be a threesome for a while I take it, so we should get to know each other." He gave Jerry a hopeful smile.

"Okay, but there's one rule I won't break no matter what. When I'm working and we're in a public setting, I will ignore you, because I'll be focused on the surroundings. If I'm distracted by conversation, then I'll miss something important. You'll just have to accept it. Oh, and by the way, I'm working right now, but since there's no one else around, I'll continue talking with you. Agreed?"

"Yes. I understand, and I wouldn't have it any other way. So, back to that question."

"I was born in Thompson Falls, MT and lived there until I was ten. My father was the town cop until he heard about a detective job in Tacoma, WA. He got the job and we moved the same week. Mom wasn't very happy about it either. She was a rancher's daughter outside of Cody, WY and didn't want anything to do with the big city. It didn't end well. They divorced when I was a freshman in high school. Dad never got over it and didn't remarry. We were pretty close during those years, but it didn't last. I bummed around for a couple of years before I met someone in Vancouver, BC. We married the next year while I was studying Criminal Justice in college. Somehow I got a job with the FBI after I graduated. I think my dad had something to do with it, because he was in a poker club in Tacoma, and one of the regulars was an FBI old timer from the 70's. Three years later I applied to the Secret Service, and here I am. Lacey and I never had children, and when I'm away working, she travels. I don't really know how our arrangement is going to go, with you and Abbey on the road for over four months. I'm sure we'll pick-up another agent halfway through. No one has said anything about it yet."

"Well, while we are palling around together, and when you're not working, consider yourself as family." A group of joggers entered the shoreline from behind them, taking Jerry's attention away. Harold stopped to pick up another shell, taking his time until the joggers passed.

"You probably just processed a dozen or so things about those folks. Tell me if I'm off base here: you scanned where they left the boardwalk, were dropped off by vehicle, checked their loose clothing for hidden arms, profiled their faces and ethnic origins for probable cause, and checked to see if they really were regular joggers by the way they carried themselves." He stopped because Jerry was laughing.

"I guess you found that amusing?" Harold said, while Jerry deadpanned him with his best Secret Service look. "Okay, I deserve that." Jerry nodded and suppressed a grin, patting his head like a good dog.

"Thanks for the laugh though," Jerry said.

"Uh huh. Anytime," Harold chuckled. "We should head back now, it's past 7 a.m."

They arrived to the smell of onions, spuds, and bacon cooking. Abbey and Ted were the cooks, while Gracie was breastfeeding six-month-old Mattie on the now folded-up sofa bed. He went straight to the kitchen to help. He and Jerry were elbow to elbow by the toaster, burning, buttering, and generally getting in the way in the narrow kitchen.

"Daddy. Got a job for you," Gracie called out.

He side-slipped past everyone and followed his daughter into the nursery. "Diaper duty?" He whined but really didn't mind at all. Gracie supervised while they chatted about the day. They were going to the San Diego Zoo in Balboa Park, a sprawling urban cultural park of twelve hundred acres. When he was done cleaning up Mattie and had botched several attempts at applying the cloth diaper, all to Gracie and Mattie's amusement, she sprung the question on him, with no notice.

"Do you miss Mom?"

The words were like a pall spread over the dead feeling in his heart, with a spike through the center of his being. Their eyes met in shared pain and loss of someone so dear to their hearts. "Terribly, Gracie." He kept a hand on Mattie's legs to be sure she didn't roll over close to the edge of the changing table, and put his arm around his daughter, pulling her in close. "I'll always miss her. She's never far from my thoughts." Gracie was wiping her eyes with a tissue.

"I like Abbey a lot. And I can see that you do. I wanted to say . . . I think it's a good thing you have each other. She told me about how she knew you when she was ten. That's so precious." Gracie wiped her eyes again. "I got really depressed for a while. Ted was so worried about me, but Mattie helped pull me out of it."

He had to take his arm back because it was hurting his shoulder. "Sorry. Still healing here." The hurt in his daughter's eyes deepened, perhaps because she'd almost lost both of her parents. "Honey, you're not going to lose me."

"Ted had to pull me away from the TV newscast because I cried so hard," Gracie said. "I understand why you did that, but it scared me so much."

"I'm sorry. I promise I won't do anything so crazy again." Harold was feeling guilty because he'd not called her from the hospital, he'd only sent a text saying he was okay.

When they returned to the living room, Ted sat next to his wife and child, holding them in the safety of his arms. It was painful for Harold to see his actions had hurt his daughter so deeply. Rushmore seemed so long ago now. He'd put it out of his mind, never wanting to revisit those images again, which smelled of death and the acrid odor of gunpowder.

Harold stepped closer to the sliding glass door and looked out at the patio area, remembering that he'd only talked with his daughter once or twice about her mother's death. It was too painful at the time and realized he'd done the same thing again after the attack. He turned to look at Gracie and her family on the sofa, so young and with their whole life ahead of them. He vowed to call her more often from now on, to try and be a better father, one who communicated. His eyes began to flood with emotions.

"Hey," Jerry said interrupting. "Breakfast is getting cold."

They were all rubbing shoulders after breakfast, getting ready for a day at the Zoo. Harold was looking forward to spending time with his daughter and her family. Besides, he'd never been to a zoo this big before.

He and Abbey rode in Jerry's black sedan, at his request. Ted had purchased tickets the previous week for a Discovery Cart Tour for the six of them to get their day started. They'd get a sixty-minute overview of most of the exhibits, and then they could choose their walking routes at their leisure. It was on the Tiger Trail that Gracie sprung the question.

"Are you really going to run for President, Daddy?"

They were in the middle of a trail through the jungle and winding their way down a log walkway with large ropes for railings, to get to the viewing windows of the enclosure. He paused, holding up their group.

"You've been listening to your Governor, haven't you? You know, she sprung that on me at the Rose Bowl fundraiser and threw it out to the whole world. Do you think she thought for one moment to ask me about it beforehand? No?"

"That's who she is Daddy," Gracie smiled.

"Guess I found that out." He put his arm around her shoulder and pulled her close. "After a while though, with seven seconds of surreal images parading in front of my eyes, I came to the conclusion that I must have decided a long time ago, in college actually, that I wanted to someday give it a shot. The difference between dreams and reality though can be a daunting challenge for the mind to undertake. So, yes, I have thought about it, but I don't feel qualified enough to consider myself running. What happened to me in front of all those people though, said otherwise; in that, if someone says they need you to do something that you've studied your whole life for, then you should take notice, and heed the calling. You know, a couple of days ago, I got a text from the President of the RNC in DC saying the very same thing. Maybe the Governor talked with him? Oh, and just as a side note, if I do run, you three can kiss your private life goodbye. The media will descend on your cottage and hound you relentlessly. I say this out of experience. Just ask Abbey. It's her job after all."

"Oh, Daddy. It's not that bad."

"One good thing about it," Harold smiled, "Ted, your private practice as a lawyer will get free advertising on air and in print." Harold turned around and continued down the log walkway, through the lush jungle, to visit with one of the top predators of the world, not unlike the media.

Chapter 25

MILBY STREET

July 3rd, 8 a.m.

Amul Al Atrash, now William Harlow, had spent the past eighteen days at 14383 Milby St. in Houston, practicing his English. The shanty two-story next to Jake's Auto Repair in which he'd been hiding out was the best that Gary Everett could afford on his meager wage stocking shelves at a large retail superstore. It did have a hot water heater and Amul used it to the fullest. Hot showers in his Damascus hideout didn't exist. He'd just stepped out and was drying himself when he heard a child's voice calling out from downstairs. A chill ran through him. In his two and a half weeks in America, he'd never left the house and spoken with anyone except Gary.

"Anybody home?" the child called out. "Hello? My dog ran into your yard."

Al Atrash finished drying and pulled on his pants, not moving a step on the creaky old floors. He heard the door slam shut and exhaled the breath he'd been holding while listening intently. He mumbled in Arabic about the rude child entering his home. He silently reminded himself to not do that again – speak only American. He wiped the mirror with his towel and didn't like what he saw. Gary had cut his hair short, cut off his beard, all of which left him feeling naked. He lathered his face with something called Gillette Foamy and removed the cheap plastic razor from the medicine cabinet. He still had nicks healing from the past two weeks and today would probably be no different. The razor tugged on his dense, black whiskers, making him want to curse again. He didn't recognize himself in the mirror. His broad jawline and deep-set eyes didn't belong to him without a full beard and long black hair. He finished shaving and pulled on a white tank top, and descended the noisy stairs to fix American coffee – which he detested – and toast scrambled eggs and bacon. Gary had insisted he learn to eat American food. He was hungry, so what did it matter. Gary also told him that prayers were only to be said in absolute privacy, with no chance of anyone seeing him. Eventually, he'd have to learn to endure the loss, if he ever hoped to succeed on his mission. These few weeks were a warmup for when he left, and if he didn't get it right here, he'd be captured in short order. He sat down to eat his American breakfast at the kitchen table next to the back door.

"Hello?" the child's voice said. "Anybody home?"

The boy was at the back door, knocking, and disturbing his cloistered world.

"Have you seen my dog? He was in your yard yesterday."

Al Atrash sat frozen, mouth half full. He chewed quickly and swallowed hastily, choking and coughing as quietly as possible. His situation was intolerable. What he wanted to do was get on the road to hunt down this American, Harold Robertson. Gary told him to have patience and wait for his time of retribution. Gary brought him newspapers to read about Harold Robertson and how he was well loved by the American people. It would be a righteous kill, one that would leave a lasting impression on America. The boy went away. He finished eating, washed his dishes, and cleaned the kitchen counters after he was done. He turned on Gary's TV and selected the cable news program, educating himself about the society he would soon enter. Al Atrash knew that Gary was right to hold him back from rushing into his mission.

Everything that he was learning would help him meld into the people and their everyday lives, thus allowing him free movement and anonymity. His victim would never know he was being hunted.

Gary returned early from work, giving Al Atrash a few extra hours to practice his English in conversations with Gary. He liked this American of Saudi descent, who had broken away from his upbringing to re-engage with the traditions of Islam but had not radicalized until he was twenty. Gary was thirty-six now and had made many connections, each carefully nurtured and protected, always keeping his profile low, and definitely not posting his true beliefs on the internet, or contacting those sites he knew were monitored by the US government. His cell phones were untraceable, having bought only disposables from big box stores, and then discarded them at regular intervals. Amul listened with great interest to Gary, learning about the man and how he'd kept under the radar through the years.

Gary told Amul that he was basically invisible, but was terribly lonely, so having Amul in his home was most pleasurable. Gary had brokered a number of small cells, training them personally, but always divorcing himself from them when they'd left to live in other cities across America. Gary never wanted to play the martyr, preferring to teach and be an important contact to brothers like Al Atrash, although he'd never had any contact with Amul before his arrival last month. And that's the way it had to be, in order to remain viable and anonymous. A knock on the front door interrupted their conversation and sent Amul upstairs to listen.

"Hi, Jake. What's up?" Gary greeted the owner of the Auto Repair shop next door. "No, I haven't seen his dog in a while. Okay, I will."

Amul came back down after Gary had said it was all clear. "That boy came earlier today – twice he knocked." Amul said, "he even opened the door to call out if anyone was home." Gary looked worried and got up to open and close the front door several times, and once it failed to latch properly. He got his toolkit and repositioned the strike plate to fix the problem.

They continued their conversation in the kitchen, while Gary made bean burritos for dinner. Amul found the smell repulsive and the taste not much better. Gary used a sauce with hot peppers, which was fiery and much hotter than the Aleppo pepper Al Atrash was used to.

That evening they spoke of family and of Gary's Saudi born mother who had died shortly after he'd left home. It was a good evening, especially since the TV news had reported Harold was on his way to Texas in the next week. Perhaps his prey would come to him, making Amul's job easier.

Chapter 26

A BOISE 4ᵗʰ
July 4ᵗʰ, 3 p.m.

Harold and Abbey were sitting on Patty Newhouse's front porch swing sipping lemonade, in Boise, ID. Patty was the organizer of the Liberty Day Parade, a twenty-year tradition, which always drew thirty thousand cheering celebrants. Patty had made room for him to ride in the bed of a 1948 Ford flatbed, behind the Marshall's car, and just in front of the Boise Highlanders with twelve pipers. The sound of bagpipes always sent chills down his spine. He rode with Abbey, while Jerry walked to one side in the ninety-degree heat. Harold kept tossing him bottles of water on the hour-long walk.

Back at Patty's, Jerry was sitting next to the AC vent cooling himself down. It was a good day to put your feet up and relax.

"Hey Harold, you gotta hear this," Jerry yelled from the living room.

He went inside to see what on earth was so important to disturb his peace and quiet. Jerry was watching a news show where one of the Presidential candidates being interviewed.

"Just wait, they'll replay it."

"Replay what?" he asked. And then he heard the words dribble from the candidate's mouth. . . an unbelievable statement coming from someone running for the Presidency. The man was insulting a United States Senator, who was a decorated veteran. His blood boiled – shear blind anger. "What an ass," he growled.

"Yeah. Don't think he'll get very far," Jerry said.

"You know, I could have lived the rest of my life without hearing something like that, and been much happier." Harold turned and walked away to cool down. "I hope the press crucifies him for that," he yelled from the kitchen.

"What's all the ruckus down here?" Patty said walking in.

"Some jerk running for office insults a US Senator who's a war Vet," Harold said pointing towards the TV in the living room. "Maybe they'll play it again." Patty walked into the living room to listen with Jerry. Harold heard an "oh my God" drift into the kitchen. "Yeah, you got that right." He huffed, still worked up about it.

He rejoined Abbey on the front porch swing. Maybe the heat would drive the words from his head. He sat quietly for a few minutes next to Abbey with the words of Governor Janet Sharp echoing in his thoughts: "When your destiny kicks you in the butt, you can't ignore it." "How right you are," he muttered.

"How right who was?" Abbey asked.

"Didn't realize I said that aloud." He repeated it for her. "Governor Janet's word to the wise, which she said to me in the Rose Bowl tunnels."

"I heard you yelling inside," Abbey said.

He repeated that too, although, he had cooled down quite a bit. "I really don't understand what would make a man seeking public office say something so un-American. If he'd said that in colonial times, there would have been a duel the next morning. I mean, really." Harold caught himself before he launched into a long, angry diatribe, which Abbey certainly didn't need to hear.

"Well, I guess you'll just have to do something about it, won't you?" Abbey smiled her all-knowing smile.

He stared blankly for a moment, his head wrapping itself around her challenge. Gracie's voice echoed in his thoughts.

Was he going to run for the Presidency? If he needed provocation, the arrogant words of a candidate would probably do just fine. But that wasn't good enough. It had to be for his reasons. Janet's statement was next in line: "Hell Harold, you've got a plan. That's more than any of the other candidates have so far." Abbey slid her hand into his.

"Everything you've worked for in your life has led you to this moment," she said. "Believe in yourself and take the next step. I'll be right beside you and so will all the people you've met and will meet on your journey across America."

Her words were a strong motivation, much more than any would-be candidate who'd opened his mouth before engaging his brain. He rubbed his chin thoughtfully, smiling at the ridiculous look he probably had on his face. But, what did he have to lose for trying?

Chapter 27

IT'S OFFICIAL
July 5ᵗʰ,7 a.m.

Harold sat up in bed rubbing the sleep from his eyes with vague recollections of a dream about a crowd of thousands in a big city – something about a death in the family. He scanned the motel room. Where were they? Flagstaff, AZ, and on their way to the Grand Canyon for the day. He threw back the covers and went to shower.

Three hours later, Harold and Abbey were standing at Yavapai Point, overlooking the South Rim of the Grand Canyon. It was warm already with the summer sun beating down on them and casting deep shadows in the canyon. This was a good place to be, a place where time could stand still, and the world could be forgotten in all the grandeur on display. Harold was feeling poetic at the moment. Who was he to think that what he did in the world could possibly make a difference? It all paled by comparison with what was here. Abbey slid her arm around his waist.

"You out there somewhere?"

He nodded. "Seeing this makes me think big. What is our place in life? And why do make ourselves out to be so important?" She pulled him in tight and pressed her head against his shoulder.

"Because we are the eyes through which all this is seen," she whispered.

"Right," he nodded, having a little 'Wow' moment. She looked up into his eyes and he kissed her on the lips, a special kiss for this special place. It was all becoming clear in his mind – his life – and he was happy with how it had turned out. "You know I love you, don't you?" he said. Her head moved against his shoulder. "And you know I want to marry you, right?" Her arms tightened around him. "And I want to do it right now, in this place, at this moment."

His right knee sank to the reddish-cream colored soil of the South Rim, and in front of: the little chipmunk foraging for food along the walk, and the birds flitting among the twisted cedars, and Jerry and the few others present on this fine morning, he proposed to Abbey Nelson, journalist from his hometown. "Will you marry me? His hopeful eyes met hers. She nodded her answer, wiping away a couple of tears.

"Yes," she whispered.

He rose and kissed her gently, turning them to face the canyon. "Good. Then I'll run for office because now I'll have a First Lady." He grinned. Abbey smacked him on his butt. The people present were applauding and Jerry was one of them. This truly was a good day to be alive.

They meandered for a while along the trails, winding up back at the Yavapai Museum after an hour, and ready to continue their journey. They were to stop in Winslow and decide to push on or stay. He wanted to stop in the smaller towns, even more than the cities because that's where he'd find the everyday Americans he dreamed of meeting way back in college. It was more fun to just pull into town and mill around, waiting to see what would transpire, rather than attend a prearranged gathering of thousands. It was up close and personal in the cafes, police, and fire stations, even once in a laundromat.

Winslow turned out to be a short stop for lunch and a chat with an older couple from Omaha, who'd come to see the Meteor Crater just west of town. Other than that, it was a quiet

Sunday on the day after the 4th of July, so they continued to New Mexico, and spent the night in a Gallup motel.

Lying next to each other that night, they talked about their journey so far, asking Abbey to marry him and throwing his hat into the ring as a candidate for the Presidency. Their sides were touching from foot to shoulder and it was having an effect on the conversation. She was fidgeting with her hands and feet under the covers This was only their second time in bed together, the first was in his daughter's living room queen sleeper.

"You know, we can't do this," she said softly, "now that you're running. I mean, it wouldn't look good to the public. They have standards, even if they say they don't mind. We'll have to have separate rooms from now on. Also, you'll need to make a formal declaration of your intent to run, so you can accept contributions to your campaign."

"Yeah, yeah. I know." He nestled closer and snatched one of her fidgeting hands in his. "No one else is here right now. Hell, no one even knows we're here together, except the night clerk, and I don't think she had the vaguest idea of who we are." He rolled to his side and moved his hand up her thigh, eliciting shivers in both of them. He kissed her gently and drew his hand along her side, and up behind her shoulder, drawing them together into a tight embrace. His phone vibrated on the bedside table, rudely interrupting them both.

"Ignore it," she murmured.

He kissed her everywhere on her face, gently stroking her cheek. He rolled on top of her and hurt his shoulder. He rolled off onto his back and breathed into the pain.

"Maybe we should wait," she said.

"You're up," he smiled. She carefully straddled him, sitting on his thighs, being careful of the flesh wound above his pelvic bone. The phone vibrated on the bedside table again.

"It's Gene's number," she sighed glancing sideways at it.

"Forget it," he said pulling her down on him. He kissed her gently on the lips, sending shivers throughout him until another burst of pain from his shoulder put an end to it all. Abbey rolled off and lay beside him.

"I'm sorry if I hurt you," she said.

"You didn't. Guess I'm not ready," he said taking her hand in his. He turned his head and kissed her shoulder. She rolled to meet his lips with hers.

"I love you," she whispered.

"I love you very much Abbey," he sighed, "thank you for today. It will always be a special memory for me. Good night."

Chapter 28

NEWS FLASH

July 6th, 8 a.m.

It was a busy morning, what with the Federal Elections Commission to call, the RNC, Gene, the First National of Clayton, and last but not least, Travis, who would release his candidacy to the media – per agreement with National. Harold called Gene last, not wanting to hear more bad news about Al Atrash before all the other business. Travis was ecstatic, practically jumping right thru the phone connection, but then said he'd known it was inevitable considering his past, and their connection with each other. It was a pretty good morning, right up until the call to Gene.

"Hi Gene," Harold said feeling apprehensive. "What's up?" Gene was in a good mood because he was chuckling when he answered.

"Harold, you old fox. Congratulations to you and Abbey. Did you see it on YouTube? I think there's been over a million views so far and it's all over every other social media channel there is."

"What are you talking about Gene? What's all over the social media?"

"You are my friend. An elderly couple got you on video with their smartphone and got every word at the Grand Canyon. They just released it last night when they got home from their vacation. Didn't Travis tell you? He should have known. He's in the news business and scans all that sort of thing. Anyway, congratulations. And it's about time you decided to run for office. I get regular reports about the impressions people have about you everywhere you go. So, good luck with that."

"Gene, why did you call me at midnight last night?"

"We've raised the threat level for Al Atrash being in the country. No real hard evidence yet though. I'm assigning you two more Secret Service agents whenever you're in a large city and speaking at well-attended events. Jerry will handle all the arrangements. You'll never even know they're there. Jerry will continue with you for another couple of weeks at his request. Then he has to take some time off – mandatory by the book. I'll get you another friendly agent to sub for him, maybe a female agent would be good for your image as a candidate. That's all I have. I'll try to catch you in Houston in a few days. I've got something to pass along to you from the President."

"He did it again," Harold yelled at his phone.

"Did what?" Abbey smiled.

"You know, hung up with not so much as a goodbye. I'm getting two more agents when we're in a dense urban area." Abbey nodded and pointed towards the door.

"We should get going. It's almost noon."

Between Gallup and Albuquerque, Abbey filled him in on what Travis, their temporary campaign manager, told her. It seems that before they left on their odyssey, she and Travis had made arrangements for people to leave their e-mail address and the amount of their intended campaign contribution, which would not be donated until Harold officially declared his intention and registered with the FEC. He had been "testing the waters" in the beginning and was allowed up to $5,000 to be accepted as donations. Travis had taken in $4,950 from several individuals, and then put a plug in it until Harold registered. Abbey said the total commitments so far was over fifteen million dollars in the past five weeks. Travis would send out the notifications to the donors and they could now deposit their campaign donations.

"Hey, watch the road, not me," Abbey said.

Harold straightened out his truck on the interstate, reminding himself to pay attention to driving. "Sorry. Got a little caught up in your explanation and the dollar amount. Are you sure it's that much?" Abbey smiled and nodded.

"Travis also wanted you to know that it's all growing so fast that he can't keep up. You need to get yourself an official team – and soon."

"I guess it's time for me to get organized, huh?" he said. Abbey smacked his thigh and pumped her fist.

"YES!"

Chapter 29

HOUSTON
July 7th, 5:30 p.m.

It's a funny thing that people do when they believe another person is famous, or on their way to being famous. They go out of their way to do all kinds of good things for that person, like give them things for no reason whatsoever, other than the pleasure they derive from associating with the famous person. What Harold was feeling at the moment was embarrassment, standing in the Radisson Hotel lobby in Houston Texas. The manager had come out of his office to greet Harold and hand him the keycard to the Presidential Suite on the 39th floor – one down from the owner's penthouse apartment. The manager told them that the owner wanted to be there, but was on a cruise in the Indian Ocean, and instructed his brother, who was the manager, to treat Harold and party as if he were going to be the next President. Harold accepted the keycard thanking Raj Bedal and signed his name in a leather-bound, special parchment book, which was filled with autographs of the rich and famous who had stayed at the hotel. Harold added his name, using the old-fashioned fountain pen, and noticed his signature was far more legible than most – something Ruth had always said was important. "Next time we're here," he said turning towards Abbey, "you can sign too, as First Lady.

"Very funny Harold Robertson."

They went up to the Presidential Suite, which had a lavish sunken living room, sitting room connected to the master bedroom, dressing room, a huge walk-in closet, hot tub, bathtub, shower, bidet, double gold sinks, and an extra bedroom with bath. Jerry would stay there, at Harold's insistence. Personally, he didn't know what to do with all the space. What he didn't like was that Abbey was in a separate room down the hall, next to the two other agents at her insistence. He wanted to sleep with her, but she said no, especially not here.

Just as Gene had promised, he met them for dinner downstairs at 6:30 p.m. Harold thought it was a little excessive that the Deputy Secretary of the DHS was taking time from his busy schedule to fly to Houston and have dinner with him, but as he found out, there was an ulterior motive behind it all. During dinner, it was all chit-chat, friendly, and informal. Afterwards, when coffee and dessert were served, Gene pushed a navy blue document across the table, which had the embossed gold leaf seal of the President's Office on it. Harold opened it and found a facsimile of the Presidential Award of Freedom inside.

"He wants you to come to the White House on July 22, for the official presentation. Abbey, you're invited as well. Another one will be awarded posthumously to Ranger McFadden's widow. He also sent this."

Gene slid a small gift-wrapped box across the table to Abbey. "What on earth? Why is the President sending gifts?" Harold said, mystified. Abbey was all smiles like she knew what it was all about.

"A small token of his thanks and congratulations on your engagement – his words," Gene said smiling. "I sent him an e-mail through channels with the video of you two at the Grand Canyon."

Harold rolled his eyes. He'd never be able to live this down. They would forever be known as the Grand Canyon couple.

Abbey opened the box excitedly to find a sterling silver belt buckle with a picture of the Grand Canyon inset in it, and a sterling silver heart-shaped necklace with a picture of it. She promptly undid the clasp and put it on. She read the handwritten note of congratulations aloud.

"Wow. I'm speechless, Gene." Harold said. "You'll have to convey our thanks. I don't know that I ever could. I mean, I'll send him a thank you note, but . . ."

"I think what he's trying to say, Gene," Abbey said, "is that you're old friends with the President, and a conveyed thank you coming from you . . .."

"Smile," Gene said interrupting and took their picture with his phone. "He asked for this."

Gene showed them the six-second video he took, much to Harold chagrin. Harold's mouth was agape, he looked petrified, mummified, or something 'fied', and all that Gene could do was laugh, because Jerry was taking one of them through it all. "Just tell him thanks, will ya."

"Yes. And give him a hug for me. This is beautiful. Thank you for bringing the good cheer," Abbey said with her smile filling the room.

"Well, I have a flight to catch," Gene said, "enjoy your evening."

****

Al Atrash was watching the five o'clock news on Wednesday afternoon, July 8th, showing a short segment on Harold Robertson at the Astros vs Rays game from earlier that day. Harold said a few words right after the national anthem played. The newscaster said that Harold Robertson would be at Discovery Green for a concert that evening at 9 p.m.

"If you're thinking about going after him, forget it. You'll never be able to pick him out of the crowd," Gary said.

"I'll do whatever I like," Al Atrash frowned.

"You don't understand. The security at these events is tight," Gary urged.

"As expected. I'll need your bicycle, backpack, and the weapon you've been hiding from me." Al Atrash stood. "Now!" His dark and foreboding face elicited fear in Gary's eyes.

"Nothing's planned. How do you expect to succeed and not get caught?" Gary rose and backed away a step.

"Now!" Al Atrash demanded.

"Okay, okay. It's your funeral," Gary said, walking to the kitchen and opening the root cellar trapdoor.

"Move," Al Atrash pushed him aside. Gary had withheld telling him about it.

Al Atrash descended the old wooden ladder. It was dark and musty, definitely not a good place to store guns or ammo. Gary pulled the chain of the ceramic fixture attached to the floor joists by the ladder. It cast dark shadows of the two men into the cobweb-laden ten foot by ten-foot room, with a dirt floor and six-foot ceiling. Gary unlocked a small newer looking metal storage box and opened the lid to reveal two 9mm pistols and a small arms tactical weapon wrapped in oiled cloths. Gary laid them on an old wood table, opening the cloths, and wiped the three with a clean towel. Al Atrash picked up the black assault rifle with suppressor, telescoping stock, and small scope – not what he'd expected. "This is the best you have?" Gary looked scared in the dimness of the cellar. "Have you ever fired it?" Gary shook his head. "Give me the ammo box," Al Atrash snapped.

"You're not going to fire it, are you?" Gary's voice wavered.

Al Atrash opened the ammo box and loaded five .223 rounds into the clip, extended the stock, pulled back the bolt and fired five times into the dirt floor. The suppressor worked well enough, and the gun didn't jam. He reloaded and fired four more rounds, with the gun jamming on the fifth. He cleared the shell and picked it up from the floor. He loaded two more rounds and fired them both without a mishap. He filled his pants pocket with a dozen or so rounds and took the weapon with him, ascending the old wooden ladder back into the kitchen. The acrid smell of gunpowder and the dull ringing in his ears made him feel powerful and ready to meet his prey. He was ready to die, if it came to that.

****

After Wednesday's baseball game, Jerry drove them to the Houston Arboretum and Nature Center to spend the afternoon walking the nature trails. He'd had enough of cheering crowds and wanted to have a quiet talk with Abbey about their future. As it turned out, it started to rain an hour after they got there, leaving the three of them with a ten-minute walk back to the car. It was funny because they said things in the rain that otherwise might not have been brought up. He learned about Abbey's childhood fantasies – which involved him – and she learned how angry he was at the government for lying to the American people about going to war with North Vietnam, because it cost his brother his life, and his mother her sanity, not to mention his own grief running rampant for decades. It was one of the main reasons he ran for a seat in the US House of Representatives, so he could make a difference. That's when his fifty-year plan began to take shape but wasn't really fully developed until after the 2007 financial meltdown, and the years of recession which followed.

When they arrived at the car, they were drenched, and their feet were sloshing around in their shoes and making squishing noises. Jerry was the hardest hit because he was wearing leather dress shoes, so he wasn't laughing about it at all.

The only reason Harold could think of, for their attendance at the Discovery Green's venue of three local bands, was that he wanted to dance with Abbey. It wasn't raining when they left, but a half hour later, there was a slow steady rain when the front man for the Lightshow band called him up on stage to greet the fifteen hundred or so people.

****

Al Atrash borrowed Gary's rain slicker and told him he'd be back in an hour, whether or not he was successful at eliminating his target. He took the cheap fifteen-speed mountain bike from the back shed and rode the mile and a half to Discovery Green, where he'd find Harold Robertson and kill him. He was not nervous or afraid of being caught because his actions were justified and righteous by his beliefs. He turned onto the street between the park and the new construction on the north side of the road. He dismounted and walked his bike on the paths to the west side of the park, stopping at the edge of the large pond separating him from the concert stage. He wiped the light rain from his face and continued along the path to find the best place for a clear view of the stage. It was 9:12 p.m. He was nervous on the well-lighted path but could see no better place. His view of the small stage, about eighty meters across the pond was unobstructed in only this one place. He was about to leave after twenty minutes when the music stopped and one of the band members was calling someone up on stage.

"HAROLD ROBERTSON," the voice called out.

A chill ran up Al Atrash's spine, hearing the name of his son's killer. He walked his bike to the darkest spot there was and into the knee-high pampas grass a few feet and stopped, straddling the center bar. He swung his backpack around to unzip it and get his weapon. His left shoulder faced towards the stage as he extended the stock, and chambered a round, his eye coming up behind the twenty-power scope, and immediately finding the stage and Harold Robertson approaching the microphone. A smile crossed Al Atrash's face as he stood alone in the rain in Houston's Discovery Park, about to have his retribution on his son's murderer. He centered the crosshairs on Harold's left temple and squeezed off a round, and then another, and another. Three suppressed, whop, whop, whops. The sound died quickly in the amplified greetings of Harold Robertson to the crowd.

****

"Thank you all for letting me interrupt the music. I just wanted to say hi and how much I'm enjoying the rain tonight." The laughter was sporadic. "Abbey and I came to dance . . ." Harold heard the unmistakable 'crack' of three rounds passing right by his head, so close he thought he could almost feel the sonic wave hit him in the face. He instinctively crouched down and covered the four feet to the edge of the stage, jumping off and rolling to his feet. He snatched Abbey by the arm and ran for the only cover in sight, to the far side of the stage to crouch behind its three-foot height. Jerry was right next to him with gun drawn, having heard the 'cracking' sound of the supersonic bullets passing close by. No one in the crowd reacted to the distant and suppressed gunshots, perhaps because they were muted by his voice over the PA.

As he and Abbey kneeled on the concrete beside the stage, with Jerry hunched over and scanning the crowd for the gunman, but the stage lights made it difficult to see anything except silhouettes. "Jerry, we're okay here. Go see what you can find away from the bright lights." Jerry shook his head, his eyes never leaving the crowd.

"Police are on their way," Jerry said. "I have to stay with you, no matter what."

Harold could appreciate how Jerry thought – like a soldier – protecting his keep. The members of the band were staring at the three of them, wondering what was going on. They didn't think to leave the stage at first until the multiple police sirens echoed off the buildings and were quite loud. Then they got off of the stage, and many of the people in the crowd began to disperse. By the time the police entered the Discovery Green, half the crowd had fled, and Harold was sure the gunman was long gone. It had only been seven weeks since the attack at Mt. Rushmore, and here he was again, being shot at out in public. "Guess that was him, huh?" He muttered to himself. Abbey squeezed his hand.

"Can we go now?" Abbey asked.

"Wait until I get you a police escort. I alerted the office to send more agents. They should be here in a few minutes. As soon as you're safe, I'm going out to the area across the pond. It's the only clear shot to the stage area, and it was far enough away to help disperse the sound. The shooter used a suppressor, I'm sure. I didn't see this coming, I have to tell you. Someone wants you dead." Jerry said.

"Yeah, no shit," Abbey said through clenched teeth.

Harold wondered what would be next. *Was this to be his way of life from now until they caught this guy?* Anger flashed through him, anger directed at himself for killing that man. He could have . . .

"You're shaking Harold. You're not hurt are you?" Abbey's voice quivered.

"I'm pissed off." He yelled, now realizing his anger had taken charge of him, just as it did in the amphitheater. Jerry shook his head and suppressed a laugh. "What!" Harold snapped.

"Someone takes three shots at you and you say you're pissed off. I don't know. It just sounded funny the way you said it, that's all," Jerry said. "Here's our guys." He pointed to the two agents in shorts, polo shirts, and sneakers, running towards them down the Green, with their guns in hand, and badges in the other – so the police didn't shoot them.

"You got your ears with you?" Jerry asked about their communications headsets.

They produced them from a pants pocket. Harold knew they'd only just arrived in Houston late that afternoon from Kansas City, and Jerry had said he didn't need them at the concert that night. *How wrong he was.* Harold thought.

Jerry instructed them to escort their assignment back to the hotel and take turns standing guard in the hallway outside the door. He said he was staying to follow up on a hunch. He and Abbey walked with Vince and Denise, to their car, parked in the middle of the street. They were done for the evening and would be confined to quarters. Harold's eyes rolled when he saw the TV news crew arriving at the hotel, probably having heard the call over their police scanners.

"Now you know what I do in my time off," Abbey said.

"Oh, you get a lot of crazy terrorists in South Dakota, do you?" Harold's deadpan sarcasm didn't elicit any smiles or laughter. They were both making light of something which was deadly serious, especially to them, having witnessed and participated in the Rushmore attack. Vince swept the reporters aside with his arm like they were branches on an overgrown pathway in a forest. Harold stopped dead in his tracks jerking on Abbey's arm and causing Denise to run into him from behind.

"I have something to say to the people of Houston and to all Americans." The lights mounted on the camera glared in his face, just as they always did. Vince was throwing him an irritated look. "Not many people know it, but the shots fired tonight were coming from the father of the man I killed at Mt. Rushmore. The Department of Homeland Security knows he has left Syria. They just weren't sure where he'd gone. Now they are. His name is Amul Al Atrash. He's somewhere in Houston this very minute and may be watching this broadcast. So, I have something to say to him. It didn't please me to kill another human being, and unlike you and your son, I don't live to kill. You may hunt me, but know that I am hunting you at this very moment. We are many. You are but one. And to the American people, I want to say that I need your help. Your country needs your help. Together, we can seek out this terrorist, Al Atrash, and capture him. If you see something suspicious, say something. There are already local communication networks in place to receive your tips and follow-up on them. Give them something to work with and together we will catch this man. Thank you for helping me and your country. Remember us in your prayers, as I do you." He patted Abbey's hand, which he'd been clutching the entire time, turned and continued on with Vince and Denise to the peace and quiet of his hotel suite.

****

Al Atrash rode hard and fast away from the Discovery Green, knowing that he'd missed his target three times. He cursed the damp night air and his bad luck. He knew the scope had not been sighted in, and if it had, it had been done poorly. Three blocks from the park, he heard sirens behind him, pressing him forward, peddling faster, the assault weapon flopping about in his backpack, which never was zipped shut. He flung the bike away from him when he got to Gary's backdoor and was greeted by Gary with a 9mm pistol in hand, pointed at him.

"Take off the backpack."

Al Atrash did as the barrel of the gun instructed. He threw it at Gary's feet. Gary backed up, shoving the pack aside with his foot, and waved the gun at him to step into the kitchen.

"Open the trapdoor."

He opened it and started to descend the ladder when Gary let down his guard and shoved the gun into the front of his waistband to descend the steep ladder. Al Atrash saw his opening and grabbed Gary's pant cuff, and pulled as hard as he could, upending and landing him on his back. He hauled him down the ladder, with both of them landing in a heap at the foot of the ladder. Al Atrash snatched the gun from Gary's waistband and struck him across the face, drawing a lot of blood from the three-inch gash. He got to his feet and dragged Gary to the middle of the space by his pant leg, where he tied his hands behind his back with copper wire from a small roll on the table. He bound him to the table leg, using the remaining wire.

"Where do you think you can run? They'll have all the main roads blocked by now. You're a dead man," Gary snarled.

"Keys to the truck and your credit card." Al Atrash kicked him in the groin. Gary puked all over himself, choking, and gasping for breath. He was ready to kick him again.

"Kitchen drawer."

He got the other 9mm pistol from the trunk, along with the ammo box, and climbed out of the cellar and slammed the trapdoor shut. The muffled curses of Gary were barely audible through the multiple layers of linoleum and thick wood sheeting. No one would hear. He found a map of Houston and Texas in the same drawer as the keys and credit card. He got his bag from upstairs, stopping at the fridge for a gallon jug of water, some leftovers and a half a loaf of bread. He loaded the truck, checking the glove box for the registration and insurance cards.

He hid the guns behind the seat and started the engine. He'd have to stop for gas right away, as there was only a quarter tank.

He took several deep breaths and calmed himself. He opened the map of the city and circled several back roads which led out of town. He checked the time on the truck's clock. It had been forty minutes since he took the shots. He drove out of Gary's neighborhood, looking to find a gas station, and being careful to observe his surroundings. They'd be looking for him now with all of their resources, but he felt a strange sense of safety and anonymity in this foreign country, a land of opportunity. He disappeared into the night with a smile of confidence to lay in wait at another location. All was right in his world. Allah would prevail.

Chapter 30

DHS – DC

July 8th, 10:50 p.m.

Gene got the call from Jerry, right at 10:50 p.m. EST. Gene thought he'd sounded a little rattled as he described what had happened at a concert in Houston. Jerry had found three .223 shell casings by the pond, but no witnesses to the shooting. Even the buildings across the street yielded no witnesses. Gene knew that somewhere, someone had seen something, and he needed to put a face to this shooter. It only needed to be coaxed out into the open through good police work and cooperation of the media in the next twenty-four hours. After that, it became harder. Gene knew that Al Atrash had fled Houston and was on his way to his next contact. He looked at the terrorists' watch map on his office wall, filled with colored pins and notes. The next two closest suspected cells were Atlanta and Kansas City, but Gene figured Al Atrash wouldn't go to the next closest city. The man needed a place to lay low and track Harold's movements, but also knew that all the major cities would be on high alert.

Above all else, Gene knew he was dealing with a professional terrorist who'd been active over the past twenty years and never been cornered or even had a good photo taken of him. Al Atrash was a mystery man in the terrorists' networks, even to his associates.

Gene got the file on Capt. Raymos that the USCG's Port Security Specialist had sent, along with the Houston office report. He had a hunch that Raymos was in cahoots with Al

Atrash and had knowingly withheld information. He read through them quickly finding no incriminating evidence, except for the lack of a photocopy of missing passenger's passport. The ship's Captain had to keep a photocopy by International Law. Captain Raymos was currently being detained by Port Security, pending further investigation. But that didn't really help Gene with Al Atrash's whereabouts.

He called Harold to give him a heads-up on what he'd planned. "Harold. This is Gene Drake. Yes, I know it's midnight, but this is important. Sorry to wake you. I'm going to need you to change the way in which you present yourself at public events, now that Al Atrash has made an attempt on your life. Jerry can fill in the details, but you're not going to be able to publicize your whereabouts in advance because Al Atrash will be following your every move through the media, and social media formats." Gene waited while Harold vented at him and then continued. "I know you don't like being told what to do, but I'm afraid it's come to that. And yes, I'll tell Jerry to take it easy on you. Okay?"

Gene had already instructed Jerry to organize alternative agendas and publicize those in advance of the real events, to throw Al Atrash off his trail. He understood how Harold felt about the whole thing, having already faced down the son while under fire – Harold would not be intimidated under any circumstances.

Gene left work just after midnight, having set up his schedule for the following day, which would begin in less than six hours, in a meeting with his boss, the Secretary of the DHS. The country was on the highest terror-watch since 9/11. Al Atrash's bold actions would embolden and set in motion all of the cells in America, and that could get complicated.

Chapter 31

RADISSON HOTEL

July 9th, 12:25 a.m.

Harold couldn't sleep after his conversation with Gene Drake. He knew full well the risks for everyone around him, especially for Abbey. She could easily become collateral damage in Al Atrash's attempts to kill him. Harold knew there would be little Jerry or his fellow agents could do to stop him if they were surprised again like they were at the concert. He was being actively stalked by a professional terrorist with associates around the world, all ready to help him achieve his goals at a moment's notice. He slept in short intervals until 3 a.m., when he finally fell into a deep sleep, not waking until 7 a.m. He opened his eyes to Abbey's smile beaming down at him.

"Morning sleepyhead," she sang. "There's coffee and Danish when you're ready."

He nodded and snatched her hand before she could leave, pulling her down for a kiss.

"Frisky are we this morning?" She laughed.

"Not particularly," he said planting his feet on the carpet. He stood and walked naked to the cart and poured a cup of coffee, taking it and a Danish back to bed. Jerry knocked on the adjoining door.

"You have a meeting in an hour," Jerry said from the other side of his bedroom door.

He patted the bed beside him, after wrapping the sheet around his midsection and legs. "Come sit with me. I need to talk about what happened last night," he said. Abbey got a cup of coffee and sat beside him.

"I'm worried that you're going to get hurt by this madman because you're around me. Gene called last night and told me that I can't publicize our agenda any longer. He's got Jerry figuring out diversions to lead Al Atrash astray. Personally, I don't think it's going to do any good. Al Atrash will stop at nothing to kill me. I'm wondering if it's even a good idea that we travel together. I couldn't live with myself if you were hurt." Harold blinked back his rising emotions. He'd never forgive himself . . .

"I understand how you feel, but I'm staying right by your side, and there's nothing you can say to dissuade me." Abbey's voice projected her inner strength.

He gathered her hand in his and intertwined their fingers. "Okay. Then that's how it will be." He leaned into her and kissed her softly on the cheek. She turned his head with her hand and kissed him firmly on the lips.

"We should get ready," she said standing up.

Harold nodded. He loved her for her strength and determination in all things. He stood and kissed her, and then went to get ready.

This morning's meeting with the mayor of Houston and the media would be a continuation of last night's brief encounter with the press. He dressed and knocked on Jerry's door, saying he'd be ready in five minutes.

The meeting had originally been planned for a small telecom room at the Radisson, but after last night's attempt on his life, it was now in the ballroom. When he walked in through the double doors with Abbey, the room was packed with no clear way to get to the lectern a seventy- feet away. Jerry, Vince, and Denise had no problem parting the waters, herding him and Abbey safely to the small stylish Plexiglas lectern sitting atop a one foot raised platform. Mayor Hector Alanso was up on the platform waiting for him, and unsuccessfully trying to control the hundreds of clamoring reporters in the ballroom. By Harold's recollection, just about every major newspaper in the country was present, along with National and local news crews, and twenty or so video cameras, all glaring in his face with their high-intensity lights, illuminating the ballroom in a fierce white light punctuated by a storm of camera flashes.

"Ladies and gentlemen, if we could have order, we'll begin." Mayor Alanso said loudly.

Harold stepped up onto the platform, leaving Abbey in Jerry's care to one side. Vince was in front and Denise was on the other side, both looking the crowd over, not that anyone was in the ballroom without an ID card hanging around their neck. It seems Gene had arranged for five or six more Secret Service to screen this morning's proceedings. They were easy enough to spot in the back of the room with their earpiece and black suits standing out from the masses.

"Before we begin," Mayor Alanso said, "I want to impress on you the gravity of this meeting. Early this morning, our local KVAN newsroom received an anonymous e-mail with a video attachment. If someone would lower the lights, I'll show you what was recorded by an observer of last night's attack."

The hair on the back of Harold's neck raised with the thought of actually being able to see his attacker. All the lights in the room, except for two small can lights in back, were turned off, and the curtains behind the lectern were opened to reveal a seventy-inch flat screen. A dark, shadowy picture taken from across the street of the Discovery Green and pond appeared on the screen, accompanied by street noise, the announcer's voice a hundred yards away, and the subdued exclamations of the woman taking the video. The picture jumped around and zoomed in on a man with a backpack, standing next to a bicycle a hundred feet away. The picture showed him pulling a long slender object from his pack and raising it to his shoulder – then three muffled crack, crack, cracks. A shiver ran down Harold's spine at the sound. The woman's "Oh, my God," clearly sounded as she dove behind a bench on the sidewalk, still holding her phone up to record whatever it was pointed at. The picture was jumbled but did catch the man riding away on the bicycle for a few seconds before ending with a view of the bench seat.

"Lights, please," the mayor said. "That, ladies and gentlemen, was the terrorist trying to take out his mark, Harold Robertson, who is standing here with us this morning. You will hold your questions until he is finished with what he has to say. It gives me great pleasure to welcome a true American hero, Harold Robertson."

Harold stood beside the mayor and waited for the room to quiet, thanking the mayor and shaking his hand. "Thank you all for coming this morning. I know you have questions just as I do, about how such a thing could happen in America with all of our security resources. Well, perhaps we can shed some light on those questions this morning.

First, I want to recognize the journalist seated in the front row, who has been documenting my journey across America. Ms. Abbey Nelson, of KIRK in Rapid City, SD. Most of you know her through her presence at Mt. Rushmore in May, where she, along with her cameraman, Chet Givens, documented the terrorists attack on that Memorial Day. She has been a guiding light for me this past month on our travels together. You probably also caught the video of my marriage proposal to her at the Grand Canyon two weeks ago." He waited for the laughter to subside.

"We do plan to be married at some point if I can keep

dodging those bullets." Again, he paused for a moment. Abbey frowned at him, shaking her head. "Anyway, what I have to say to you today is a continuation of what I said last night." He motioned to the tech woman in the back of the room to play the fifty-second recording from last night before he began his remarks.

"What I am asking of the American people is to unify on this one thing, to catch a terrorist in our midst who is still faceless, but his name is Amul Al Atrash, from Syria. He has been a terrorist for over twenty years, but his reign of terror will end here in America because the American people can never accept what he has to offer.

A man such as him, which would subjugate us all to his beliefs, to his brand of government by force, and to the will of his god, who he says will reward him for his actions against the evil Satan of Western Culture. If we as a people allow such men as this Al Atrash to purvey their brand of terror in our midst, then we will lose what we have fought for long and hard with our blood, our Freedom.

He doesn't understand the concept of freedom any more than he understands us as a people. His only aim is to make us afraid and to dominate us, to subjugate us to his god's will. I believe it to be a worthy cause to unite us as a nation, just as we were united against the aggression and oppression of Nazism. I know myself well enough to know that I am fiercely independent, and not one to follow a cause unless I see the worth of such a cause. And, I do see the need for us to unite as Americans, for whatever time it takes to defeat this man's brand of terror.

We are many. He is one. In the meantime, I plan to go on with my life while I work to defeat him, as should you all. I am not asking for anyone to give up anything or any belief. I am only asking us all to unite on this one cause and see it to its end. Thank you for this chance to address you. I'll be seeing some of you on my journey in the days and months to come. I plan to shake as many of your hands as I can and to sit and listen to what you have to say about our country, and about your hopes and dreams for a better life for all of our children. God bless you all and God bless America."

He stepped back from the lectern feeling a stillness in his soul, a quiet strength he'd come to know at different times in his life. He nodded to the people in the ballroom that he was ready for questions. The room erupted in voices calling out all at once. He stepped back up to the lectern and held his hands up, and waited for silence. "Yes, Ms. Jordan," he pointed to the third row back.

"Will you attend the debate next month?" She asked.

"Yes, if they ask me." He pointed towards the back of the room, to a tall slender man whose hand was raised in silence. "Yes, sir. The tall man who isn't yelling at me. What's your question?"

"Jay Weeks, Denver Press. Have you decided on your running mate?" His voice crackled through the room.

Harold smiled with a thoughtful nod. "Good question, but I can't answer it just yet. In any case, it probably won't happen until next year at the Convention in July. Can you wait till then?" The reporter shrugged his shoulders, drawing laughter from those around him. Harold pointed to a young woman on the far side of the room, buried by the men around her. "You guys want to make some room for the lady to ask her question?" He pointed towards them.

"Suzie Bullock, Memphis Times. Will you and Ms. Nelson be married in your hometown?"

"Great question." He turned towards Abbey with a hopeful face, seeing that hers was turning pinkish as she nodded a yes. "She said yes. But, we don't have a date for you yet." He was feeling the heat on his face too, as his eyes met with Abbey's again, before he pointed to Mel, from his home state.

"Mel Goodfellow, Springfield News. Were you afraid last night?" Mel nodded his 'knowing nod' to his friend.

"Did you all hear the question? Mel asked me if I was afraid last night. Damn straight I was. But I think I was more pissed off that someone was shooting at me again. I am thankful that no one got hurt and that Al Atrash missed his mark. I heard all three bullets pass by my head though. It's a sobering sound if you're not familiar with it. A speeding bullet breaking the sound barrier next to my ear –Crack, Crack, Crack. Yes, Mel, my heart jumped up into my throat for a half a second." Abbey raised her hand at his last word. He nodded at her.

"Abbey Nelson, KIRK reporter. What message do you have for the terrorist, Amul Al Atrash?"

He nodded at her knowing why she'd asked. "Why, yes. I do have a message for him, and it's this: The American people are hunting you, and there is nowhere you can hide."

The questions went on for another twenty minutes, and he was happy to answer to the American people through the media. They deserved to know the truth, no matter how difficult it might be; armed with the truth, he knew they could make the right decisions for their country.

Chapter 32

RNC

July 8th, 2 p.m.

James, are you listening to the news?" Sally asked, leaning in his doorway. "You'll want to hear what Harold Robertson just told the American public."

"Where is he?"

"Houston. Where the Syrian terrorist took a shot at him."

"I'll catch it online. Thanks, Sally." James Picford wasn't surprised at all when he brought it up on his screen. Harold Robertson, leader extraordinaire, rallying the people to a meaningful cause. He'd been meaning to speak with the man, but it really wasn't his place to recruit for the Party, at least he didn't think it was. Besides, Harold Robertson had already thrown his hat into the ring. The way James saw it, he'd be hard to beat. He was hands down, the people's choice, and everywhere he went he gathered followers in droves, so much so that some of the candidates were thinking about calling it quits before the first debate in August. Harold had already surpassed everyone in the fundraising department, except for Oliver Plunkett, the Silicon Valley billionaire who was, by and large, funding his own campaign. James looked up Harold's number and called him.

"Harold, this is James Picford over at the RNC. I've been meaning to call you and wanted to convey our support for your candidacy. You can reach me at this number during the day. Looking forward to meeting with you when you're in DC."

James set his phone down on his desk and pondered calling

the FOX News Network, which was sponsoring the first debate in August, to make sure they included Harold in the ten candidates on stage – there were seventeen running. Since Harold's popularity had skyrocketed so recently, he may not have been included in the polls used for the selection process. The thought of Harold not being on stage just didn't register with James, as he was the best man for the job as far as he was concerned. He punched in Jim Smyth's number at the network and leaned back in his chair, knowing his old college buddy was on the same page as he was – finding the best man for the job.

Chapter 33

CHICAGO
July 15th, 9 p.m.

Amul Al Atrash was lost on the south side of Chicago, trying to find an address using a map he'd brought with him from Damascus. He had eight such maps of cells in different cities, and this one seemed to be leading him astray. He was looking for 34586th S Evan St where his contact, Jack Amos lived. He didn't particularly want to ask for directions, but it was almost dark, and he'd have little luck finding it when it did get dark in fifteen minutes or so. He stopped at a corner grocery on Calumet and ran inside to ask. The old man pointed and told him three blocks east and one south, and then ignored him. Al Atrash tried to follow the directions, but wound up in an alleyway with no name, behind some beat up old homes with sheds and garages that looked to be falling down. A couple of kids were playing in the dirt-backyard of one, so he stopped and asked, showing them the address. The kids pointed across the alley to a similar looking tenement, with a basement apartment and stairs to the second story, just like most of the buildings in the alleyway. He left the truck and went to knock on the basement door. A forty-something dark-skinned, Middle Eastern woman answered. He showed her the map, noticing the fear in her eyes.

"Jack Amos. I'm looking for him," Amul said. Her eyes narrowed as they examined him. He didn't like the feeling he was getting, like she knew who he was.

"Yes, my husband's name is Jack Amos. Who are you?

And what do you want?"

"I knew your father," he said, which was the code phrase to identify himself. She gave him a blank look for a moment and then nodded, and told him where to park his truck, closing the door before he could say anything else. He had to park on the next street over in the only spot big enough for the truck. He emptied some of his clothes to make room for the three guns from inside the truck's cab, looking over his shoulder for anyone watching in the fading twilight. He shouldered his duffel and counted four sets of eyes following him as he passed their residence, making him feel uncomfortable. A narrow sidewalk between structures led to the back of Jack's building and the three steps down to his door. He knocked and was let in.

"You'll have to wait for my husband to come home," she said pointing to the small kitchen table with three wooden chairs.

Amul sat down alone in Jack's kitchen and waited for over an hour. The wife would not talk to him or even stay in the same room with him. She disappeared into the dimly lit living room with the sounds of a TV tuned to a news channel faintly entering through the kitchen doorway. The kitchen was tidy with pots and pans hung on the wall above the stove and fridge. An AC unit was blasting away from the ground level window in the cramped kitchen. The view out the top portion of the window revealed a wooden staircase to the second floor. The woman had been cooking but had cleared any sign of it away, while he had parked the truck. The room smelled of chicken and bulgar spiced with turmeric and onion, he thought. Four days on the road, with only drive-through fast food, made the smells in the kitchen familiar and inviting. A little before 10 p.m. there was the sound of a key unlocking the door, and as the door swung open into the small entryway attached to the kitchen, a slender man with a full head of black hair appeared. Al Atrash stood to greet Jack Amos, his contact in Chicago. His eyes were met with uncertainty. Jack had no way of knowing who this man was in his kitchen.

"I knew your father," Amul repeated the introductory phrase and waited for Jack to respond. Jack nodded his approval after a moment.

"Welcome to my home. Tell me your name." Jack said.

"Meechum," Amul replied, giving the second part of the code phrase. Jack nodded his final approval, latching the door behind him. He offered his hand and the two strangers shook hands and sat down together at the table.

"Lamir, come greet our new friend," Jack called out to his wife.

She stood in the kitchen doorway with folded arms. Al Atrash knew in his heart that she did not want him in her home. He was not welcome, but she would follow her husband's wishes to take him in, at least for a few days. "Thank you for letting me stay with you," Amul said to Jack, but also looked up at Lamir's questioning eyes seeking approval from his host's wife. She was an American after all, there was no doubt in his mind about that, and American men must also have the approval of their wives to have guests in their home. "Thank you, Lamir. I won't be here long." Her face softened and her arms unfolded, but her eyes still had doubt in them.

"Lamir is a very good cook and you have arrived on a Wednesday, so we are having chicken, pan bread, and tabbouleh. I am famished," Jack said getting up to help serve.

Al Atrash couldn't remember the last time he had such a good meal in the nearly two months since he'd left his home. Gary certainly didn't know how to cook Middle Eastern foods, and the boat ride over had nothing but Greek fare, which was okay with him but wasn't as good as this simple meal. He must have sighed after a few bites, because both hosts looked at him, pleased that he was enjoying the meal.

After supper, Lamir served tea in the living room and went to bed without saying a word.

"You'll have to forgive her," Jack said. "We're not used to having visitors such as yourself."

"No need," Amul said, "I understand and will only be a few days." He lowered his voice to continue. "What news has there been about Houston? I've been traveling and sleeping in the truck for four days." Jack's eyebrows both raised, surprise spreading across his face.

"They still don't know anything about you," Jack said in a hushed voice. "But they are looking with all their resources. You will be safe here. I have not had any contact with anyone in the past year, and we are not being watched that I know of. The man you seek will be here in two weeks. That is what I've heard on the news. He is traveling the country and meeting the people on his campaign for President."

"Really? He's campaigning for the Presidency? I didn't know." Al Atrash rubbed his forehead with the fingers of both hands. That will make it more difficult." Jack gave him a knowing look.

"You must be tired," Jack said standing. "You will sleep here on the sofa. It's quite comfortable."

Jack disappeared into a hallway and came back with a pillow and blanket. The sofa already had a soft cover throw. Al Atrash was more tired now than he'd been in the past four days of catnaps in the cab of the truck, perhaps because of the good supper he'd eaten, and because he was in a safe place for a few days. "I am very tired," he said spreading the blanket out and moving his duffel from the entryway to beside the end table by the sofa. One of the guns clanked against the wood table, making Jack stare curiously at him and the bag.

"Sorry, I don't mean to pry. I'll say goodnight then."

"Thank you for your hospitality," Al Atrash said. Jack walked to the bedroom door and closed it behind him. He would be here for this one night, because something didn't feel right about it, especially with Lamir's display of disapproval.

Chapter 34

CLEMSON SC

July 21ˢᵗ, 1 p.m.

Harold and Abbey had landed in Atlanta six days ago, abandoning his truck with Chet and the news crew temporarily. Jerry had told him it was all part of mixing up his mode of travel and his plans, in case Al Atrash was following them more closely than they thought. The three of them had rented a car in Atlanta and driven to Clemson University for the day as part of the decoy agenda. He was advertised to be in Augusta, GA today, ninety some odd miles to the south of Clemson. The first place they visited was Fort Rutledge, just south of campus by a lake. Abbey wanted to see the DAR marker placed there by the Daughters of the American Revolution, of which her mother was a member. Abbey never took the time to join. What Abbey did find out about South Carolina was that this subtropical climate bred interesting spiders, mainly the pretty red variety, whose web she walked into on the way to the marker. It had spun a web between bushes eight feet apart, and the morning sun obscured it from view quite nicely. She had screamed so loudly that Jerry had almost drawn his weapon. Harold removed the unwanted visitor with a stick, which was leg-to-leg an inch and a half across, and held it up for her to see, knowing full well what her reaction would be. He and Jerry got their laugh and then separated her from the web, and continued down the narrow path through the bushes and trees. Abbey walked behind them, not wanting to encounter another web. And that's how their day began in Clemson. It got better later on, after her disappointment with the DAR marker and the five walls of stones, which substituted for the fort that was long gone.

They drove back into town for a late breakfast at a small diner just off campus. They'd no sooner walked into the 50's style café than a man and woman in their forties came over and introduced themselves. It turned out to be the President of Clemson University and his wife. They had their picture taken and chatted for a few minutes, thinking nothing of it, until they returned to Atlanta that afternoon for a meeting with the mayor and some local business owners for an early dinner. The mayor said their visit was all over social media – an unexpected visit by a Presidential candidate to a small college town.

It had never really occurred to Gene or Jerry, that social media could blow their cover story in short order. They learned something important that day about creating diversions and the folly of believing that it would work. They were due in Chicago in five days and after that, Harold and Abbey were going home for a week before the first debate on August 6th, plenty of time to rethink their strategy.

Chapter 35

CLEVELAND

July 31st, 8 a.m.

Al Atrash sipped his tea in the backyard of Yamen, his longtime contact through Beirut, and a friend of his wife's family. Yamen had moved to America in the late 80's and taken his oath of citizenship in 1999. He had a Ph.D. in Middle Eastern Studies and was a tenured professor at Case Western University, not far from his very modest home on East 81st Street in Cleveland. Al Atrash was spending this Friday morning purely for pleasure. Amul was not staying with Yamen and would not return to his home again. He did not want to risk compromising his friend's standing in the community, since associating with a person such as himself, would only lead to prison. Yamen had picked him up from his hideaway close to downtown and brought him straight into the garage in his backyard. No neighbors could have seen his entrance, and that was as it should be.

They did not speak of his presence in America, nor of his mission to avenge his son's death. Rather, they spoke of their youths and of family visits to their homes in Lebanon and Syria. It was a pleasant morning of sun and conversation, reminding him of a life he'd lived long ago, but was no more. Even though Yamen understood why his friend Amul had chosen the life he had, he did not agree with his methods, but would never question him about his faith and commitment to Islam. They lived in different worlds but believed in only one faith. Yamen had followed the path through education, whereas Al Atrash had radicalized in his early twenties, never looking back or longing for the carefree days of his youth. His path was rigid and unyielding to outside influence. Yet, here he was, speaking of those days spent under the Middle Eastern sun, a light like no other in the world, because of who and what it shone upon. When they parted, Al Atrash would lay those precious morning hours to rest, and not think of them again.

"Goodbye, my friend," Yamen said.

"Peace be upon you my friend," Al Atrash said and closed the door of Yamen's black Audi, walking away quickly towards the backdoor of Faheid's apartment on Pelton Ct, in a decaying house that smelled of mold.

He'd left one world and entered another. This had been his home for the past ten days and was the place where he plotted his next move against his son's killer. He never looked back to watch Yamen drive away on the narrow red-bricked drive. Amul was no longer in that world. His few hours of respite from being a fugitive were over, and in their place was the reality of his life, where he was hunted by nations all over the world, none of which, had ever come close to catching him.

He was not a proud man, but he looked every assignment over with scrutinizing eyes, knowing that one mistake would cost him everything. In that, he took away a sense of great fulfillment, because his Faith told him the hard and fast truth about life would always see him through to the end. He would always win with God on his side. The world was but a proving ground for faith, one in which he excelled.

The screen door slammed behind him, announcing his arrival to Faheid, who was preparing the afternoon meal in a kitchen that was in need of repair at every turn. Al Atrash found this fetid structure offensive in every way and hated having to spend even one more minute within its walls. He went straight to his room and opened the old wood frame sash the few inches it could and lay down on the smelly cotton mattress atop a sagging metal bed frame, and thought of the upcoming debate in six days.

He had studied the Quicken Loan arena from every angle and was certain he could set himself up for a kill shot from the parking structure across the street. He'd been there three times in the past few days, examining the layout, exits, where he could lay in waiting for the best shot, and then how he could escape. His plan had uncertainties, which he had no way of knowing ahead of time, like where Harold would exit, and how many people would be blocking his shot if he did see him on the short distance from the arena doors to his awaiting car.

He'd laughed at the American's attempt at deception, when Harold was discovered at Clemson, instead of being where his announced meeting was supposedly being held ninety miles away. Stupid American Intelligence Services. They didn't know anything about the tactics of deception.

He'd come to Cleveland, because of the political debate, scheduled by a major network. No one could fake that. He'd even thought about buying a ticket, but that was too risky and would place him among tens of thousands of pleasure-seeking Americans, rubbing shoulders in the cramped seating. He had no stomach for such things – he never had. Sometimes his aversion worked against him on an assignment, making him skirt around such situations, and change his tactics. He much preferred to work at a distance, sending his message at the tap of a phone, or squeeze of a trigger, always observing from a distance to witness the carnage he'd created, and the chaos which ensued, all in the name of God.

Tomorrow he would park Fahied's old 90's Toyota 4Runner on the third level of the parking structure, angling it just enough to hide his presence at the edge of the structure. He would keep back a few feet in the shadows to hide his

sor would mask the reports of shots
fired in quick succession. He would collect the brass casings
and quietly drive out of the structure, which dumped him onto
a street on the opposite side of the structure. He had it all
worked out in his head, and he had driven the route, parked,
squatted in front of his vehicle, then exited the structure all
with precision. Start to finish, after the shots were fired, it
would only take him three minutes to exit and drive at least a
half a mile away, including stopping at intersections. The
police would take at least that long to respond. He closed his
eyes and dreamed of his success, arriving home from another
completed assignment, his ears embracing the welcome sound
of his native tongue.

Chapter 36

THE FIRST DEBATE

August 6th, 7 p.m.

They'd arrived early at the Quicken Loan arena, because Jerry said he needed some extra time to instruct the six agents on the logistics and timing after the debate concluded. There were certain unknowns with the interaction of the ten candidates and their families afterward. Jerry said he needed to be sure the agents understood the threat level which existed with Harold Robertson, and that he was positive Al Atrash was close at hand, lurking in the shadows, waiting for the right moment to strike again, just as he had done in Houston. Jerry was insistent with Harold.

"And so it begins," Harold said mounting the stairs to the stage, his arms spread wide. "Here is where the words shall fall upon the country's ears, and here is the beginning of each of us as candidates for the office of the Presidency, and here also lies the demise of all but one." He whirled around to face the empty arena. "What I mean is, each of us will express our aspirations and intentions within these few moments, and those lasting impressions will define us throughout the campaign. Make no mistake about it, only two shall rise above the rest tonight to continue through the Primaries and into the early summer, at which point, one will yield to the will of the people, and fall in line to support their candidate." He looked down at Abbey, who was sitting on the front edge of the stage with her legs dangling, and had an amused look on her face as she peered over her shoulder.

"Are you going to be this longwinded, philosophical, and prophetic with all your answers? Hmm?" She smiled while stifling her laughter.

"Yes dear, if I must." He laughed when Jerry started clapping his hands slowly from the seats way in the back. "Thanks," he said, waving Jerry off with a brush of his hand. "Thank you for your support." He went to sit with Abbey while Jerry finished doing whatever it was that he was doing with all those agents. "He seems to think Amir's father will show up here tonight. He'd have to be crazy to do that with all the police and Secret Service agents posted everywhere. But then, he was crazy enough to make it into the country and get off three shots in Houston." Abbey elbowed him in the arm.

"It's not a joke you know. He came very close to killing you that night. Let Jerry do his job. He's good at it."

"You're right. I shouldn't joke about it. They're spending a lot of the public's money protecting me. I should be more grateful. After this, I want to go home and finish those five days we said we were going to have. Who knows, maybe we'll even have time to get married?" He tickled her ribs.

"Harold Robertson, you're terrible." Abbey's tone belied her real meaning.

"Oh, so you think it's a good idea," he said. He waited for her stoic, slow burn reaction, something she used to deflect his sarcasm. Never was there a time in his life when he felt surer of himself; he was in love for the second time in his life, and he could hardly wait to see what the next moment had in store for the two of them. Abbey's eyes were searching his, extracting his innermost desire to gather her up in his arms and walk away from all this candidacy hoopla. He wanted to run away with her. She smiled as if she knew his thoughts, catching him off guard, and sending a shiver down his spine. *How was this much happiness possible?* he thought.

"Do you have any idea what you're doing to me right now?" She nodded and kissed him softly. "How does she do that?" He mumbled to himself.

"We can continue this later," Abbey said. "Right now, you need to focus on how you're going to conduct yourself during the debate. You and I both know there's bad blood between you and Oliver Plunkett over his insulting comments to a war veteran. You don't want to lose your temper with him because he'll turn it back on you, and tell you that you're wrong, and make you out to be the angry Congressman who can't control himself."

"Yeah, I know," Harold said. "But if he starts down that road, then so be it. I won't back down, just because he's behaving irrationally and childish, and will probably do me more harm than not. The American people need to see him for what he really is, a selfish tycoon, who didn't give a hoot about all the people losing their homes during the recession, while he leaned back and profited handsomely. It's who he is, and it bothers me that he's even in this debate. He's not Presidential material, but he has the right to be here because of the way the system is structured – bamboozle enough people into believing you on a grand scale, and you can run for President." He could go on, but by the looks of Abbey's face, he was preaching to the choir again. He laughed. "Sorry. I'll try and be good." She shook her head and kissed him.

"Sir, it's time to get ready."

Harold looked up at the tall slender man with a headset and a fist full of papers in his hand. "Gotta go," he said to Abbey. He followed the man around the stage and through the curtain to the waiting area for all ten candidates. No matter how many times he'd played the waiting game in his campaigns for Congress, it didn't change the level of nervousness which slowly crept into his mind.

He knew his platform by heart; it was the same thing he'd fought for in Congress for the eight years he'd served the people of Illinois's 16th District. He'd taught it to his high school students, instilling in them the American Values most prized, and wholly essential to the success of America as a Nation indivisible. He, and all the other candidates, no matter their platforms, believed in America; otherwise, they wouldn't be here tonight for this debate. Even Oliver believed in these values, no matter his outward boisterous, condescending, and totally abrasive attitude towards others. Harold did respect him as a citizen, despite his shortcomings, because he also had a long laundry list of flaws – ones he'd readily admit to holding.

"You know, I'll probably sweat your work off in the first ten minutes," he told the young makeup gal when it was his turn to have his nose powdered, and the sheen dampened on his cheeks and forehead.

"Waterproof," she'd said.

He laughed, knowing he could flush it off his oily skin in no time. It was time to chit-chat with the other nine candidates in the minutes before they were called to the stage. He knew most of the men, some veterans of the Hill, others state governors, but the businessman, he didn't know much at all – no reason for him too.

Harold had never accepted any campaign contributions from special interests, like Oliver. All his funds came straight from common working men and women because that's who he'd represented, no matter what economic class they came from. He barely nodded to Oliver Plunkett when he walked past him as they proceeded from backstage to mount the steps, and take their places behind their lecterns – something to hold onto for dear life in times of trouble. He might get a chance to do just that tonight because he was positioned next to Oliver at center stage. The poles that were taken to choose the ten candidates had shown his rapid ascension through the ranks, to where he was now, second only to Oliver.

If there was to be a sparring match between them, then it would take place within arm's reach of each other – perhaps not the best place for either one of them. When one is hurling insults, it's best to be out of reach. He covered a chuckle by clearing his throat. "Careful," he murmured to himself.

"Ladies and gentlemen, candidates, welcome to the first Republican debate." The female moderator said in a firm voice.

And so it begins, Harold said to himself.

After the introductions, and at the midway point of the discussion on the economy, the first barb was thrown, latching onto a former governor, and beginning round one of a six-round fight to the finish. Harold was surprised by some of the comments and innuendoes being said. Clearly, there was an ensuing dogfight coming if the moderators didn't intervene quickly – which they did, of course. He got his feathers ruffled several times, but Oliver had cautiously circled around engaging him on much of anything of importance. Harold made it his business to avoid engaging as well, especially with the look Abbey cast his way from her seat in the second row.

All that ended when Mr. Oliver Plunkett got into it with the female moderator about things he'd said to the media. Harold had to fight back the urge to laugh aloud at the absurdity of what played out between Oliver and the moderator.

Not long after that, when the questions on America's fight on terror came to the forefront, everyone else on stage had some semblance of an answer about the war with the

Islamic State, but Oliver chose to open his mouth and spout some platitude about closing the borders – an idea so completely against what America stood for. It had drawn a mixed reaction from the audience, encouraging him to elaborate – and then Oliver's foot got in the way of his mouth. In the heat of the moment, Harold opened his mouth, against his better judgment, and interjected a question, running over the man's ridiculous dictum.

"What would you have America do, sir?" Their eyes met squarely for the first time that night, and much to Harold's surprise, Oliver curiously wanted to engage with him on this issue. The moderators didn't interfere, at least not at first. Oliver laid out his plan, and it was apparent to all that he thought it was a smart and clever one. Oliver turned towards Harold from time-to-time with a challenging demeanor, and his curtly smile.

Harold was never one to miss out on an opportunity to clarify a man's beliefs, who was seeking or currently in public office, so he quietly entered the ring with Oliver, casting a glance towards the moderators for approval, which he got.

"Mr. Plunkett, would you please explain to the American people how you plan to be the Commander in Chief of our Armed Forces when you insult a war hero in the public forum of broadcast news?" Harold folded his arms tightly across his chest and was frowning at Oliver, demanding an answer with his forceful delivery. He quietly stared him down in those few moments of utter silence in the arena. Oliver's face was turning red and he looked flustered but ready to charge his aggressor.

Silently, Harold willed the man into battle. He wanted to show this man up for what he really was: a shrewd businessman with no leadership skills to offer as the

Commander in Chief of the American military. Oliver's blustery responses drew cries, cheers, and boisterous boos from the audience; mostly he had nothing of consequence to say, so Harold launched the second of his two questions.

"Will you apologize to Senator James Still?" He literally threw the words at Oliver with his body and eyes. He found himself halfway between their lecterns and away from his mic, which emboldened him all the more, knowing that what he said would not be heard by anyone else but them.

"By insulting one veteran, you have done so to all. You are not worthy to hold the Office the President." Harold's words surprised even him.

He was angry and ready to fight and that scared him. He quickly stepped back, having immediate regrets about his actions, but his eyes never left the man.

"Gentlemen, please refrain from . . ."

"You couldn't hear what he said, could you?" Oliver's words rang over the moderators. "He threatened me. I can't debate with an angry man who issues threats . . ."

"Answer the question," Harold said firmly into his mic, feeling the heat on his face. His worst nightmare was to lose control in a public debate, and he'd just done so in front of millions of viewers. Adrenalin would always cause confusion in the mind, a fog of non-thinking, and he was struggling to keep his composure, while his thoughts cleared.

"Not to you I won't," Oliver snapped.

By now, the audience was murmuring loudly, as were the other candidates on stage. Everyone knew Harold Robertson was a patriotic man and had lost a brother in the war.

"Answer the question for the American people, sir." Harold's demanding tone made Oliver nervous. He could see it in his eyes.

"Gentlemen, we're moving on now," the female moderator interrupted.

Harold took a deep breath of regret, knowing he'd committed the cardinal sin in a debate. He'd gotten angry and hurled an insult. And even though only he and Oliver had heard what was said, it was still a mistake to have done so.

Most of the remaining time he spent in regrets, all because of one unfiltered statement made in anger. As the evening wore on, he missed a lot of the crosstalk on stage and didn't engage with Oliver. He answered the questions asked him by the moderators, but his heart was not in it, and it showed.

Chapter 37

KILL ZONE

August 6th

A l Atrash had spent half the day lying in the back of the 4Runner SUV waiting for the appointed time when his son's murderer would emerge from the arena. He was following the debate on the internet with his smartphone, paying little attention to what was being said, merely waiting to take his revenge. From his position in the parking structure across the street from the arena, he had good views of two exit points. By the looks of the commotion at the front entrance around the corner, he expected Harold and his Secret Service men to exit through one of these two sets of doors. He would be hidden from view behind an architectural panel between the concrete posts, designed to hide the vehicles from view. His SUV would hide him from anyone passing by, leaving him free to focus on the task at hand. This time he would not miss.

Around six o'clock in the evening, he heard male voices approaching. He slid off the back seat onto the floor and covered himself with some of the large shopping bags, and a raincoat, made to look as if it were hastily thrown into the backseat. The men were checking vehicles. He hoped the darkened windows would obscure their view of the contents enough to make his camouflage look authentic. He laid perfectly still until a metallic sound against one of the windows made him flinch. Sweat poured down his face as he clutched his 9mm pistol by his side.

"Hey, what time do we get a break?" one of the men said, as

they moved onto the next vehicle.

Al Atrash released his breath, having held it the entire time. He waited ten minutes before moving to peer out the window. Seeing that the coast was clear, he stretched his legs and moved about in the backseat. He was uncomfortable and tired of his confinement in the vehicle.

He broke off a piece of cheddar cheese from the two-pound brick and took a bite from the day-old loaf of French bread, chewing the tasteless mass that Americans passed-off as cheese. His hunger needed to be satisfied, just as his hunger to kill Harold Robertson needed gratification. His water was warm and his patience grew thin. He'd endured enough and wanted to make the kill and go home – if he lived. There were no illusions in his business. Bullets ripped through bodies and people died. He'd never considered it a thing of beauty, this business he'd chosen, but it was ordained and needed doing.

When he finished the remainder of the bread, he covered himself and continued to watch the debate on the floor, fighting off sleep. He'd already nodded off several times in the afternoon while sitting in the backseat. The time for his destiny was growing closer and he couldn't afford any errors, especially one as stupid as falling asleep and getting caught. He didn't mind the notion of being caught after he made the kill, but before was to shame both his family and himself. He hunkered down and watched the inane display of American politics, completely unable to grasp its importance, because there was no glory to God in any of it. As to the man he hunted, he did respect Harold for his bravery, especially since he knew he was being targeted and could lose his life at any moment. Al Atrash laughed when Harold stepped towards the man next to him on the stage, challenging him to answer truthfully – that he could respect.

Thirty minutes later, Al Atrash opened the cloth shopping

bag which held his assault rifle and assembled it while lying on the floor. The debate had concluded and the men on stage were with family members and shaking the hands of the other candidates. He uncovered himself and looked out the window, making sure no one was nearby. He locked in the twenty-round clip and chambered a shell, making sure the safety was on.

He opened the side door and slid to the concrete floor, latching the door quietly behind him. He was backed into the parking place and three feet away from the concrete column, and the panel used to hide cars from view from the street. The narrow four-inch slot between the two was the perfect cover to hide him from view. He lay on his belly and watched closely for the first group of candidates and their families to exit. One of the exits he was covering had a steady stream of people from the audience exiting, so he ignored it to focus on the closer set of doors, which had the waiting security vehicles lined up on 6th street. He had no way of knowing what Harold's vehicle looked like, so he observed everyone who exited the arena. Each person loomed large in the 20-power scope, making it an easy shot, and guaranteeing his success.

After twenty minutes, he rubbed his tired eyes and stretched his cramping leg muscles. The long hours of waiting were having a toll on him and the blurriness, which came and went, was affecting his ability to identify faces clearly through the scope. When he thought he recognized two Secret Service agents, his heart pounded in his chest, sharpening his attention. He followed them as they exited, but Harold wasn't completely visible. Three of the largest men were directly in front of Harold, and his head only bobbed into view for a second, but certainly not long enough for him to squeeze off an accurate shot. They were halfway to the vehicle when he thought he had to take a shot now or risk losing the opportunity because of the poor angle of the shot. The narrow slot he had to work with was interfering with him following his target, making him have to shift his body to the left in order to keep up with the quickly moving targets.

Harold's chest appeared suddenly between the shoulders of the lead men and he took four shots in quick succession. Harold disappeared from view, but the man behind him fell to the sidewalk. The three agents in front already had their pistols drawn and were scanning the parking structure, as they rushed Harold to the vehicle, leaving the man lying where he fell. They were gone within seconds and he had no further shots.

Al Atrash withdrew and jumped into the SUV, and fled down to the exit, ramming through the plastic gate and out onto Bolivar Rd. From there, he'd connect to Interstate 90 in two miles, and be out of the city in less than fifteen minutes, giving him at least a small head start. He would get off the freeway after ten miles and drive on the county roads all the way to New York City. It was there that he had the best chance to survive, hiding among the large diversity of people.

It was of little consolation, as he'd failed again. It wasn't over yet. Harold was still alive.

Chapter 38

HOME

August 7ᵗʰ, 4 p.m.

There was no way to describe the feeling of desolation in Harold's heart. Jerry was dead; shot three times, with one of the bullets grazing Harold's temple before entering Jerry's heart, and blowing it apart. Jerry had hit the sidewalk already dead. There was a report of four shots, with that many casings found on the third level of the parking structure in the northwest corner, later that afternoon. Abbey cried in his arms for hours, on the way back to their hotel, and then lying in bed together. She couldn't stop. Harold remembered only a feeling of helplessness.

At the time, he didn't even know Jerry was dead. They'd left him on the sidewalk in a pool of blood for the TV news crews to record his epitaph for all the world to see. It should have been him, he'd thought as they sped away to safety.

His feelings of complete helplessness grew, eventually encompassing far more than just the death of Jerry. It included his brother Alex, the eleven immigrants, but the most painful of all was his wife, Ruth. That's when the feeling of utter desolation began to form in his mind, its malignant roots finding their way into every part of his body and mind. He preferred death to this feeling because at least with death, there was a resolution. He had no way to resolve this madman's agenda. Wherever he went, death followed. How many people would die because of him? The responsibility was all on him. It was, after all, he who had killed the man's son. When Abbey had finally stopped crying and fallen asleep, he lay there as if in a prison, devoid of any feelings, and unable to sleep. How lucky she was for sleep to come and take her away from all this misery.

"Sir, there's a call for you," Denise said from the doorway of his bedroom. "It's Deputy Secretary Gene Drake of DHS."

Denise placed the phone in his right hand and then retreated to the doorway. Harold's mind was incapable of comprehending anything at the moment. He heard Gene's voice, but the words were gibberish. He heard Jerry's name and something about a plan for tighter security, none of which made any sense. And then there was a deafening silence.

"Harold," Gene said quietly, "I need you to talk to me. Tell me what you're feeling, anything."

Again there was silence. Harold tried to find the words, but his emptiness kept them at bay.

"Harold, Jerry's dead. You know that, right?"

"Yes," Harold's shaky voice replied. It didn't even sound like his voice.

"I'm sorry. I know this is hard, but we have to move on and focus on your safety." Gene said firmly.

Something inside of Harold heard those words and comprehended what had happened on the sidewalk. The image of Jerry lying in a pool of his own blood wouldn't leave his mind.

"He was my friend," Harold whispered. As he spoke those words, all those images of being hustled away by hands gripping his jacket and shoving him into a vehicle came back with a vengeance. They bore the truth. And driving away with the image of Jerry lying crumpled on the sidewalk in the window, that was the point at which his feeling of desolation faded, and the truth took hold. He sucked in a shaky breath and got himself sat up against the headboard.

"I'm sorry Gene," Harold said drawing in a deep breath, "I didn't really hear anything you said. You'll have to repeat it for me." He listened to Gene repeat the message as best he could, and apologize for the incident ever happening. Harold's mind was still a little numb, but he heard every word, and he understood for the second time, just how fortunate he was to be alive.

His hand holding the phone fell to the bed, feeling lifeless and heavy. Across the room, Denise was standing in the doorway still wearing the blood-stained white shirt, and her drawn and tired eyes were looking at him. She walked over and pocketed her phone, her eyes never leaving his.

"I'm sorry," he said. "Were you friends?" She shook her head.

"I'll be right outside," she whispered, and walked away.

Harold felt cold and began to shake again. That was the last thing he remembered before falling asleep and didn't wake until ten o'clock the next morning. Abbey was gone. His mind had cleared and he felt mostly rested. He sat up, finding he was still dressed in the same clothes from last night. When he ran his fingers through his hair, he noticed a sore spot above his left ear, where the bullet had nibbled off some hair and skin.

"That's twice, you son of a bitch," he mumbled in front of the bathroom mirror. This was his life now, traveling from place to place, having to watch over his shoulder for this madman hunting him. What kind of life was that? He showered, shaved, and changed clothes, before entering the living room area of their suite. Abbey was sitting with Denise on the sofa, with a breakfast cart parked by the dining table. He poured himself a cup of coffee and took two of the Danish rolls, and sat next to Abbey. "Morning," he said quietly. Abbey lay her head on his shoulder and uttered a barely audible, "morning."

"Sir," Denise said, "Gene has canceled all your planned

stops for the next week. He told me to tell you to take some time off and go home. Vince and I will accompany you, and we'll be met by two other agents when we arrive."

Harold took an enormous bite of the roll, stuffing his cheeks to the max, and nodded towards Denise. He chewed for a minute and sipped his coffee, while the two girls stared at him.

"Okay, that sounds good," he said swallowing the last wad of Danish. "At the moment, anything sounds good after last night. I'll want to send a personal note to Jerry's parents with some flowers, and regrets that I cannot attend his memorial service." The words were so matter-of-factly said, that even he felt their coldness, but that was how he felt at the moment – cold and dead. Abbey squeezed his hand and drew it into her lap. He couldn't help but feel her warmth of spirit trying to cheer him up. Even in this state of mind, she could still reach out to him and connect. What an amazing woman she was.

"You know, we could get married now, and even have a honeymoon. My folks have an older, but nice RV. We could park it out by the old oak tree next to the pond at their place." Abbey's eyes shone.

Her hopeful eyes were searching inside of him. He kissed her hand, clutching it with both of his. "Sounds like a plan." He mustered up the best smile he could. "Can we leave now?"

His question was directed to Denise, whose eyes were drinking in the scene playing out before her. She had told him of a lost marriage because of her work. "Can we?" He repeated. She replied with a nod and stood, walking to the door to inform Vince, who was in the hall, keeping watch. They were on the road within the hour, and that seemed to lift him out of his gloominess. They'd be at her parent's home by supper.

As they turned off the main highway and onto the county road leading to the Nelson's farm, the last of his heaviness lifted from him, leaving him clear-headed for the first time. It was all of twenty-four hours since the shooting and here they were in Clayton – home at last. Nothing could compare to the feeling of being home, especially the farm smells and humidity mixed in with summer heat. He breathed it in like it was an elixir, capable of curing most anything.

The old farmhouse looked the same as it did when he'd met Jimmy to practice. Denise parked the truck by the barn next to Vince's black sedan. He and Abbey had ridden a lot of the way in the camper but had sat three abreast in the cab when they were getting closer to home.

He bailed out of the air-conditioned truck and into the sweltering heat of a fine August day in Middle America. Pete and Sharon Nelson were already out the door and headed straight for them, covering the two hundred feet with quick steps. They were in their mid-seventies but moved like they were thirty years younger. Abbey and Sharon were dead ringers for each other, so much alike, they could have been twins, less the twenty-something years difference in age. He vaguely remembered them, but that was a long time ago.

Pete reached them half a step ahead of his wife, thrusting his hand into Harold's, and clamping down with a vise grip. He gave his best effort in return. Sharon and Abbey were practically dancing in the barnyard, they were so happy to see each other.

"We saw you last night on the TV," Pete said. "Terrific, just terrific."

"Daddy, you don't know do you?" Abbey said with a sadness in her voice.

"Know what?"

"That man tried to kill Harold again. He missed, but he killed Jerry, our Secret Service agent." Abbey wiped at a tear that was filling her eye.

"My God. No, we hadn't heard," Pete turned towards Vince and Denise. "I'm so sorry."

"I'm sorry, I don't know what I was thinking," Abbey said. "This is Denise and Vince. We were all together last night in Cleveland."

Pete pulled his daughter into his arms and stroked her head. He looked hurt like he was feeling her pain. Sharon's eyes met Harold's, searching much like her daughter's eyes had.

"Twelve hours ago, we were both a mess. Being here helps." He said in a reassuring tone. Sharon's eyes answered for her, filled with deep concern. Even though he tried to sound reassuring, he knew in his heart it wasn't true. He couldn't protect her any more than Jerry could. Abbey could have been just as easily shot as any one of them.

"Let's go in out of the heat," Sharon said. "I made iced tea this morning and baked some oatmeal-raisin cookies before the heat of the day set in."

They left their bags and followed them into the two-story farmhouse. It was like stepping back in time. The living room was filled with fine furniture from the turn of the century, right down to the drapery and oriental rugs. It was an eye opener for Harold. Abbey grew up in a home which had been in the family for one hundred twenty years. It was complete with some of the best Americana style furniture he'd ever seen.

It must have shown because Sharon took him straight over to the prized piece, an 1880's Davenport desk with burl wood top. Harold smiled, running his hand over every inch of it. He caught Sharon's eye and asked where it came from. She said it was her great grandmother's wedding gift to her daughter. He nodded. "You have a beautiful home, Mrs. Nelson. I see now where Abbey gets her discerning eye for traditional values."

They sat and talked for an hour about politics and the need for unity in America. It was the most relaxed he'd been since leaving his home nearly three months ago. They had barbequed chicken legs and potato salad on the back patio, right before a sunset to remember. Then Abbey and he walked out to the pond and sat under the huge oak tree, which was planted in the mid-nineteenth century. There was a swing hung from a large branch twelve feet above the ground. They stayed there and talked until the last of the twilight faded. They would spend the night in the house and set up the RV tomorrow morning.

That night he dreamed of baseball and woke up the next morning feeling rested and happy, something he'd not done in a while.

Denise and Vince helped them clean the RV and charge the batteries, fill the water and propane tanks, and wash the windows. It was twenty-five years old, but nicely kept, and everything functioned except for the TV – fine by him. The RV sat behind the barn and thirty feet from the pond and oak tree. Sunrise shone through the oak and sunset was directly behind the house and four elm trees that shaded it all day. They were having lunch on the patio when Gene called.

"You'll want to hear this news," Gene said.

"Okay, I give."

"We got a clear video of Al Atrash leaving the parking structure and then another at an intersection with a traffic cam. It's not perfect, but at least now we have a make, model, color, license plate and partial on his face, enough so a facial recognition program can pick him out from a crowd. Pretty good, eh?" Gene's excitement swept through the phone.

"Yeah, that is pretty good. Only a matter of time now." Harold's face flashed with anger, but it was good to hear some positive news. "Thanks for passing that along. You need to talk with the guys?"

"Already have. Enjoy your time on the farm." Gene chuckled and hung up.

"Well, it looks like they're gonna corner this terrorist soon. They got some pictures of him." Harold shared with the Nelsons. That was the point at which Pete started probing his daughter for answers, much to his wife's dismay. Sharon wanted them to have time away from the terrible events they'd witnessed, but the man needed answers because it involved his daughter. Harold could appreciate his feelings, having a daughter himself.

Harold let Abbey speak her mind to her father and mother. She didn't mince any words either, laying it all out there on the table that afternoon. It was indeed quite the story, hearing it come from the one who had experienced it all. Her journalistic approach helped her father not dip too deep into the emotions of his daughter's life being in jeopardy.

The defining moment was the announcement of their plans to be married by the local justice of the peace. Pete was excited while Sharon was disappointed that they wouldn't be having a church wedding. Abbey was diplomatic about it all, saying she'd already been that route, and didn't need a big to-do this time. Harold was happy he didn't have to say one word until the end when Sharon's quiet, piercing eyes spoke worlds about her concerns with the man hunting him and the two close calls. He understood and shared her concerns.

"The DHS will be upping my security from now on until the man is caught or killed. Gene Drake, the Deputy Secretary is seeing to it personally, and I trust his judgment." Harold hated that he had to lie to put Abbey's parents at ease. They deserved better, but the truth was, no one had been able to protect them against this madman. And now, his friend Jerry was dead. In his heart, Harold knew how worried Sharon was for both their lives and rightfully so.

They ended the afternoon with Abbey showing her parents the video from the Grand Canyon on her phone, and that changed the mood and set the tone for the next few days.

They arranged their wedding with Judge Simmons for the following day at noon – the only time available in the Judge's schedule. It gave Abbey and her mother time to find the family heirloom wedding dress in the attic. Its fine linen had yellowed a bit over the years, but Abbey was dead set to wear it this time. She'd had a modern dress for her first marriage. Harold minded his tongue and stayed out of it.

Later that day, Abbey explained to him that she was at her grandmother's bedside when she passed in the middle of the night. They'd talked for hours the evening before and had the dress out for her grandmother to help her recall her wedding day – Alzheimer's disease had taken away much of her past. Abbey had cried till dawn. Grandma Nelson was the one who had instilled the journalist's bug in her at a young age, reading her children's mystery stories when she'd visit her at the nursing home in town. Grandma Nelson always helped her to find out the secret or uncover the mystery.

It came as no surprise to Harold and Abbey that half the town showed up at noon outside the courthouse. There were reporters from: the local paper where Abbey had worked after high school; the TV news crew from Rockford where Abbey had her first journalist position; George, an old time friend of Harold's from Chicago who'd followed him on the campaign trail numerous times and submitted articles to the AP; and most importantly, their personal friends and families dating from childhood to the present. After greeting hundreds of old friends and wading their way into the courthouse with the help of Vince and Denise, they sat in the Judge's chambers and talked of old times and current events for a half an hour before getting to the civil ceremony. Judge Simmons rushed out afterwards, saying he was late for a hearing, waved and left them in the hallway outside his chambers.

"Well, now we've gone and done it, haven't we?" Abbey tickled his ribs and laughed.

"Yeah, that was the easy part. Now we get to face the crowd," he pointed from the second story window at the end of the hallway. He waved because one of their friends spotted them in the window. "Shall we?" Harold offered his arm and they walked down the original marble staircase and out the front doors. There on the steps of the Clayton County Courthouse, with Abbey in her Grandmother's wedding dress and him in a rented black tuxedo, they greeted the now sprawling crowd of perhaps five or six hundred people. The female TV reporter walked down the steps next to them, with the cameraman nearly tripping as he walked backwards down the twenty-two steps. She kept pushing questions at them about the shootings and his run for the Presidency. He fended her off until they reached the sidewalk and then he turned to face her and smiled. "I'd be more than happy to answer questions about . . ." He paused and waved to the crowd, lifting his and Abbey's hands up high. The cheers drowned out the reporter, leaving him the option to walk away or stay and see if she would honor his request. She smiled up at him, almost laughing, and nodded.

"Congratulations Mr. and Mrs. Robertson." She said when the cheers died down.

"Thank you," Abbey responded. "We'd like to say that we will be honeymooning for the next couple of days. Love to tell you where, but then that would spoil it for us, wouldn't it?"

"I'm sure all of America wishes you the best. Is there anything you wish to tell the American public?"

"Yes," Abbey grinned. "Please vote for my husband."

Harold laughed at Abbey's frankness, knowing that she was toying with the reporter. He kissed her on top of her head.

"That's my gal," he whispered in her ear.

"Hey, Harold. You gonna kiss her or what?" A loud male voice came from the crowd.

"Yeah," he laughed. They both turned to face each other and executed a long drawn out, 'sailor's goodbye kiss' from the 40's, where he leaned her backward in his arms, and dove in for the kiss. The crowd ate it up, cheering, howling, and the like. He was having some fun for a change and Abbey didn't seem to mind, so long as he didn't damage her heirloom wedding dress. He held the kiss for as long as his aging back could, standing her back up, both with flushed faces.

"Now that's what I call a real kiss," Abbey teased him. "We should do that more often."

Harold's face was hot and he was feeling more self-conscious at the moment than he had in some time. *Was it the hometown crowd, or was it because he was in love for the second time in his life? he wondered.*

Abbey's eyes were dancing with love as the crowd quieted and her lips formed the words, "I love you," sending his heart into flip-flops.

He laughed and hugged his bride, turning them both to face the hometown crowd, whose faces clearly wanted more. As he waved, the sheriff worked his way up to Denise and Vince and handed them a wireless mic. Denise handed it to Harold and gestured with her hand to say a few words. Her eyes were gleaming with pride for the newlyweds. He took it and forgot to click it off before he cleared his throat, hearing the sounds echo off the brick buildings across the street.

"Thank you all," he said. "Thank you from the bottom of my heart. Abbey and I are so happy to be home in Clayton . . ." The applause drowned him out for a few seconds. "We are so happy to be home and thank you for the warm welcome. I have missed my home over the past few months, but I have been busy fulfilling a dream of meeting the people of our great nation. And I am thrilled to say, 'there's no place like home'." He waited for the cheers to quiet. "When Abbey and I are on the road again, I will remember this moment, cherishing the love we shared here today and drawing strength from it in the days to come, with whatever they bring." He paused because he was at a loss for words. "Ah, I think Abbey has something to say now." He handed her the mic. She clasped his hands and the mic in hers for a moment with tears in her eyes, and an angelic smile painted on her lips.

"I have dreamed of this day ever since I was nine years old, and Harold would come to my home to teach my brother the ins and outs of baseball. That's how long I have loved him. And God willing, I will go on loving him for the rest of my life . . . and then a whole lot longer after that. You all know what has happened in the past few months, but what you don't know is that one of our dear friends, Jerry Isaack of Montana, who also happened to be protecting us, died several days ago right before our eyes. You need to know that the men and women of the Secret Service lay down their lives for those who they would keep from harm's way. Denise and Vince are two such individuals, and I truly value their dedication and willingness to serve our nation, the same as our men and women in the armed services."

The people of Clayton gave them a thunderous applause which lasted a full minute, and from the looks of Denise and Vince, it was taken to heart. Harold was so proud of Abbey, always thinking of others and their dedication in service to the country. He laced his fingers together with Abbey's, knowing what a strong leader she'd be as First Lady – an inspiring leader for every woman in America.

"Now, if you'll excuse us, we have a honeymoon to begin." Abbey waved.

They departed as the applause faded, waving, and followed Denise and Vince to the car parked behind the courthouse. Harold was walking on air.

****

Harold and Abbey disappeared into the Nelson's RV for three days straight, venturing out only for morning and evening walks, and campfires by the pond. They turned off their cell phones and no one came to their door. It was the best and most memorable three days of his life. They did what all honeymooners' do: they searched the depths of each other's souls, got lost in their lovemaking, and talked into the early morning hours, both of them eager to learn more about each other. He didn't remember ever feeling quite like this, not even on his honeymoon with his high school sweetheart, Ruth; similar, but this much more intense as seasoned lovers on their second time around.

It was on the evening of the first night, he realized how unprepared he was to fall this deeply in love again. Gone were his excuses and intellectual reasons for being satisfied with the life he'd lived. They couldn't hold a candle to this level of meaningful love, founded in gentleness and depths of a romantic ecstasy, which far exceeded any youthful lovemaking. It was like falling into a deep sleep, filled with every dream he'd ever had being fulfilled beyond his wildest expectations, only to wake and begin again throughout the night. The windows into Abbey's soul were thrown open and so completely alluring, he found it nearly unbearable. She took him places within himself that he never dreamed possible, and still there was more.

And then came the third night, with its mellow glow of a dream come true. All that had come before, had gently unlocked the doors of his heart, leading him into the surreal vision of what life was really all about. Together as one, they were both reborn in each other's arms that night, falling into the abyss of love too deep for anyone to find their way out – and yet, they awoke in the morning, not the same two people who had entered the night before. His mind was a shambles, his body vibrating strangely, but his heart was strong and bright. Life had taken on new meaning for him.

He woke at three o'clock in the morning, more awake, more aware of himself and life than he could remember. He stepped outside to sit in the cool morning air just before dawn and waited for the sun to rise. Inside the RV lived another world, a world foreign to him until three days ago; a world he credited to Abbey, for it was she who had opened him to himself with her wealth of love. He always thought of life as a mystery, a puzzle to be solved; but now, he knew it was so much more than that, having fallen into its cathartic embrace so full of love, the kind of love, which only two individuals can share. He'd seen a small part of the meaning of life, something he'd searched his whole life for, not truly finding it until this moment. And as he waited for the dawn of a new day, he knew in his heart that their journey together in life would bring both change and understanding. He was filled with the knowing that there was so much more to life than he'd experienced so far, and it carried with it a peace of mind, a clarity like no other.

"May I sit with you?" Abbey's soft voice carried from the RV door.

He turned to see her in robe and slippers, standing at the open door. He got up and walked to the door and wrapped his arms around her buttocks, lifting her to the ground. The very smell of her was intoxicating, making him dizzy with desire. He sat beside her under the massive oak, almost afraid to say a word, not wanting to break the spell, which had settled on them for three days of utter enchantment with life.

"Harold Robertson, I experienced more of life in the past three days than in all the days previous. Are you to blame for that?"

The sound of her voice wrapped itself around him, leaving him nearly mute, eventually summoning the words to his lips. "No, I think it's the other way around. I have never loved like this before and I think you are the responsible party. I feel as you do, as if all of life has lived through me in the past few days."

"Imagine if this was only the first step," Abbey's eyes gleamed.

Abbey held his hand to her breast, stroking it, and hummed quietly to herself. "I wish I could feel this way more often," he almost whispered, "but I know it will fade as time goes on." He leaned across to kiss her cheek.

"Perhaps the memory will suffice. These three days were a gift I shall always cherish," Abbey said rising from the chair. "I'm going to make coffee."

Harold watched as she walked towards the RV, searing her image into his memory. In the moments just before dawn gave way to the sunrise, his gaze fixed on the horizon, knowing that she was his sunrise and the dawning of a new day in his life. He would become a better person because of her.

Chapter 39

NEW YORK CITY
Sept. 11ᵗʰ

Sept. 11th

The call came at the perfect time. Harold was flipping through the news on his phone, and eating breakfast with Abbey in Central Park, a boxed meal from their hotel, when his phone rang. It was Gene. Harold put it on speaker and was about to say hello when the phone blared out Gene's words.

"We got him," Gene said.

Harold's mind was blank for a brief moment, wondering who he could be talking about, but then it registered very clearly with him that Amul Al Atrash was in custody, and no longer a threat to him. Such feelings of freedom are rare in life, so he took a moment, and drew in a long deep breath of the exhilaration, which quickly spread throughout his body. "Gene, that's great news," he said, but Gene had only called to say those words, and hung up. "Hump," he grunted.

"What?" Abbey's inquisitive eyes found his.

"You heard him say 'we got him,' so I think it's safe to assume they have Al Atrash in custody." His downturned mouth and nod spoke of his thoughtful recognition of this turn of events. "It comes at a good time for New Yorkers, because this is where he's been hiding the past month."

"How do you know that?"

He showed her the headline he'd just scrolled to on his phone, of the CNBC report from twenty minutes ago. "The South Bronx. He was holed up in an apartment of a long-suspected cell

216

operative."

"So it's finally over. We can feel safe again." Abbey's excited tone resonated in the air.

He nodded, smiling. "Yes. What a great feeling, of freedom, I mean." Abbey's tears ran down around her mouth and fell into her open breakfast container. He wiped her cheeks with his napkin and slid his arm around her gently shaking shoulders. He knew how relieved she was because he felt the same way. He held her and waited as she emptied herself of all the stored fears she held for both of their lives. Denise was watching from nearby, probably having already heard the news from her boss.

"I'm better," Abbey sniffled, wiping her nose and face with a wad of napkins. "I feel hungry all of a sudden, really hungry."

"Well then, let's eat. If we want more, we passed a coffee and croissant vendor a ways back." Abbey wouldn't eat the cold scrambled eggs, so he shoveled them in, letting her have the bacon, potatoes, and toast. Even their coffee was getting cold. He waved Denise over. As she hustled over to them, he got his wallet out and was about to hand her a couple of twenties, when she waved him off, saying she was alone with them for a half hour. Vince was sick and a replacement would take that long to get there. "I take it you heard Al Atrash was captured."

"Yes, but that doesn't change our coverage for you, especially in this park early in the morning. Rules are rules. You know that." Denise's piercing eyes conveyed her message.

"Right. Then let's walk together, shall we?" He stood and threw the trash in the container next to the bench. "Did you get any specifics on the capture?" He asked as they walked along the path.

"It wasn't pretty. The FBI raid, with NYPD support, took a lot of fire. There were five males in the apartment, and each had an assault rifle close by. Two of them managed to get a dozen rounds off before they were taken down. One agent was injured in the leg. Other than that, the raid went smoothly. This was an important cell in the area, which had been under surveillance for some time. The fact that Al Atrash was there, came as a complete surprise though."

"I'm sorry an agent was hurt." He said, stopping behind two people in line at the coffee stand. Denise took up her position several steps away, scanning the area with her trained eye. He liked watching her work, taking in so much and accessing it so quickly. She was alone at the moment, so she was being extra vigilant. He stepped up to the cart and ordered enough for four, in case the new agent was hungry too. He mixed sugar and creamer in Denise's cup, and handed the coffee to her while placing the croissant in her jacket pocket. They returned to the same bench and sat together, with Denise getting up every thirty seconds to scan the surroundings.

"Roger that," Denise responded into her lapel mic.

She sent a text off and then sat with them.

"He's two minutes out. I sent him our location," she said stuffing the croissant in her mouth.

"You know, I really admire how efficient you are. I timed it. You ate that croissant in less than fifteen seconds, and only tied up your weapon hand for oh, six seconds." He laughed, as did she. Both women elbowed his arms, laughing. Denise was all business the next moment, taking up her position to observe, as the new agent rounded the bend in the path, jogging up next to her. They spoke for a moment before he moved into the position Denise pointed to across the path. They would say hello later.

****

Later in the morning, he arrived at the 9/11 Memorial for short talk as part of the proceedings, nothing fancy, just a few words to lend his support. He chatted with the Mayor, Police & Fire Chiefs, and several survivors beforehand. It was a small gathering of several hundred, but the TV news crews would carry the message to the nation and world later in the day. Fourteen years had passed, but in his mind, it was only yesterday, after listening to some of the survivor's personal stories. The seven people he spoke with each added their story, lending itself to a complete emotional picture of the chaos on that morning. He felt their strength, their pain, their resolve, but most of all he got to know their hearts as survivors. He would hold their stories as close as he did his brother's because remembering was important for the generations to come. Vigilance always came at a price.

****

That evening, Abbey invited Denise and Vince to join them in the dining room of the hotel for dinner. It took some convincing on their part because both Denise and Vince said it violated protocol to sit with their assignments, something about not being able to surveil the room while engaged in conversation. They sat at a table next to a wall so that Denise and Vince faced the room. It didn't become awkward until a protestor entered the dining room and began ranting and raving about the ills of the world, and that 9/11 was justified because America was the aggressor in the world. Well, Vince had moved swiftly across the room and subdued the man, while Denise hustled them out through the kitchen, and was ready to get them back to their hotel room, when Vince radioed her that the police were hauling the guy away. She holstered her 9mm and apologized to the kitchen staff as they returned to their table. It was then that the conversation became lively, and Denise was on the cutting edge, wanting to know more about them personally. Vince didn't rejoin them, instead, taking up a position next to the kitchen door to better survey the room.

"Well, I'm glad that's over with," Denise said, pushing the cold steak around on her plate. "Sorry if I was a little rough getting you out of the room."

"No need, you were merely doing your job, and we are most grateful you're so good at it," Harold said. He hailed the waiter over and asked to have their food warmed.

"I didn't want to bother you on your honeymoon, but was curious if you two grew up together and were sweethearts in high school," Denise asked.

"Yes and no," Harold responded. "I coached her older brother in baseball, but other than that, we really didn't interact with each other. There's nine years between us."

"Maybe he didn't interact, but I did, every time he came over. You just don't remember Harold. I'd fetch the wild throws when I wasn't being too shy. You see, Denise, I had a crush on him, and he didn't even know it."

"Typical guy," Denise said. "I practically stalked this one football player during high school. He was clueless until I cornered him at a school dance, and kissed him. He about fell over, but at least I got his attention. He said I embarrassed him in front of his buddies when really, he was glad I'd kiss him in front of all his jock friends. I was pretty athletic and strong compared to a lot of guys. So, what became of you two after high school?"

"We both married and had families. We didn't meet up again until I ran for Congress after I retired from teaching. Abbey was a local journalist and she covered my campaigns. We'd meet up from time to time later on, but only when I was newsworthy. She covered my run for governor and then we didn't see each other until the attack at Mt. Rushmore. She was there dodging bullets like everyone else, only she and her cameraman got an exclusive of the shooting. While I was in the hospital, she interviewed me, and it was then that we really connected."

He looked to Abbey to see if he'd left anything out, which of course, he had. Abbey continued filling in the important details for the next ten minutes, and before she was done, Denise and she were fast friends. He was astounded at how quickly women could become friends.

He'd watched his Ruth do just that, even when he saw no way over what he considered to be, insurmountable obstacles – at least it seemed that way to him. One thing he'd learned in his first year on the Hill was to be cautious about trusting lobbyists and Representatives who were overly friendly – there were always strings attached. Abbey elbowed him in the side.

"Hmm? What?" he mumbled, looking clueless at her and Denise.

"Harold, are you paying attention? Denise asked you a question."

"Ah. Sorry. What did you ask?"

"I asked if being in love again was easier than the first time?"

"Oh, I don't know about easier. Different yes, but just as intense, if not more so than the first time." Harold paused a moment, looking at Abbey, wondering how in the world they'd wound up together after all these years. It mystified him still. "I think maybe I'm more in love this time because I'm older, and therefore my body's not going berserk – not that it isn't though – just different." He scratched his head, a bit bewildered. "What do you think Abbey?" He said, looking for help. She leaned into him, laying her head against his arm, and then punched him in the arm.

"Men," she laughed. "So clueless about love."

221

He didn't know what to say, so he managed a pleasant smile and continued eating his cold steak. One thing he'd learned with Ruth was to not say anything if he knew it would get him in hot water, which happened more often than not.

"I'm just teasing," Abbey smiled.

He nodded and continued to chew. The smirk on Denise's face made her appear ready to join in with Abbey, instead, she glanced around the room.

"Let me guess, you're working now?" He chuckled. She frowned and looked away.

"Okay, so you're not pretending." She threw him an annoyed look. "Just teasing, you know." He grinned. Denise acknowledged him by looking away with a smug look on her face. He was having fun.

"Very funny," Abbey said.

"Hey, all's fair. Right?" He set his plate to one side and hailed their waiter, who was watching their little banter session. He came right over.

"Yes, sir."

"We would like to order dessert now, apple pie a´ la mode I should think." He glanced at them both for approval. Denise waived him off.

"I'll have a bite of yours if that's okay," Abbey said.

"One apple pie alamode it is then," he said, just as Denise pressed her hand to her earpiece to hear Vince's message.

"We need to leave through the kitchen right away. Vince says there's a few demonstrators out front of the hotel."

"My pie," he groaned, and followed Denise into the kitchen. "Now what?" he said, irritated.

"Service elevator's this way," she said walking ahead.

Harold saw their waiter and walked away from Denise and Abbey – he wanted his pie to go. Denise was clearly not happy with him but waited while the waiter fixed his pie alamode in a plastic container.

On the way upstairs in the service elevator, Denise told him that if he became President and tried to pull a stunt like that, he would be hustled away against his wishes, because that's the way it had to be. The Secret Service agents have that right when called for. She was nice about it, but he got her intent. This is the way it was to be for the next fourteen months until Election Day.

Chapter 40

TRIAL DAY

December 8th

Harold had dreaded this day from the moment Amul Al Atrash was arrested in the South Bronx, three months ago. It meant that he had to relive the Rushmore attack all over again in order for the jury to understand the intent of Amir, and therefore, the revenge sought by his father, Amul Al Atrash. It would also bring to the forefront every emotional trauma involving guns he'd experienced in his life, the final one being the death of his friend Jerry in Cleveland. In the months leading up to the trial, Gene Drake had assigned him one of the DHS's legal staff to coach and prepare him for the ordeal. Gene said he didn't want to leave it up to the US District Prosecutor's Office. He knew how cool they could be to witness's emotional needs, expecting them to be strong under cross-examination. Harold's head was spinning from the moment the whole process began in early November. He told himself he could deal with it, but that was a lie, one huge miscalculation on his part. He'd admitted to Abbey how unsure of himself he really was at breakfast in their hotel room, and then he'd thrown-up.

All that didn't matter now because he was sitting in the courtroom of the US Southern District Court of New York, waiting for his world to collapse around him. From the moment he'd entered the courtroom and seen Al Atrash sitting next to his counsel, his mind had gone on the rampage. He finally wound up focused on his brother Alex's death in a fire-fight nearly fifty years ago. The smell of death still haunted him at odd moments, and this was one of those unwelcome moments, lending its bottomless pit of despair to the trial of a heartless killer. It was all tied together in his mind – one memory begat the next until the dance of death was all-encompassing in his mind.

"Mr. Robertson," Frank Olscamp said. "Harold."

Harold was oblivious to the US District Prosecutor's hails. He was in the amphitheater at Mt. Rushmore, charging the madman in front of him, with the sharp cracks of automatic weapons fire lodged in his memory, drowning out the real world. In midair, en route to his objective in his mind, he had already wrenched the neck of Amir Atrash, so that when they'd collided, there was no thought as to what to do next – it was already done. The pit of his stomach sent a wave of revulsion through him. He was on trial here, not the man who had hunted his son's killer. Not the one whose thoughtless murders throughout his life had taken hundreds of lives in dozens of nations

"Harold!" Abbey's urgent voice broke the still courtroom air.

His rubbed his face with trembling hands, wiping away the surge of emotion. Their eyes met and drew him back into the courtroom.

"Harold. Frank was speaking to you." Abbey pointed at him.

He swallowed the sick feeling in his mouth and tried to gather his thoughts into some semblance of order, taking a deep breath, and leaning forward towards the Prosecutor's table on the other side of the low wooden wall.

"Mr. Robertson, I'll be calling you to testify in a moment. Are you alright? I can ask the Judge for a brief recess to confer with you," Frank said leaning over the dividing wall.

"No. I'll be fine." He lied, his gaze wandering over to the defense's table. He wasn't fine. Fine and dandy didn't exist in his world at the moment. The only thing occupying his world was death, its stench and cold clammy grip were his reality. The sickness returned to his stomach, launching a cold sweat that saturated his shirt beneath his jacket.

"Harold," Abbey squeezed his hand, "Come with me. Now."

He grabbed her arm and stood on shaky legs. She led him out into the hallway and to a drinking fountain, where she told him to splash some cold water on his face. She never let go of his arm and he clung tightly to hers. She pushed the lever to start the flow. He took small sips at first, before plunging his face into the cool arch of water, all-the-while clinging to her arm. Between the cold sweat and the cold water, he shivered, wondering if he would even make it to the witness stand without falling on his face. How sad, he thought, that a man who would be running for the Office of the Presidency, would be in such a state, over . . . "over memories, for the love of God," he choked. He pulled his face from the stream of water and sputtered. But, it did snap him out of his stupor. At the last cough, he rolled his eyes at his wife, and almost felt like laughing at himself. It was comical after all that *the man running for the Presidency would be so lame and to allow himself to descend into such a state of mind – definitely not a Commander in Chief moment.* He did laugh at that thought.

"That's better," she said hugging him. "We should get back if you're ready."

He nodded and they returned to their seats in the front row of the courtroom. The US District Judge was seated and the court was already in session. Frank's assistant motioned to him that his chief witness had returned. Frank was speaking with the Judge in an aside and then addressed the jury briefly, explaining a statement he'd made in his opening remarks from several days ago. Harold didn't catch much of it, just something about his course of action to prove the United States case against the defendant, Al Atrash, a known terrorist, and Syrian citizen. Frank's assistant, Julie Kurtz, leaned towards him, passing a note, which simply said to relax, that he'd do just fine. Her eyes conveyed confidence when he looked up after reading the message. He managed a weak smile.

"Mr. Olscamp, your first witness, if you please," The Judge said.

"Yes, your honor. The government calls US Congressman Harold Robertson to the stand."

Harold stood on shaky legs and left the safety of his visitor's seat to be sworn in by the Clerk of the Court. His hand trailed behind him with his fingers slipping from Abbey's as he sidestepped his way into the aisle. In the surreal moment of the Clerk swearing him in, his thoughts went immediately to his being sworn in nine years ago as a US Representative for the state of Illinois. He stared blankly at the Clerk, who was waiting for his answer. "I do," he said after a moment.

"Please be seated," the Clerk said.

Harold stepped up into the witness box beside the Judge and readied himself, shuffling a bit and clearing his throat.

"State your name and spell your last name for the record, and speak into the mic for all to hear." The Clerk said.

"Harold Robertson, R-O-B-E-R-T-S-O-N." He answered, again clearing his throat. His mind was clear now, no longer ranting and raving in the emotional memory department. He fixed his gaze on Abbey and gave her a little nod to say he was okay now.

"Good morning, Congressman Robertson." Mr. Olscamp said.

"Good morning sir." He was uncomfortable with the use of his old title, always had been. He preferred a more common title but was used to hearing the more formal term.

"Please tell the jury where you were on May 25th of 2015, and what you were doing there."

"Objection your Honor. What relevance does this have to the charges against my client?" Ms. Williams stated.

"Objection noted and overruled. This was already addressed. Please continue Mr. Olscamp. You may answer the question," The Honorable Judge Millford said.

"Thank you, your Honor."

Harold gave what he considered, a short explanation of the Rushmore Incident, during which Mr. Olscamp played video footage of the attack and then segments of interviews done on site. The words rolled off of his tongue, neither embellished nor diminished. He told it like it happened. All of the video clips came from Abbey's cameraman, Chet.

"Congressman Robertson, I'd like you to tell the jury your former occupations and describe them for us if you would please."

Harold summarized his teaching days and then his eight years in the US House of Representatives, including at the end, his run for Governor of Illinois.

"Thank you, sir. Now if you would please, tell the jurors about the incident in Houston on July 11th of 2015."

Now, he began to feel the tension in his body, a tension which had been building slowly while he was on the stand. He looked down at his hands, which were clasped tightly together with fingers laced. "I was called to the stage of a concert at the Discovery Green. It was raining that night, so everyone in the audience was hunkered down under umbrellas and ponchos. I said a few words before I heard the distinct 'cracking' sound of bullets passing close by my head. There were three in all. I crouched down immediately and jumped off of the stage to take cover to one side of it. Jerry, our Secret Service agent, met me there with gun drawn. He had called for backup and had called 911, so police were on the way, as well as more agents. I think we waited all of three minutes before hearing sirens. No one there really knew anything had happened until the police arrived. The suppressed rifle shots weren't really heard by anyone. We left and returned to the hotel."

"Now, tell us what happened in Cleveland on the evening of August 6th, 2015."

"We were at the first Republican debate at the Quicken Loans Arena. Afterwards, we left through the south exit, across the street from its parking structure. There were four shots, with one of them grazing my left temple. The sound was muffled and not all that loud. Jerry was hit and fell to the sidewalk. The other three agents hustled Abbey Nelson and me to the waiting SUV. We left Jerry lying on the sidewalk and sped off to the hotel. It was all over in less than thirty seconds."

"If it please the Court, may we see exhibit 33B on the monitors." Mr. Olscamp said.

Harold's monitor showed a video of Al Atrash's black SUV ramming through the exit gate; the next video clip was from a traffic cam and it clearly showed Al Atrash's face. The face of the man seated next to his counsel at the Defense table, a mere fifteen feet away. Al Atrash was facing him, watching him, still surveying his prey with the look of a killer, not the man shackled and handcuffed to his restraint belt. It sent a shiver through Harold, a cold shiver of death waiting for its time of delivery. Harold looked away for a moment before returning the steady gaze of the man whose only purpose in life was to kill him.

"Is this the same man seated at the Defense's table?"

"Objection your Honor."

"Overruled. You may answer the question."

"Yes, it is," Harold said in a deep and firm voice.

"Have you ever seen the accused before?"

"No, only in photographs provided by the DHS."

"Please explain what DHS stands for."

"Department of Homeland Security," Harold said leaning into the mic, making the words clearly heard by all – even a bit too loud. They were a challenge to the defendant. You have violated American soil and must bear the consequences.

"So, the first you ever saw or knew of the defendant, Amul Al Atrash, was in a photograph and a report by the Department of Homeland Security?"

"Correct."

"Can you tell the Court why you were being targeted by the defendant?"

"Objection your Honor. The witness cannot answer to another's intentions."

"Sustained."

"I will rephrase the question, your Honor," Mr. Olscamp said. "Do you know why you were being shot at on two separated occasions?"

"Yes, I do. I killed a man's son. That is why I was being targeted."

"Objection your Honor. The conclusions of the witness have no supportive evidence."

"Sustained. Mr. Olscamp, Ms. Williams, a sidebar if you please," Judge Millford said motioning with his hand. Both attorneys approached the Judge's bench, opposite to where Harold was seated in the witness box. They conferred for a minute and then Ms. Williams returned to the Defense table, and Mr. Olscamp returned to the lectern where both Plaintiff and Defense attorneys addressed the Court. "May we see Exhibit 4B at this time. This is a ballistics report submitted by the FBI on the July 11th shooting in Houston, at the Discovery Green concert. Are you familiar with this report, Congressman Robertson?"

"I've seen it."

"It states that the Browning semi-automatic assault rifle found in the defendant's possession at the time of arrest was the same rifle which fired three shots on the night in question. Ballistics matched them to this shooting and also to the shooting the night of August 6th in Cleveland, at the Quicken Loans Arena. In both instances, the .223 shell casings were recovered at the scenes with the defendant's fingerprints on them. Ballistics also matched the rifle to the bullet which killed Secret Service agent, Jerry Isaack. The FBI lab also found the defendant's fingerprints on the weapon recovered from his duffle bag at the time of his arrest. Is this why you are drawing the conclusion as to who was targeting you on two separate occasions?"

"Partly. My assumption is based more on the fact that I killed the defendant's son, and that he is a known terrorist, associated with many attacks and deaths worldwide. I find it reasonable, because I am a father myself, and understand his hatred for me."

"Objection," Ms. Williams responded.

"Overruled. Testimony of the witness is relevant," Judge Millford said.

"At this time, I have no further questions for this witness, but I reserve the right to recall him at a future time."

"Very well. Ms. Williams, you may cross-examine," Judge Millford said.

"Thank you, your Honor," she said stepping up to the lectern. "Good morning, sir."

"Good morning," Harold said returning her greeting.

"Sir, do you wish to be addressed as Congressman Robertson, or would you prefer a less formal title?"

"Less is fine." Harold almost smiled at the tall woman behind the lectern's mic.

"Mr. Robertson, did you ever see who shot at you in either of the two incidents?"

"No."

"So, you don't really know if it was the defendant?"

"Correct."

"No more questions, your Honor."

"The witness is excused for now, but subject to recall at a later time. I will instruct you to not discuss your testimony with anyone except your attorney."

"Thank you, your Honor," Harold mumbled on his way out of the witness box. It had gone better than he thought it would, although he was still very uncomfortable being in the same room as the father whose son he'd killed with his bare hands – a total act of rage on his part. Justifiable? Most definitely, but that could never change his emotional reaction to such an act under any circumstances. Revulsion was the word he used to describe the way it left him feeling.

He sat down next to Abbey and blindly stared out into the courtroom, his eyes darting over towards Al Atrash every few seconds. He was ready to bolt out of the room.

"We should probably go, don't you think?" Abbey said.

She stood and walked him out into the hall, just as she'd done before, and he was thankful she did. He went straight to the drinking fountain and cupped his hand in the stream to splash some on his face.

"I'll be right back," Abbey said.

She left him to give a note to Mr. Olscamp's assistant that they'd be at the hotel if needed.

Chapter 41

IN A NEW YORK MINUTE
Radisson Hotel 1 p.m.

From the minute the keycard had opened their door, Harold's head was spinning wildly, embroiled in a stew of long-forgotten guilt – survivor's guilt. The moment his head hit the pillow on their bed, he was flip-flopping between age fifteen and twenty-two. He was a sophomore in high school when the telegram delivered the unmitigated devastation to the Robertson family, especially his mother. When Harold left the Air Force at twenty-two, it was then that he began to suffer bouts of guilt. Why hadn't he died instead of his brother Alex? He was in a war zone. He'd had close calls at times and was injured in a rocket attack. So why was he alive? It became an obsession at times like it was now. His mind was racing to a finish line which didn't exist, he'd never arrive, never have the satisfaction of a life well lived. All because he'd lived and Alex had not.

"Harold! Open your eyes and look at me," Abbey's words commanded.

His eyes opened, but not to the image of his wife. He only saw what he was feeling, no matter what his eyes were telling him about his surroundings. Abbey shook him by the shoulders.

"Tell me what's happening with you?"

"I don't know if I can. Everything's all jumbled up in my head. I always felt bad about why I lived and my brother died. I don't think I ever got over it, kinda like my mother, only I could function in the world, and she couldn't. I feel guilty Abbey because I lived and he didn't. Seeing Amir's father in court today

234

brought it all back to life. I feel ugly inside. I killed another human being. It doesn't matter how evil he was, I still killed. And with my bare hands. You have no idea what that's doing to me. There's no way I can go on with my life until this is settled once and for all. I can't live with it any longer. The trial's brought it all out in the open again. I haven't felt this way since I was twenty-two and returned home to live my life without my brother or mother." He got himself sat up and leaning against the headboard. Abbey slipped a pillow behind his back and head.

"Tell me about it," she said. "Begin with today and tell me what you were feeling." She sat down beside him.

"I love you," he hugged the woman he loved more than any words could say. "I guess I never really got over Alex's death. He was always better at everything – didn't matter what. He didn't flaunt his abilities with anyone. He was a born teacher who loved to help people. He didn't care that he was good at something, he just shared what he knew and reveled in helping others."

"And then he died in an awful firefight," Harold said in an angry voice. "For what? For some politician's ideals for America. They lied to the people to justify going to war. And Alex died – I lived."

"Today when I was on the stand," he said calming down, "somewhere way back in my mind, all this was brewing. Every glance at the defendant opened the door a little further. Sure I was calm on the outside, but I could feel the impending storm. You know, when I was lying there on the amphitheater's cold concrete with Amir's head and neck in my hands, I felt horrible, less than human. And even though I knew what I had done was right, had saved lives, and rid the world of a trained killer, I still felt less than human. I killed that man's son, and I would do it again if need be, but seeing him today brought all the jumbled emotions to a head. It just didn't happen until I entered the hotel room. Probably a good thing for me; no one would want me as President if they'd seen what a mess I am."

"You know that's not true, so don't you dare say it again," Abbey said shaking his shoulders.

He winced in pain from both his shoulder and her emotionally laden words, which drilled right into him, delivering what they needed to say: *Don't you dare talk down about yourself around me.* Her hand rubbed his aching shoulder.

"Sorry," she frowned, "it's just that I can't stand to hear you say such things about yourself. And no, people would not think the less of you for having real feelings about traumatic events in your life. Just the opposite, Harold Robertson. It's what makes you so darn likable. You can't change the past. You can't bring back your brother. But, you can change the future if you want to. The man on trial is a known terrorist. He deserves what he'll get in our judicial system. You, well you need to prove to yourself that you're worthy of holding the Office."

The people want you in there," she said in a stern voice sitting beside him, "so what's the holdup? You've been thinking about this all your life, haven't you? Sure it's just a dream, but you have the right answers and knowledge to make a strong leader. We all need you to do this." Abbey wiped the tears from her face. "For that matter, so does the world. It needs the kind of America that you can help its citizens give to the world. Use what you felt today, it's a part of you, it's one of your strengths. You have nothing to feel guilty about. You're a good man Harold Robertson. Believe it."

Abbey leaned her head against his shoulder and let her tears stream down her face onto his shirt. This woman, who loved him so deeply, was the only person who had ever reached this deep into his hidden fears and trauma. She was stronger than anyone he'd ever known.

Chapter 42

CAMPAIGN TRAIL

San Diego, July 10th 2016

Harold was never called to testify again. The trial had drug-on for two more weeks before the jury handed down a death sentence, which the Court pronounced on the accused on March 21st. Al Atrash was to die by lethal injection on the same date in 2017. He was remanded to the Federal Penitentiary in Terra Haute, Indiana, where he would remain until his sentence was carried out. The world was rid of the man who'd long terrorized, killed, maimed, and otherwise lived a miserable excuse of a life in their eyes. Harold had put it all behind him shortly after he'd testified. Abbey had helped him realize things about himself he'd been neglecting for decades.

That day in the hotel room, when he'd completely lost it, she'd shown him the way forward and given him a swift boot in the rear to get started. He thought about it often during their long days on the campaign trail. He was doing well in the polls, even though he'd not won enough delegates to be the presumptive nominee at the Republican National Convention, just eight short days away in Cleveland. He'd have to battle with Oliver Plunkett for the nomination, who was neck and neck with him in the polls and delegates. Harold wasn't worried because Oliver had yet to reap the harsh criticism he deserved from all of his nasty campaign attacks on character, record, and alleged wrongdoings, by everyone he'd encountered on his run for the nomination. It had gotten ugly more than once, and the man didn't know how to apologize, even when he knew he was wrong. It had angered Harold more often than not, but Abbey was helping him to let it roll off of his back. He'd even laughed at some of Oliver's attacks on candidates' character. The man had no sense of shame in him.

But this week was to be a rally 'round the campfire,' with some of his most supportive members both in the House and the Senate. It seemed that Capitol Hill was choosing sides and being public about it, which irritated Oliver to no end, and was probably why they did it. Harold would get to see his daughter Gracie and his granddaughter, Mattie. Nothing could please him more. Mixed in between was a mishmash of meetings, public events, serious strategy sessions with the powers that be on the Hill, and some down time for him and Abbey. He wasn't real happy about having to fly to DC for the sessions on the Hill, but he needed all the help he could get – Oliver Plunkett was not going down without a fight.

But first on the agenda was family. Today was a beach day, much to Denise's and every other Secret Service agent assigned to him, objections. Security was impossible, they'd said. His reply was that his enemy was in the 'pen', so why worry. Their entourage had grown considerably since the last time. Now he had four agents instead of two, plus a campaign team of five, who'd been with him for the past few months. So, things were a little more complicated when he was out in public. He and Abbey would meet Gracie and Ted at their beach cottage with just Denise and Vince, leaving the rest of his crowd to mill around on the beach while they waited the hour he'd set aside for his family. They arrived at ten o'clock in the morning in their black SUV – nothing too obvious about that. The press had followed them from the hotel in downtown San Diego, shadowing their every move right up until they pulled into the alleyway, to enter through Gracie's back patio. Vince got out before they'd even stopped, and taken up station in the alley, blocking the press van from getting any closer. It made Harold laugh, seeing the mountain that Vince was, arms folded, legs straddled, like he was biggest, baddest man around. Even Denise got a chuckle out of it.

"Daddy."

Gracie's voice called out as they entered through the gate. It made his heart skip a beat, he was so happy to see her. He flung his arms around her and lifted her up and twirled her around twice, just like he used to do when she was eight. He planted a big kiss on her cheek and set her down. "So good to see you kiddo."

"You too. Is this Denise?" Gracie's hand extended. "Daddy's told me sooo much about you. I'm so sorry about Jerry. He became a part of the family during your visit last year. Let's go inside. I know Mattie will be pleased. She loves visitors."

Gracie led the way through the sliding glass door. It was just the same, except Mattie was walking now, and came clip-clopping across the living room wood floor. She latched onto Denise's pant leg and looked up at her, melting her heart. Mattie squealed with delight and moved onto Abbey, who squatted down to receive a hug and kiss. Harold was beside himself, he was so happy and amazed at little Mattie's behavior. She was getting to be all grown up, and she was only a year and half old.

"She's such a cutie." He said sitting on the sofa to wait his turn. Ted came in and scooped her up and together they landed next to grandpa on the sofa. Mattie climbed into his lap and snuggled like she'd known him forever. He laughed way down in his belly he was so happy. "You, little girl, are getting so grown up, and so much like your mom." His gaze met Gracie's, bringing a happy tear to his face. And just as quickly, Mattie crawled out of his lap and into her daddy's. It was the best beginning of any day he'd had, ever.

"I made some coffee and we got croissants from the bakery this morning," Gracie said from the kitchen.

"Sounds good," he replied, watching Abbey eye her new family. She was beaming with delight. He scooted over to make room for her in the middle, next to Ted and Mattie. He put his arm around her shoulder and jostled her a bit. "I'm so happy now. I don't think anything could ever top this moment." He kissed her cheek and lay his head on her shoulder. This is what life is all about – family. The rest of the world could wait in line.

****

Flying back to DC, he thought about those special moments with his daughter's family a lot, trying to ease his mind about what lay ahead on the Hill. The power brokers of the House and Senate would have their way with him. They were the establishment which reigned in candidates such as himself. He'd gone through a similar beginning during his first year in Congress. Young, innocent of the ways of politics, he'd come with ideals, and within the first year, he saw firsthand how difficult it would be to put those ideals to work. Sure, he was right to have them, everyone who was elected to office had them in some form, but the reality of the Hill was contained in the power of the establishment's hold on the way things got done, a lesson every new freshman Representative and Senator learned from the gitgo. He'd done that like everyone else had, and now he was the new candidate, back in the same position once again, only this time the stakes were much higher. He'd gotten everyone's attention in the past year, but now it was time to listen to the men and women with whom he'd have to deal.

The President was the Commander in Chief, but the Senators and Representatives were the ones who passed all the bills and wrote all the laws for America. And to them, the Office of the Presidency was but one person to deal with, albeit the Boss, but still only one up against the many. They'd seen Presidents come and go, some better than others, but always, the business of the country passed through their halls – as it should be.

He was about to get his feet wet and he was excited and scared too. Some of the people he'd meet with today were unknown to him, other than by reputation. His eight years in the House was only a part of the whole machine of government. So, he was barely broken-in to their ways of doing the business of governing and financing a country.

When he stepped off the Delta flight and into the Baltimore-DC airport, it was like coming home. This town was his second home for eight years, and it was good to be home. There was a car arranged for him, which he found waiting with a Secret Service escort's SUV. He climbed into the Lincoln Town car and rode to the Hill to meet with the Senate Majority Leader and his team for the next three hours – a very long meeting by his standards.

Harold was escorted into Senate Majority Leader Michael P. Howell's office suite feeling a bit intimidated, but feeling at home being back in the Capitol Building. Michael introduced his three staff members and had him sit at a small conference table with eight burgundy leather armchairs. Michael's Chief of Staff, Marjorie Smyth sat next to him and filled him in on the Senator's agenda for the meeting. While she did, the Speaker of the House entered and sat across from him. He was engaged with Marjorie and turned the opposite direction, so he never saw him enter. She motioned that they were ready to begin, at which point he straightened his chair and saw his old friend Representative Charles Barker sitting across from him.

"Charlie, how are you? It's good to see you." Harold stretched across the table to shake hands.

"You're looking well, Harold. I'm so sorry for your loss. Susan and I will dearly miss Ruth. But, I hear you're married again. And to a journalist!" Charlie's voice raised on the word journalist.

"Yeah, go figure. We knew each other back in Clayton. I used to coach her older brother in baseball. Small world." Harold's eyes found solace in his old friend from Iowa.

"Shall we get started gentlemen," Michael said, sitting at the head of the table. "I want to welcome Harold Robertson back to his old stomping ground, in the other wing of course. What I wish to accomplish today will be the framework for our strategy at the Convention next week. I believe we are all agreed that Oliver Plunkett is not our first choice. Hell, he's not even on my list." Michael chuckled. "But he's done a bang-up job of corralling some of the American public and their delegates. It won't fly at the Convention though. After the first vote, many of his delegates will switch camps and vote for Congressman Robertson here, a man who understands America and how its government works. I can't say how strongly I feel about this. Plunkett would be a disaster if he were elected to office. I think we all know that to be true. So, I've laid out some strategic points to help Harold have a smooth nomination at the Convention. First on the docket is a short list of VP running mates. I can only assume you have a list started." Michael said looking at Harold.

"Um, yes, as a matter of fact, I do have a list of one. Senator Regina Lawford of Illinois. She's respected, sharp as a whip, served two terms and is beginning her third this year, on board with good solid conservative values, but open to compromise, which she excels at as you all know, and she's a trial attorney formally with a top Chicago Law Office, Marshall & Marcel I believe." He raised an eyebrow in hopes of an agreement, his eyes glancing towards each.

"Good choice," Marjorie whispered.

He smiled at her as Michael cleared his throat a bit gruffly. Their eyes met and he could see that Regina was not his first choice. "Who's on First?" He made everyone laugh at the old running line joke of the '40's.

"Regina's third on my list, but a good choice. I believe our strength lies in Senator O'Connor of South Carolina. He has the ability to carry the Southern States with ease, and has served four terms in the Senate, sits as Chairman of the Ways and Means Committee, and has great sway with over half the members of the Senate. He would be hard to beat, both in the nomination process and during the general election. He's well-liked by the American People." Michael's brow furrowed in its signature entrenchment.

"Well, he's certainly a fine Senator. I don't know him well, as we've only met briefly once or twice before, but I'm open to all of your recommendations." Harold leaned back in his chair, planted his elbows on the armrests, laced his fingers together, and pressed his thumbs into his chin just below his lips.

"Good choice," he said raising an eyebrow. Michael didn't know him all that well, so he would not be familiar with his own signature look, a look he gave whenever he disagreed but was not ready to enter the trenches. He glanced at Marjorie's, supportive looking face that also appeared to urge caution. He waited while the silence gave way to further discussion of the matter.

And that's the way the rest of the three-hour meeting went, attack and parry, merge and disperse, regroup and move on to the next subject. In the end, all were pleased with their meeting. It was time well spent in strategizing Oliver's defeat, that and Harold got his way with Regina Lawford as the VP nominee, something Marjorie had backed him up on by launching a campaign on her boss to see the wisdom of Harold's choice. There would be many more meetings after the Convention; he was, after all, a newbie on the scene of the time-honored process of electing a President.

It came as no surprise as they left the Capitol Building to find a small army of TV journalists and cameras on the steps, all ready to launch a thousand questions at the two most powerful men on the Hill about this candidate, Harold Robertson, slayer of terrorists, and dear to the hearts of most Americans. It was three against thirty or so, fair odds in the world of politics. Senator Howell silenced the mob with a calming hand.

"Now I know you're all intently curious as to our meeting today, and we do have a statement, which we'll get to in a moment, but first I have something of a more personal note." Michael's voice drew them in as he placed his hand on Harold's shoulder. "The man you see standing here with the Speaker of the House, Charles Barker, and myself, is something of a legend in his own lifetime. This decorated veteran, public servant extraordinaire, and newly married last month, is a man who stands before us as a living example of Jeffersonian ideals, and Lincoln's tenacity, of service to America. Now I know you all think I'm playing this up a bit for the media, but Harold is the real deal. If you don't believe me, go to Clayton High School archives and view the productions he orchestrated in every American History class for more than twenty years. Include clips with your stories, I guarantee your ratings will go up ten points. Now that I've said that, Charles Baker has some words about our meeting.

"Thank you, Michael. Well spoken words about a man I came to admire and respect during our time together in the House. More than anything else, I want to tell you how confident I am about Harold Robertson's character, bearing, and political savvy. He will lead America into a brighter future, one built on the foundations of our Forefathers' examples and ideals. If you want to know this man, go inside the Rotunda and look up at the murals on the dome. They depict every characteristic about Harold Robertson, and he will deliver those values to the American People on every day he's in the Office of the Presidency. America will never find a better man for the job than Harold. Today, we put our heads together to plot out Harold Robertson's successful run for the Presidency. He makes it easy on us because he is everything we could ever want or need in a candidate. Before Michael reads our statement, perhaps we should let Harold speak." Charlie wrapped his arm around Harold's shoulder and gave him a good squeeze.

Harold was embarrassed, to say the least, by everything they'd said about him. If they could have seen him in action at the Federal Courthouse, coming unglued in the hallway, and having Abbey pick up the pieces, they'd be singing a different tune. He tapped one of the six or so mics shoved at him, looking at it in an odd manner, causing laughter.

"Listen, you all know me. I'm just a small town history teacher who loves his country. I've got some good ideas for all of us as Americans to work on if I'm elected. There's nothing really new about them, just plain old common sense values, which founded this country. They're just as true now as they were when they were written into the Charters of Freedom, better known as, the Declaration of Independence, Constitution, and Bill of Rights. You've heard me talking about some of them in the past months and there's more to come.

In our meeting today, these two great Americans who have served our country for over fifty years combined, gave me some tips on how not to screw up, something I seem to have a knack for." More laughter erupted from the now calm, bright and shining faces of the men and women of the media. His eye scanned the crowd, expecting to see Abbey, but knowing she was home waiting for him to return.

"You know, I married one of your group." More laughter. "And she's the best thing that's happened to me – ever. She's gonna knock your socks off when she's First Lady." More laughter. "Now, I want to thank the Speaker of the House and the Senate Majority Leader for giving so generously of their time. I'm sure we'll have many more sessions in the weeks to come." Harold stepped back, forgetting he was on the steps of the Capitol, grabbing Charlie's shoulder to catch himself. He shrugged his shoulders to the cameras and laughed. He couldn't wait to fly back to California to be with his family.

****

Abbey was waiting for him on the beach in the hours before sunset, leaning back in a beach chair, reading the latest western romance novel. Her straw hat covered her shoulders and extended over the back of the legless chair, its red ribbon bow fluttering about in the breeze. He didn't see how life could get any better than this. Denise was milling around some twenty feet away, speaking into her lapel mic, probably with Vince, who was plowing the way through the Sunday crowd. He was flanked by three more agents, with one final one hanging back close to their SUV. Pacific Beach got very crowded this time of year, so Vince had insisted on parking where the Lifeguards patrol vehicles accessed the beach. Harold didn't care. There was no one out there hunting him any longer. He snuck up behind Abbey and whispered in her ear. "Did ya miss me?" Abbey flinched a little and then reached behind her and pulled his head next to hers.

"You're back in one piece I see. The ravenous wolves of the press didn't eat you up on the Capitol steps?" She laughed. "Denise and I watched your interview on her phone today. You were terrific. Did those two Hill people treat you nicely?"

"Yes, of course. We had a productive meeting. They told me what they wanted, and I told them how I saw it playing out. The Majority Leader wants the South Carolina Senator, O'Connor, as VP. He gave me his best 'trench warfare look.' In return, I offered mine. Regina's going to be the nominee."

"Good, dear. I like her a lot. Senator O'Connor is very old school, so it makes sense they'd chose him." Abbey smiled. "There's another chair," she said pointing towards the cooler and beach bag of goodies.

He set up next to her and grunted, as he lowered himself to the sand. "Whoever invented these things, did so for younger people." He leaned forward to get a can of iced tea from the cooler and waved to Denise.

"Miss me?" He grinned at Denise, and almost as automatically, Abbey elbowed him in the arm.

"Not in the slightest," Denise laughed. "Abbey and I had some quality 'girl time' together. Your name never came up."

Denise threw him the same look he given her, only she accentuated it with more body language. "You're teasing me, right?" Denise turned away with a look of aloofness, almost haughty. Abbey was tittering, trying to bury it in her book. "Hey Vince, they're making fun of me," Harold said over his shoulder.

"Not my problem. Why don't you ask Denise about the time she got caught naked in the men's showers, during training exercises last year." Vince chuckled.

Denise glared at him. Vince was smirking and catching glimpses over his shoulder. Harold was getting a crick in his neck, trying to see Vince behind him. Things were heating up, he could tell. Vince came around to the cooler and got an iced tea, taking it to Denise. As a peace offering?

"Here, chill girl," Vince said pushing the can up against Denise's chest.

Denise smiled, taking it and dropping it to the sand. Then the antics ensued like they were almost rehearsed. It was a Laurel and Hardy, ala-Secret Service karate, eye poking, face slapping, noisy affair, ending with Vince turning away with a big smile on his face, only to have it knocked off by Denise's head slap. Harold was coughing and sputtering, having taken a sip of tea right before it all started. Abbey, ceremoniously whacked him on the back several times. It was a show. And it had an audience – fifty or so to be exact, who were clapping, laughing, and closing in on the entertainment, bringing the other three agents rushing in. Harold jumped up to hold them off.

"Boys." He waved them away with the back of his hand. "It's an act."

"Pretty good one too." Came a voice from the crowd. "Got it all on YouTube already." A young lad said.

"There, you see. Entertainment, Secret Service style." He laughed with Vince and Denise, while the other three grumbled and returned to their stations.

"Welcome back Harold," Denise said covering up her smile.

"Thanks. I haven't had such a good time in a while." Then it was like nothing happened at all; everything returned to normal, samo-samo, boring agent watches out for the bad guys thing. He sat back down next to Abbey and brushed the sand off the sides of his can of tea, which was knocked over when he got up. "Miss me," he whispered in Abbey's ear. She turned her head and kissed him on the lips.

"Sure," she said rolling her eyes. "Gracie will be down shortly. Denise called her when you showed up."

She planted another kiss on his lips and returned to her book. He leaned back in his chair and laced his fingers behind his neck to watch the sun blazing through the mountainous bank of clouds. The crowd had thinned after the entertainment ended, but it was all available to see countless times on social media. He was relaxed and ready for a couple of days off.

Chapter 43

RNC CONVENTION
July 18th

They arrived in Cleveland the day before and prepared themselves for an extraordinary event. National Conventions were normally a well-orchestrated production, all designed to deliver the Party's winning nominee for the General Election in November, full of pomp, traditions, surprises, and behind the scenes logistics.

This year's convention, however, was marred by two police shootings and the retaliatory targeting of police in two different cities, killing five officers and wounding eight. Security at the convention was stepped up ten notches, with Cleveland becoming the temporary home to over one thousand extra law enforcement. Protests were expected both inside and outside of the Quicken Loans Arena, the "Q", as it was known.

His battle was with Oliver Plunkett, the bombastic billionaire, who had stormed onto the scene a year ago, touting change on all fronts for American politics. Harold cringed every time he heard the man's voice on TV because he knew some personal slur, political contrivance, or just plain out and out rude comments were about to be unleashed. The sad part was, many were buying into the rhetoric, supporting his call for radical change on all fronts. Harold had been on the receiving end many times, and he still couldn't get over the fact that the media would take his lies and run with them because they boosted ratings or some such cockamamie line. In any case,

Oliver had secured enough delegates during the primaries to make him a formidable opponent.

Not since 1976 had there not been a clear nominee going into the RNC convention, and it was a wild ride back then, so Harold thought this years just might go that way too. Back then, Governor Reagan had challenged the sitting President, Gerald Ford, for the party's nomination, and the close primary fell into the convention in a near tie, with both sides cultivating behind the scenes shenanigans. Phone lines had been ripped out of the walls to keep delegates from communicating during the early hours. It was chaotic, loud, and very much an all American political affair.

Today was shaping up to be a similar kind of day. They were going head to head on the first day and hopefully, Oliver's lies and deceptions would be seen for what they were, unfounded rhetoric driven by money and the media. Harold knew that factual and truthful campaigns had been buried more often than not in the past. Politics was all about perceptions and the one with more money bought the most airtime, and therefore the most in-your-face, perceptions to persuade the public.

Both he and Oliver had popular governors and senators warming up the floor for much of the day, with their speeches coming in the early evening, followed by a vote. Harold was not looking forward to listening to Oliver before it was his time to address the delegates and woo their votes to himself. Oliver would employ every worn-out lie he had in his arsenal, slinging dirt and hearsay like confetti. It pained him to have to listen, but he had to in order to answer some of the accusations. This was all warm up for the Presidential Debates in the Fall, when his platform would be assaulted by the Democratic nominee.

She would be a formidable enemy to confront on stage, a former US Attorney General and Senate Minority Leader, Victoria Hemstead was a forty-year veteran on the Hill. By comparison, Oliver was a lightweight billionaire businessman, banking on the party's past twelve years of contentious rankling at every level.

Harold listened with Regina and Abbey from the lounge at the "Q", until it was his time to walk the plank. Oliver drew rounds of cheers from the floor, but nothing overly rousing.

He kissed his wife, winked at Regina, and proceeded to the stage to address the state delegates. He would be introduced by his old friend, Charles Barker, the Speaker of the House. Standing backstage, Harold thought he'd never stop with the history lesson of Harold Robertson's 'patriotic' life, and experience as a Representative in the US House. Harold glanced down at his few notes as Charles was winding down, stuffing them in his pants pocket, and walking past Charles to the lectern. He looked up at the enormous screen above him and chuckled. The first words out of his mouth were to make fun of himself.

"I forgot to comb my hair," he jabbed his thumb up at the screen, catching the attention and laughter of the twenty-something thousand people. He launched into his twenty-minute speech, almost entirely focused on his platform and what America needs from its leaders. He saved his comments about Oliver for last because he didn't see the need to cut the man off at the knees if it wasn't necessary.

"It has always been my hope for America to realize all of her dreams for the world. America needs strong and unified leadership from every level of government. The policies I have addressed here tonight will get the ball rolling. They are the first steps and will open the door for all Americans to participate in the growth of our nation. When the vote is called tonight, I want you all to cast your vote for all Americans, and for what is best for our country. Thank you." He stepped back and waved.

The delegates on the floor were waving a sea of banners, flags, and hats flung high into the air, all to the deafening cheers of the other fifteen thousand people seated above and behind them, Abbey surprised him from behind, took his hand and waved along with him. He kissed his wife and raised their hands together. He was pleased with his talk and knew he'd done all that he could. Now, it was up to the delegates.

The vote came in after an hour, and to the cheers of the crowd, the RNC President, James Picford announced that Harold Robertson had won with 1,956 delegates. He and Abbey returned to the lectern and he accepted his nomination, quite possibly the second best day of his life; the first being his marriage to Abbey.

Now it was time to go home and rest before the all-important final three months of campaigning and debating the Democratic nominee. It was game on.

Chapter 44

THIRD PRESIDENTIAL DEBATE

October 19th

Long before Harold had ever dreamed of participating in anything political, he'd passionately devoured American history books, and biographies of American Patriots, before, during and after the Revolutionary War. It had all begun in fourth grade with his principle's short lesson on the story behind the National Anthem. He remembered hanging on every word as if his life depended on it, never being sure why, but always remembering the feeling of expansive freedom that had settled upon him. It was a feeling that never left him, even though all the years of teaching the subject, and then serving in the US House of Representatives.

When he was a Congressman, he'd sit in his office behind the Capitol, staring out the window at its gleaming white dome, reliving the feeling of that day in fourth grade. It was the same feeling he had now, the day before the final debate with Victoria Hemstead, the seasoned veteran of forty years on the Hill.

She had won the first debate hands down in the eyes of the media. He'd held his own during the second debate a little over a week ago. And now, he was preparing to do battle once again, at Nevada University in Las Vegas.

They were barely twelve feet apart on the stage, he and

Senator Hemstead. She smiled at him, but it was a hungry smile, of a predator ready to devour its prey. He returned a pleasant nod and turned his focus to the moderator, Allen Erickson, a longtime national news anchorman, who'd seen the best and the worst that the world had to offer. And judging by the look on the Senator's face, he'd get a little of both tonight.

"Good evening ladies and gentlemen," Allen began. "We are here in the Artimus Ham Concert Hall of the University of Nevada, Las Vegas, for the third and final Presidential Debate. I'd like to welcome our two nominees, Senator Victoria Hemstead and Congressman Harold Robertson."

Allen droned on for a few minutes before beginning, giving him time to settle in and calm his nervousness. Abbey was in the front row with her parents, which pleased him. It was hard to see with the bright lights illuminating the stage, but it was comfort enough just to know that they were there, thirty feet away. Allen was shuffling papers, so he took a sip of water and prepared himself for the duel with the good senator. The first question went to his opponent, and spoke to National Security issues, and the protection of our nation's borders – no small subject by any means. He focused on Senator Hemstead's answers, paying close attention to openings and flaws in her platform's answers. She said nothing new, merely drawing different shades and textures of the same agendas she'd held for years. She was pleased with her aggressive tone, challenging him on several issues, boarding on open hostility with her interjections of political correctness. He had two minutes to give his reply.

"While Senator Hemstead has made some valid points, I do take issue with her ability to be an effective leader and accomplish her plans. She is well known to be combative with members of the other party, both in the Senate and House. I don't see her as the person who can foster goodwill and dialogue across the aisle.

That being said, my eight years as a Congressman were spent getting the votes needed on progressive legislation, without regard as to party affiliation. I sold ideas and programs that were needed, even if it was at my own expense with members of my own party. It's called politically shooting yourself in the foot to save the legislation. It got me a reputation for being the go-to man because I wasn't afraid to lose important allies in order to win a war. I know how to get things done in the House and I will take what I have learned there, and apply it to my dealings on the Hill, and with world leaders.

As to the Senator's views on National Security, they are all well and good, but my intent as President, is to enforce International Laws already on the books, which call for sanctions against any nation which exports terrorists, either knowingly or unknowingly, nations such as Iran. The deal made with them was done so without the support of Israel, our most trusted and important ally in the region. This was a totally unacceptable outcome, even though we managed to reach an agreement with Iran. If we abandon allies such as Israel in order to make deals, then it better be ironclad and be worth risking a long-held and very deep friendship, otherwise, we are only hobbling our own influence and credibility in the eyes of the world – not a good thing to do.

We are also not going to bear the bulk of the burden when it comes to such matters. All those nations in an affected region will pay and do their part. The world is a smaller place now and we need to learn that we can work together. The UN Security Council can step up their role as well. There are no easy fixes to the world's problems, but that doesn't mean they are unfixable."

His two minutes were up and Allen made sure he knew it by flashing the bright red light on his moderator's desk twice. It was a difficult question, one which didn't have easy answers. He was okay with what he'd said going into the rebuttal phase and then open discussion if time permitted. Fifteen minutes to solve America's problems, that's what they were given; make a show of determination and force for the American people, throwing caution to the wind as to whether it was even possible to do what was suggested. Political promises, which mostly would all be forgotten after taking office. It was always the same story, we can't do that, it's not possible, we'll attack that problem next year, the list was long and worn out. It was what he disliked most about debates, promises made and then broken.

He breathed a sigh of satisfaction at the closure of the last question. He'd done his job well he thought. Summations were next and he would be the last one to speak. He was quite sure that the good Senator Hemstead would lay into his party's antique, obscure and derelict platform, her words during the primaries. He listened closely as he had the past hour and a half. He thought she did a decent job, right up until she laid a trap for him to fall into at the very end. "How can you trust a man to be the leader of the free world, who's had no experience at the international level?" She then preceded to lay out her leadership skills, having served eight years as the Chairwoman of the Senate Foreign Relations Committee and mentored two Secretaries of State at their requests. And, then it was his turn.

"Ladies and gentlemen, I want to thank you for listening to many arduous questions that do not have simple answers. You have been entrusted with the task, as set down by our Forefathers, of selecting a leader for our nation, one who will set our sights on the future, both for our children and for the world. The good Senator Hemstead said that I have little experience to do the job vs. herself. Truthfully, she does have more, but what about these Presidents who had little experience when they took office:

Abraham Lincoln – with only 8 years in the Illinois House; he led the nation through the Civil War and signed into law, the Emancipation Proclamation.

Woodrow Wilson – with only 2 years as the New Jersey Governor; he was the WW I Commander in Chief, presided over creation of the Federal Reserve, and won the Nobel Peace Prize for his sponsorship of the League of Nations

Franklin Delano Roosevelt – with only 3 years as the New York Governor, and 2 years as N.Y. State Senate; he was the WW II Commander in Chief, and led the nation out of the Great Depression with his New Deal.

"That's just to name a few. The Office of the President is open to any American who has the leadership skills to serve our great nation. I stand ready to serve America as President, because I have listened to her citizens all my life, and I have a plan to set her on a course straight and true, one in which the Founding Fathers would be proud. We are Americans, unique in all the world. Let us stand together, unified in our purpose to lift America up, that our children may prosper and carry on her tradition of freedom and equality for all. Thank you and God Bless America."

On the way back to their hotel, he asked Vince what he

thought of the debate. Vince turned his head towards the back seat, smiling.

"Bully," he said.

Harold laughed at his use of Teddy Roosevelt's term for 'Superb.'

Chapter 45

ESCAPE
October 23ʳᵈ 9 a.m.

Amul Al Atrash's only recollection of the beating was the first blow struck, which came from an inmate and had knocked the wind right out of him. He remembered nothing more than that. When he woke, he found himself handcuffed to a hospital bed in a small room. He hurt all over. His eyes scanned the room, thinking that he was still in the prison in Terra Haute, Indiana, but there was a window with no bars on it to his left. He tried to sit up and discovered a strap across his chest held him tight to the bed. The steady beeping was coming from a small white box next to his bed, which had plastic coated wires leading under his garment. There was an IV tube in his left hand, the one not handcuffed. He guessed he was in a hospital outside of the prison walls. Blue sky with puffy clouds shown outside the window. He stared a long time at their beauty as they passed by the small opening to the outside world. He was tired and closed his eyes.

He woke sometime later to a nurse checking his readings on the machines and taking his blood pressure. She never spoke. Behind her, stood a stocky, middle-aged man in a white shirt. He wore a badge that said, FBI, on it. He also never spoke to him. The nurse finished her work and stopped to make notes on his chart at the end of the bed, and then left with the FBI man.

He closed his eyes again and dreamed of his family and home in Al Bab. His son, Amir, was six years old and they were celebrating his birthday at his grandparents' home, the same one Amul had grown up in. He'd given his son a new laptop so that they could explore the world together, and read stories from Syria's past. Sometimes his wife would join them in Amir's room and they would read together, each taking a character from the story. Those were good days in his life, ones which mattered more than his missions to purify the world around him, through violence if necessary. Amul's father, Mohammad Al Atrash, never agreed with his son's use of violence, saying that in their family's history, violence was always a last resort used to accomplish a task. Now, he was the six-year-old, looking up at his formidable father's face, being admonished to follow family traditions. He was a troubled child, one prone to anger and vengeful acts while playing with other children where he lived.

He was woken by a different nurse and guard this time. It was dark outside his window now. "What time is it?" he asked the nurse. She pointed to the tiny numbers at the bottom corner of the white box that beeped. It was 9:30 p.m. This guard did not have an FBI badge. He was dressed in a hospital security uniform with a different badge clipped to his shirt. He was hungry, apparently had slept through dinner time. "May I have something to eat?" he asked. Nothing was said, not even a look of recognition from either of them. It was like he didn't exist for them. He could live without having food for days when he was working intently on a mission, but this was different, he hungered, and it caused him great discomfort for some reason. He closed his eyes and forgot about food and tried not to think of his family because their deaths still filled him with raw emotions.

He woke several more times during the night, never noticing the sandwich on a tray beside his bed. He found it the next morning, when the sun shone through the window, warming his face and providing a brilliance to the sterile room. He reached over for the sandwich and ate it slowly, sipping water from his cup to wash it down. His mouth was dry and his lips were fat and tender from the beating. He remembered blacking out early in the beating from a blow to his head from behind. Maybe that's why he was here – from that blow.

The morning nurse came in with the same FBI man as the day before. She brought a tray of food with her and set it on the table next to his cup, which she refilled with cool water. She was young, maybe twenty-five, with jet black hair and large brown eyes. She reminded him of his wife, Syri. He could hear a man's voice out in the hall, speaking to her after she'd left the room. The man from the hall entered the room. He was dressed in a white coat and had a stethoscope hung around his neck – a doctor perhaps. He checked the charts and then left without saying anything. He was alone again.

Two days passed with the same routines playing out. In the evening of the third day, the same nurse with the black hair came in just before dark. She did everything the same, except that she checked his electrical leads on his chest, pressing them with her fingers for a better contact. Her hand slid down his arm and placed a small piece of paper into his free hand, and then she left. His heart pounded in his chest, making the monitor beep wildly. His fist held a note, the first contact he'd had with another person since the beating. He waited for a few minutes to see if anyone else would enter, before opening the folded note.

"Tomorrow night"

That's all it said, but he knew what it meant. It spoke of friends who were coming for him. His weary mind yelled back at him – you have no friends in this country – only enemies. But, there was the note, proof of a friend. How did they know he was here? How could anyone know, except for the people at the prison? He didn't sleep much that night, thinking about the possibility of a friend, his escape, and his freedom. He dreamed once during the night of returning to his homeland on a cargo ship, the same as what had brought him to America. The night nurse had startled him awake, sending him frantically searching for the note with his free hand, not remembering for a moment that he had swallowed it right after reading its message. She didn't seem to notice anyway. The day passed so slowly, he could barely stand it, napping when he could, eating all of his food, and drinking as much water as possible. By 8 p.m., when the shift changed, he was feeling ready for anything, pain, failure, death, it didn't matter to him. Anything was better than going back to prison to await execution.

His nurse with the black hair and brown eyes returned after her rounds on the floor and spoke with the guard outside his door. He listened intently before she entered with the man and changed his leads on the heart monitor, nodding at him while she did so. Soon, he said to himself. After they'd left, he began to stretch his legs and tighten the muscles to get the blood flow up, doing the same for every muscle in his body, even the ones which brought him pain. He still had a bandage wrapped around his head, which was changed only once. He wondered what was underneath of it, and if he would be dizzy standing for the first time in days. Could he even walk? His mind raced for a while before he forced himself to calm down and remain alert. The clock on the white box said it was close to midnight. Soon he thought.

When she came in just after midnight, his heart raced, making the monitor beep rapidly. She frowned at him and then turned around, saying that she'd forgotten something, and would be right back. The security guard remained standing just inside the doorway, his arms folded across his chest. He looked bored and tired, his eyelids drooping every few seconds. She'd drugged him – he knew it by the signs on his face. So there would be no struggle, no loud voices, no gunshots, just a sleeping guard. She returned and finished her work and left with the guard, having to hold the door for him, he was so sleepy. He waited those long few minutes, worried that something would go wrong.

She entered with two other men dressed in white coats, like the doctors who had visited his room. She undid the heart monitor and shut it off, shut off the flow of his IV and unhooked him from the tree. The two men wheeled his bed out of the room, passing the sleeping guard by his door and then down the hall to the elevators, which they took to the basement. When the elevator doors opened, he had a strange sense of freedom, free, but really free. The two men wheeled him down a long hallway to a door which led to a large maintenance work area.

"Time to get out of bed," she said quietly.

The two men helped him get up, swinging his legs over the edge of the bed to the concrete floor. He felt dizzy, but not so much as to be a real problem. She pushed his head down into his lap and held it there for a few seconds.

"Let's go." She said.

The two men walked him outside to a waiting car, helping him into the backseat, and then they all left together. He was laying down with his head on her lap, while one of the men drove, and the other checked the GPS on his phone to be sure they were on the right roads.

"You can call me Rema. We will take you to a safe place, where you can finish healing enough so you can leave the country. It will be a long road ahead after they know you've escaped. The Feds will have everyone looking for you."

"Thank you for freeing me, all of you," he said in a weak voice, still dizzy from all the exertion. "Why?" he asked.

"Because we believe in your cause, our cause. You should rest now."

He closed his eyes and slept.

****

When Amul woke from a long string of confusing dreams, he was in a dark room with log walls, lying on a cot, and very thirsty. There was an IV bottle hung on a floor lamp by his cot. "Hello?" He called out. He heard a door close and then Rema entered, dusting herself off, and putting on a warm smile.

"Good, you're awake. I had to give you something to sleep because you were uncomfortable after the car ride. You're in a cabin in the woods. No one uses this place any longer so we are alone. There is no electricity or cell service here. It's just you and me. Are you feeling better?"

"Yes. I'm very thirsty. May I have some water?" Rema returned with a bottle of water and pulled the IV out of his hand, placing a band-aid over the leaking vein.

"That will be a little sore for a few days. Are you dizzy at all?"

She helped him to sit so that he could drink. "No, not much." He answered. "Who are you? I know your name is Rema, but who are you really?"

"Just a friend who believes as you do. When you were caught and then sentenced to death, a number of us in the Midwest talked about ways to free you. The man who hit you in prison, he's one of us. It was the only way to get you out of the maximum security prison and into a place we could deal with. I applied for an RN position two months ago at the hospital where you were taken. We gambled that you'd be treated there because they have neurosurgeons. You would have died if they hadn't operated to relieve the pressure in your cranial cavity. We gambled and you won, but you still need to take it easy for a few weeks. You're still healing. We'll be fine here."

"Thank you, Rema. Tell the others thank you. I am most grateful. I'm hungry." Al Atrash laughed at himself and the way he said the words.

"Come on, I'll help you to the other room and I'll make us something to eat."

****

Harold's phone rang just as he and Abbey were about to board a flight to Chicago. "Yes Gene, what's on your mind." Harold stumbled on the ramp connecting the aircraft to the jetway.

"He escaped last night." Gene flat tone resonated concern.

"You mean Al Atrash? How could he?"

"He was in a hospital in Terra Haute for surgery after he was beaten by a prisoner. He had help." Gene's words sounded hollow in Harold's mind.

"Does Denise know yet?" he muttered.

"Yes, I just told her five minutes ago. You'll have extra security when you're out in public, at least until he's caught, which shouldn't take long. He was in bad shape."

"Any other good news for me?" Harold's tone was semi-sarcastic.

"Don't worry, we'll get him."

"Yeah, that's what you said the last time he took a shot at me." Harold realized he was talking to a disconnected line – Gene had hung up already, as usual. He slid the phone into his jacket pocket and stopped Abbey in the aisle. "We're not alone

266

again. He's escaped."

"I heard. Let's go sit down, we're in the way here." Abbey's brow furrowed.

Denise led the way to their three seats in the middle of the MD 80. They sat in silence during preflight, each knowing the gravity of the situation.

****

Rema was taking good care of him in their hideaway. The crisp autumn air was refreshing his spirits on the early morning walks they took together. They'd return to the small two-room cabin and cook breakfast in the fireplace, with the wrought iron pans. She'd stocked enough dehydrated food for several weeks, and had medical supplies to serve his needs. He'd taken a severe beating and ached pretty much everywhere, but it was the head injury he'd received when he was knocked into the corner of a metal table, which had landed him in the care of a neurosurgeon – not exactly the planned outcome, but it had worked. His dizziness was gone by the second day and his strength was improving, as was his growing desire to leave this safe haven to hunt his prey before he was caught again, which he considered inevitable.

"What will you do when you leave here?" he asked Rema, concerned about her welfare.

"I don't really know. I can't go home and I can't continue nursing, and I don't want to go to prison. So, that gives me only one option. I have to leave the country."

"I have connections to help get you out, but you'd probably wind up going to my country. At least there, you wouldn't be hunted." He knew it would be difficult for an American born woman to adapt to a country at war, one which lay in shambles most places. Her face brightened at his offer of help.

"You would do that for me?"

"You saved me from certain death at the hands of my enemy. For that, I will always be grateful. Can you get a car? We'll need transportation."

"Yes. One will be here day after tomorrow. But, it's too soon for you to leave. You're still healing inside your head and you don't want to risk reinjuring the blood vessels that the doctor fixed. You were lucky the first time that you didn't go into a coma for days or weeks. It's important for you to stay here and rest quietly."

"Yes, and you're doing such a good job of it. What day is this? I've lost track completely."

"It's Friday I think. Why?"

"Nothing just wondered. Where are we again, I forgot what you told me the first day?"

"We're in Indiana, about seventy miles southeast of the prison, in a National Forest, Hoosier, I think. This hunting cabin dates from the eighteen hundreds I'm told. We found out about it from a story a friend of mine heard in a class at Indiana University in Bloomington."

"You are a very resourceful person Rema and are the first friend I've had in America. Most of my contacts wanted little to do with me, except to see me on my way. You remind me of my wife. She too, was a resourceful person, often making do with very little, yet still remaining a loving and happy woman."

"What is she like? If you don't mind my asking." A warm smile filled Rama's face.

Amul's face went dark and angry, his eyes burning with the revenge he'd been seeking for years. "She is dead. Killed in an air strike by an American led attack on Al Bab. Her name was Syri. My daughter was killed too, alongside my mother and father. I was not there." His mind went far away, to another time and place, one of mourning and grief, hatred and rage; all things that lived within him now.

"I'm so sorry," Rema said extending her hand across the small wooden table they ate at.

He leaned back in his creaky and loose-jointed chair, wanting no part of another person in his life, let alone a woman. His hand waved her off, his lips tightly sealed in bitterness.

"I didn't mean . . ."

"It's not you. It's me." He got up and paced across the cabin, turning to face her. "I swore I would not care for another woman." He walked outside to breathe in some cool fresh air and calm himself. Why had he lost control so easily? Was it the injury to his head? He walked down the trail in the lush woods, now ablaze with fall colors. He must be on his way. He had a mission to fulfill, a prey to pursue. He needed to kill Harold Robertson before he was killed or caught.

****

"Rodger, I'm not going to argue with you. Abbey and I are going to her parent's farm for a few days, and that's the way it's going to be. Besides, what more can we do on the campaign trail? I'll do a short interview at the farm if you insist, but that's all." Rodger Atwood, his campaign manager, was pushing him to do three more stops in California, New York, and Florida, before Election Day. But, he'd had enough. He'd done all that was humanly possible to convey his message and present himself as the absolute best candidate for the Presidency. The Democratic Senator from California was a strong candidate, but she'd angered too many on the Hill in her ten years in office. Her stubbornness towards a more conservative approach to rebuilding the economy would be her downfall – of that he was certain. He'd heard enough talk with the powers that be on the Hill, to know when someone was beaten. The media may have played it down to help her out, but the American people were rallying against her views on the economy. Old school didn't work anymore, and she was most definitely old school.

"Vince, did you get us two vehicles for the trip?" he asked, knowing it was already taken care of. He did it to put an end to Rodger's rant, once and for all.

"We're good to go. Denise and I will ride with you and Abbey. Al and West will follow," Vince said.

"Good deal," he said walking across the living room of their suite overlooking Lake Shore Drive and Lake Michigan. "Anyone up for a walk to the Museum of Science and Industry?" Only silence ensued. "Okay, how about a stroll on the lakefront trail?" Abbey smiled at him. "Good, it's settled." He turned towards Rodger, who was looking a bit sullen. "Room for one more, if you like." Rodger eyed him warily, shaking his head no. Harold grabbed Abbey and headed for the door before anyone could change their mind. Denise opened it for them and gave him a look. "What? It'll be fun, won't it?" He teased her. So, that's how they spent their last day in Chicago – ditching the campaign manager.

HALLOWEEN

Clayton 8 p.m.

Rodger Atwood had dutifully tagged along, wanting to be in on the taped interview with the local TV station. He was a good sport and doing his best to enjoy the downtime before Election Day, which to him was most certainly not the time to rest. They were at the local Community Church's Halloween party, mostly for children under ten years of age. The basement was the hallowed sanctuary of creepy stuff, and he and Abbey were dressed for their parts: he as a ghoul and her as a fairy. Denise got to be the damaged FBI agent with bloody scars on her face. She was having a blast with the kids. He'd never seen her so happy as she was in a crowded room of giggling, screaming, wild kids. It all ended around nine o'clock, and they'd grabbed some handfuls of candy for the ride back to the farm. West had stayed at the farm to guard the home-front so that no boogieman could sneak in while they were gone. He was milling around the barn when they parked.

"Hey West," Harold greeted him and shoveled some candy into his pocket. "Booty," he grinned. They laughed. He walked Abbey to the RV, where they were sleeping. Vince and Denise were in his camper close by, and West and Al, well, they got to take turns patrolling the grounds all night, sleeping in shifts in their SUV. Rodger was at a motel in town. Harold built a small campfire by the pond in the stone fire pit. They set up chairs and huddled together under a blanket against the cool fall evening, listening to the silence around them.

"Warm enough?" He whispered.

"Hmm," she turned her head and kissed him on the cheek.

"I'm glad we took this time away. I told Rodger we'd make two of those stops after we leave here. He was happy about that. The man would have me turning cartwheels on the moon if he thought it would help us win the election." He laughed quietly.

"He's just doing his job honey."

"Yeah, I know. But after Oliver's meltdown at the Convention, and Senator's Hemstead's dive in the poll numbers last week, he knew we'd win. He even told me in so many words in a text the next day."

"Can we not talk about this right now?" Abbey snuggled closer. "You know, I used to sit under the oak tree at night and dream about kissing you. Bet you didn't know that." She lay her head against his.

"You had it bad, huh?"

"I always knew we'd be together, maybe not at first, but someday. I could feel it right down to my toes on warm summer nights under that tree. You and I had a good life, didn't we?"

"Still do. Why did you say it like that? We have a terrific life ahead of us, Ms. First Lady Robertson."

"I guess I'm tired and feeling kinda melancholy. Can we go to bed early tonight?" She yawned.

"Sure." He got a bucket of water from the pond, doused the fire. They were in bed before 10 p.m.

****

Al Atrash had lied to Rema, more than once. She never guessed that all he wanted to do in his remaining days was to hunt down his son's killer. He'd questioned the two men who'd driven the two cars to within a quarter mile of the cabin. One of them had read in the Indianapolis Review about Harold and Abbey being at home in Clayton for Halloween. He knew right where Nelson farm was, having researched it online and found it on maps. He knew the layout of the farm and even studied an approach which would be mostly undetectable until he entered the yard area around the house and barn. All he was lacking was a weapon.

Neither of the two men had a gun, but did volunteer a hunting knife with a seven-inch blade, sheathed and attached to a leather belt. He demanded their cash and took the late model Mazda sedan, leaving while Rema was busy talking with her two friends – said he was going for a short walk. That was late in the afternoon on Sunday. He'd driven on the back roads, until dawn, making several wrong turns in the confusing array of country roads in Indiana and Illinois, and parked in a hay field behind a large round bale because he was low on fuel.

Midmorning, he pulled into a café and truck stop just outside of a small town, bought gas, used the restroom, and then drove the remaining twenty-something miles to Clayton. He went straight to the old abandoned farmhouse he'd found on a real estate website when he was in New York. It was a mile outside of town and he could park out of sight behind the two-story clapboard house to wait for dark. He didn't dare approach the Nelson's farm in daylight for fear of seeming suspicious if he passed by more than once. He sat quietly, going over in his memory, the layout of the farm.

He didn't know what time he left, but it had been dark for several hours. He drove to the dirt turnoff used between fields, turned off his headlights, and crept down the rutted access road, until he felt he'd gone far enough. The Nelson home was about a quarter mile across the field to his left. The house was dark, so he waited some more, hoping to see lights when they returned. He fell asleep several times for a few minutes. His body ached and his head was throbbing at the site of his wound. He nearly slept through their arrival, and if he'd not heard the faint sound of a car door closing hard, he probably would have. He rubbed his eyes and saw the house lights come on downstairs. He got out and started to walk across the plowed field, tripping over the deep rows of dirt clods left after plowing.

About halfway to the barn and pond, he hesitated, crouching down because the two utility lights in the barnyard were illuminating him. There was one man patrolling around the house and yard, two SUVs parked in the front yard of the house, a truck and camper next to an RV back of the barn close to the pond, and no lights coming from the house or RV. A dim light in the camper shone through its side window. The man walking was about to go around the house, so he kept walking towards the pond, circling around it to get to the SUVs. He waited in the shadows by the far edge of the barn, needing to see the man on patrol move away across the driveway, to the other side of the yard.

Again, he hesitated to proceed because he was entering the area illumined by one of the barn lights. He walked as quietly as he could to the two SUVs, stopping between them and then looked in through the windshields for an occupant, and most importantly, a weapon. He was exposed as he gaped into the two vehicles, both of which had darkened windows. He had his knife at the ready and was about to move away because he'd seen no one inside, when he heard a man snort and cough loudly.

He peered in the one where the sound came from and saw a man lying in the backseat. He chose a side where he thought the man's head would be, and carefully depressed the latch button, and pulled the door open in slow motion. When it was halfway open, he covered the man's mouth with one hand, and slit his throat all the way to his vertebra, muffling one faint guttural sound before the man was dead. He glanced around quickly for the man on patrol, sheathed his knife, and reached in to unlatch the holstered 9mm from the man's hip. He clicked off the safety on the weapon, feeling around for the spare clip, locating it and extracting it from the gun belt. He crouched between the SUVs and looked again for the man on patrol, he would be coming this way soon.

Behind him, he heard a man clear his throat and call out.

"Hey Al, wake up. It's your watch."

Amul squatted in silence, listening intently for any sounds from the other man.

"Come on Al, I'm tired and want to get some sleep."

The man on patrol was on the other side of the SUV rapping on the window. The sound of a door latch sent rushes of adrenalin to Amul's throbbing head, making the pain worse. He had to act now before the body was found, and the man drew his gun. He reached up and grasped the door latch, and flung the door open, firing three volleys in quick succession. He didn't wait to see if the man was still alive, instead, rushing towards the camper, where he thought more agents would be sleeping. The camper was a hundred feet away, and he'd only made it halfway, when the camper door flew open and a person emerged in midair, touching down with a foot, rolling up into a kneeling position, and fired four or more shots his direction. One of them found its mark on his left shoulder before he returned fire, emptying his clip. As he frantically ejected the spent clip and loaded the other, more shots were fired by the person he'd just shot. Al Atrash was hit again in the left side down by his hips. He fell to one knee and took careful aim at the shooter on the ground, and squeezed off one round, seeing the person crumple to the dirt.

He turned his attention to the dimly lit camper door and waited for some movement in the shadows of the interior. The sound of breaking glass inside the camper confused him. Was the person trying to climb out the opposite side? The cab of the truck was facing away from him at a sharp angle, but he still could make out slight movement of the truck's suspension. They were climbing through the pass-thru window and into the cab, he thought. He crept towards the rear of the camper and crouched down in pain, glancing back at the motionless person he'd shot. He sprawled on the ground, nearly crying out in pain, and watched towards the front of the truck for feet to slide to the ground.

Instead of feet, he was blinded by a high-intensity flashlight, causing his sight to go very dark for a few seconds while his eyes adjusted back to the dim light cast by the barn lights. He bolted towards the RV thirty feet away with his eyes still adjusting, when four more reports from behind him found their mark on his legs and lower back. He hit the ground hard, clinging desperately to his gun. He rolled and returned fire, very aware it was his last clip. In the dim light, he saw the person rolling on the ground, and holding their midsection. Amul knew he had one last chance to kill the man who'd taken his son from him. His legs were useless to him and the pain in his lower back was sharp and debilitating. He rolled on his stomach and faced towards the RV and fired one shot through the door, then another towards the rear of it.

Across the yard three hundred feet away, the house light came on, and then three floodlights, essentially blinding his view of anyone behind the lights. The report of a high powered rife followed dirt flying up in his face. He knew the man wouldn't miss again. Al Atrash emptied his clip into the RV, spreading the remaining four shots about midway between the door and the rear. He never felt the .308 bullet strike his shoulder and blow his heart apart. He was dead the moment of impact.

****

Harold was crouching with Abbey limp in his arms in the dark, narrow hall between the bedroom and the living room. He was afraid to turn on a light, not knowing that Al Atrash lay dead twenty feet outside the RV. He was numb and shaking, so afraid that Abbey would die right there in his arms. He rocked her gently in the silence.

"Harold," Vince's pained voice called out. "He's dead."

It took a moment for the words to sink in, but when they did, he lay Abbey on the carpet and stood to turn on a light. He found blood on his shirt and hands, and Abbey's head was oozing blood from her left temple.

"Oh God, no." He jumped over her to get his phone and dial 911, bringing it back and laying it on the carpet, and speaking loudly when the operator came on. "Nelson farm, three wounded, send two ambulances, they're all gunshot wounds. Do you understand?"

"Yes, the Nelson place on Briar Road. Is the shooter active?"

"No, he's dead. Please hurry, one's a gunshot wound to the head."

"Stay on the line sir, the first ambulance is on its way."

Harold looked up from Abbey to see her father standing in the RV's living room with his hunting rifle in hand, his face filled with pain. Pete opened the hall closet and got a first aid kit. He opened it and pressed a large gauze pad to his daughter's head, and placed Harold's hand on it.

"Is she hit anywhere else?" Pete asked.

Harold shook his head, looking down at his wife in horror. "I don't see . . ."

"I need to check on Vince. I'll be right back." Pete said.

"Abbey, don't you leave me," Harold choked out weakly. "Don't you die. You stay with me." He began to sob, stroking her hair and holding the gauze to her temple. Pete came back in and kneeled next to them, his face lost in pain. The minutes passed like hours before the first police car roared to a stop, with the ambulance right behind.

"In the RV," Vince's voice yelled outside the RV. "I'm okay." Harold's pain filled mind could barely comprehend the voice coming through the open door.

Two EMTs came into the living room, one opening a kit, and the other moving to the opposite side of Abbey, doing a quick triage.

"Sir, are you hurt?"

He shook his head with his eyes never leaving Abbey.

"I need you to move now," the EMT said. "We have to get her to the ER."

Harold scooted back towards the bedroom on the carpet and watched as his Abbey was quickly examined and taken away. He couldn't move, his mind was so numb. When she disappeared through the door, he just sat lifeless against a hallway cabinet.

"Harold," Pete Nelson shook his shoulder. "Are you hurt?"

He looked into Pete's face and shook his head, no.

"Come on, I'll take you to the hospital."

Pete helped him to his feet, and stepping out of the RV, Harold saw Denise crumpled on the ground, and Vince was walking towards the ambulance with a policeman's assistance.

"Is she dead," his voice weak and cracking.

"Yes," Pete answered.

Chapter 46

SHATTERED DREAMS
Clayton Regional Medical Center

Abbey's father never said a word on the way to the hospital. Harold was thankful for the silence because he had no words for what had happened to the man's daughter. She was not the target, he was, which made him responsible in his mind. This was the third time he'd been targeted and it was always someone else who got injured or killed. The tape played over and over in his mind, from the first gunshot to the final high powered rifle report. He'd draped himself over Abbey in the hallway because that's where he'd found her. She was walking to the kitchen for a drink of bottled water from the fridge, and he'd sprung from bed at the first shot, and tackled her in the hallway. And that's where they'd remained through all the gunfire outside. He didn't have a weapon in the RV – he saw no need. The image of Pete standing with a rifle in hand, aghast at the sight of his daughter crumpled on the floor filled his mind, overpowering all else. It was the final frame of the endless loop tape. Pete had shot the terrorists, not him. It should have been him protecting his wife. Pete's profile was erect and strong as he drove them to town. The man was closing in on eighty years and still a tower of strength.

"You know it's not your fault," Pete said turning into the Regional Medical Center.

"Yes, it is." Harold's words sounded hollow and dead inside his head.

Those were the last words he spoke to Pete that night. He

sat in the ER waiting room in silence, answering only a few questions from the police. Apparently, Vince had called Gene and given a report, because at 5 a.m., three agents arrived at the ER and took up posts, not that he cared. The madman was finally dead, and it had taken a father to do the work of the Secret Service. The agents had asked him questions, but he had no answers. They waited for Vince to come out of surgery before they got any real answers as what had happened. But, what was there to tell. Denise was dead. Vince was wounded. Abbey had slipped into a coma. And daddy had taken out the bad guy. All he'd done was call 911 and hold a gauze pad on her wound.

"Mr. Robertson?" The nurse called out to the waiting room. "The doctor wants to speak with you. Please follow me."

She led him and two of the agents to a small consultation office, where he met with the ER doctor who'd attended Abbey.

"Mr. Robertson, we have to move your wife to Chicago Memorial. I've done all I can to stabilize her condition. I removed some of the bullet fragments, but a neurosurgeon will have to go after the two in her temporal lobe. Life Flight is on the roof and you'll need to sign some forms to release her. We can arrange for you to go with her, but there's only room for you." Dr. Moss said pointing at the agents.

"Thank you, doctor. I'll have to ride with them." Harold's shaky voice made the doctor frown at him.

"Have you been examined?"

He nodded yes, looking down at his pajama top. It had two bloody bullet holes in it where it had passed through and then struck Abbey in the head. He walked out of the office and back to the waiting room.

"Pete, they're moving Abbey to Chicago Memorial for surgery. I'm going with them." He pointed at the agents standing nearby. "Abbey is stable for now, the doctor said."

"I'll go home and get Sharon. We'll meet you there in a couple of hours."

****

When they arrived at Chicago Memorial, the neurosurgeon had already shuffled his schedule to accommodate Abbey Robertson, wife of Presidential candidate Harold Robertson. He sat in the waiting area with several other elderly people, mindlessly thumbing through every magazine on the tables, while Abbey waited for the surgeon to finish a surgery already in process. Harold was not a patient waiter, stalking the nurses station and hallway in between magazines. He'd tried to ask about the case, but no one seemed to have the right answers for him. Finally, the doctor had sent his assistant in to talk with him and allay any fears. The young man was very understanding of Harold's position, but could not say one way or the other about the long term outcome. Comas, he said, were difficult to predict as to their duration. Dr. Harlow took him into to see Abbey a few hours later, after she'd left post-op recovery and been assigned a private room in the ICU. He only stayed three minutes, but reassured Harold about her condition. He said they'd know better in a day or so, but for now, she was stable and breathing on her own. The doctor left Harold to wrestle with his demons.

"Abbey, what are we going to do? It can't end like this. It just can't." He held her hand and stroked it gently. "I don't know if you can hear my voice, but I need you to decide right now that you're going to fight this and wake up. We have so much to do." He stopped suddenly when an alarm sounded and a nurse slid open the glass door a moment later. She checked the leads and reattached one which was loose. She patted his shoulder on her way out.

"She's doing fine, Mr. Robertson."

He returned her smile. "Thank you." He pulled up a small vinyl and metal chair and sat next to his wife, and continued stroking her hand through the safety rail. One of his agents knocked on the glass door and held up his phone, pointing to him. He opened the slider and asked who it was. Gene the agent said.

"Hello, Gene. This is not a good time for me."

Gene proceeded to say how sorry he was that Abbey was injured, and then strangely went silent. For Harold, it said everything about how Gene felt. He knew him well enough to know that much.

"Thank you, Gene. The doc says she'll pull through, maybe in a few days. Thanks for calling." Harold hung up on Gene first, for a change. He didn't particularly want to talk with any one at the moment, but he knew he had to call Rodger and tell him to cancel all the engagements, which he did before returning to her side. Rodger was understanding about it all and said Regina would attend as planned.

Harold sent a text to Abbey's parents, saying she was doing well, but still not awake. He didn't use the word coma, because it spoke to the possibility of death. They responded and said they were on their way and would be there around noon. He pocketed his phone and slumped in his chair, his whole life felt like it was in limbo and the upcoming election didn't even register with him as being real. Around noon, he had to get out of the ICU and walk off his looming depression. It was getting out of control. His three newly assigned agents followed him on his walkabout, as he meandered in the corridors as if he'd find some magic elixir lying about. Eventually he stopped and turned back towards his shadows, to talk to the nearest man to him. He needed to get out of his head, because it was in wild disarray.

"You have family?" he blurted out. The look of surprise on

the man's face seemed to help break through his moodiness. "I'm really sorry about Denise. She was my friend. Did you know her?" It didn't even occur to him to ask about West and Al. Just two more bodies added to his list of casualties for whom he was the responsible party – he was the prey of Al Atrash, not them.

"No. We never met. But, I do know Vince, and he spoke well of her courage and dedication."

Their eyes met for a brief moment, before he looked away. "Are you hungry? I am. Let's get some sandwiches from the cafeteria."

When they returned to the ICU, Pete and Sharon were in with their daughter. He waited outside the glass door, not wanting to disturb their privacy. He approached the ICU nurse's station and spoke with the nurse seated behind the counter, asking about Abbey's condition. She queried the computer and interpreted the surgeon's notes for the ICU staff. He'd repaired a minor tear to subdural tissues, removed two small fragments of the bullet, installed a drain, and repaired the cranium.

"He's the best neurosurgeon in the area, Mr. Robertson. Your wife's injuries, as far as gunshot wounds are concerned, are minimal and will heal. She may have minor issues with her memory and feel confused for a while, but in my experience, she will fully recover. She's not in any danger and will wake soon. A few days for such injuries is typical. You can go in if you like."

Sally Grayson, it said on her nametag. "I wanted to let her parents have some alone time." Harold returned her pleasant smile and walked back to Abbey's unit. Sharon motioned for him to come in and join them. He opened the glass slider and went to the opposite side of the bed, where all the bedside medical equipment was. Pete's soft-spoken eyes met his, filled with the pain of his little girl lying in a coma. It brought all of his hidden fears to his eyes and it hurt terribly to be there with them. He was responsible. Al Atrash was his madman. He'd brought him here by killing his son. His eyes fell to Abbey's hand with the IV taped on top of it, such a gentle and yet strong hand.

"It's not your fault." Sharon's gentle voice spilled out into the room.

He lifted his head slowly to meet her tear filled eyes. Abbey was so like her mother, strong, gentle, and always outspoken. He wanted to say how sorry he was that he hadn't protected their daughter from harm, from the madman who'd hunted him for over a year, but the words wouldn't come out. He hung his head in shame, so wanting to comfort their pain.

"What did the doctor say?" Pete asked. "When will she come out of this?"

"The surgeon said she'll be okay," he mumbled raising his head, surprised by the sound of his words. "It may take a few days before she wakes though." The words didn't come out very strong, but at least he'd said something useful. Pete nodded and motioned that he wanted to talk outside. He followed Pete out and slid the door closed.

"Your man at Homeland Security called and apologized for their failure to protect you and Abbey. He sounds like a good man. Anyway, then he thanked me for doing what they couldn't and said he'd be recommending to the President, some medal or something. I need you to talk to him. I don't need a medal. I just need my daughter to be well again." Pete's eyes spoke his words louder than his lips.

Harold nodded and hugged his father-in-law, whose courage and love for family, far outweigh his once, large physique. "The ICU nurse reassured me that in her experience, Abbey will be fine." Harold felt better saying the words aloud, feeling like he was the one who really needed to hear them more than anyone else. Pete nodded and rubbed his chin.

"You're going to keep to your schedule, right? Abbey would want you to, you know. Sharon and I can keep you up to date on her condition. Besides, she'll be awake in a day or so, you said, and if she wakes up knowing you didn't finish your campaign stops, she'll be mad. But, you already know that." Pete smiled at his son-in-law and future President.

Harold almost laughed. Pete could have that effect on people, he was such an easy going guy, with the strength of an ox, and heart of a lion. "Yeah, you've got a good point there." He looked back in at Abbey, finding Sharon watching them through the glass. No wonder he loved Abbey so much. Her parents were so strong and loving – just a couple of American farmers, making their way in life.

Chapter 47

THE FINAL SIX DAYS

Los Angeles, November 2ⁿᵈ

Harold stayed with Abbey until noon the next day, then flew to California to meet with his VP, Regina Lawford. Rodger was elated when he'd called him, saying these were the most important days in any campaign, a time when many were just getting to the point of making up their minds. The way politics worked these days, a large number of the independents didn't make their final choice until the day before the election, and independent voters were quickly becoming a majority in America.

The last eight years had taken its toll on both parties, because the American people were angry that they weren't doing their jobs, spending much of their time fighting among themselves, increasing the national debt, and risking our nation's future by not addressing the fall of the nation's middle class over the past thirty years.

Rodger reminded Harold of all these points, because these and others, were the reasons he'd decided to run in the first place – his dream and all. His campaign manager had reminded him often about his dream of gathering the people under one roof, with one unifying cause to follow, one in which all Americans could be proud of what She stood for in the world. Rodger said that this was his time to roll up his sleeves and get to work. And Harold had believed him because it was what he wanted as an ordinary American – to feel proud and unified again.

So, when he stepped off the Delta flight at LAX and entered the main part of the terminal after the TSA security checkpoint, he was greeted by several thousand people who had just arrived or were about to leave, or perhaps those who'd come to see the Presidential Candidate arrive on a commercial airliner.

In any case, Harold took a moment to shake hands and greet people as he and his three agents made their way to his awaiting SUV. The agents weren't happy about it, but they were gentle as they made a path for him in the throngs. He was to meet with Regina for a press conference downtown in the LA Hotel Downtown, close to the Staples Center, where he and Regina would address a full house of twenty thousand plus.

This was one of Rogers' crowning jewels he'd planned for since the RNC's Convention. Harold was tired, but knew the importance of this one event, because it was being recorded and broadcast locally that evening, and would be out on the internet immediately. It was a big deal and he knew it, because the usually Democratic state of California, was a must-win for him, at least that's what Rodger had said.

He sent Pete and Sharon a text that he'd arrived and they replied back that all was quiet at the ICU. Harold walked down the hall to Regina's suite and knock on her door.

"Harold," her energetic voice rang out. "Oh, Harold," her tone softened. "I was so sorry to hear about Abbey. Come in."

His agent, Ted, stayed in the hall as he entered her room, and her agent joined Ted in the hallway. "Abbey is doing as well as can be expected. The neurologist who did the surgery said she'd be awake in a few days, that all went well."

"Thank God she's going to be okay. I know how hard it must have been to leave, but we do have our work cut out for us." Regina sat on the sofa.

He sat in the overstuffed chair across from her and began discussing his prepared speech, which Rodger had provided as a framework for him. Rodger knew he'd only follow it part of the time because he liked to think on his feet and react to the crowd's energy, something he'd always done in public speaking.

Regina was comfortable with what she'd be talking about, as she was already familiar with his plans for the first year in office because they'd worked closely during previous years on the Hill, he in the House and she in the Senate. They had similar views on how to move the American economy forward among other things. They had a light dinner brought to the room and invited the agents in, all four of them.

Ted, the agent in charge of his three, informed them of some logistics at the Staples Center, the usual comings and goings, and what to expect if there's a problem close to the stage. They left the hotel at 7 p.m. primed, pumped and happy to be working together again. She would precede him at the lectern, doing what she loved to do, energize the crowd and drop him into the midst of it all. She reminded him of the Governor of California, Janet Sharp, both bulldogs in disguise.

In the brief time he had alone in the hotel room, Harold had explained to himself the dialogue he wanted to have with the packed arena, boiling it all down to a plain and simple approach, as if he were sitting in a living room with friends, talking about family matters. Rodger had told him that this was a fundraiser for their after-school programs in the LA school district, with half of the twenty-dollar ticket sales going to those school district programs, and the other half paying for the rental of the arena. A popular local band opened for a famous all Latino rock band, currently rated sixth in the nation for sales, and up for a Grammy Award. When Rodger had approached them, they jumped at the chance to have the American hero, Harold Robertson, speak for a few minutes.

Rodger's directions would have him address cultural issues key to the local Latino community, but Harold wanted to talk to them as an everyday American, about what they wanted for their children. He extracted the key points and put them in terms that would mean something to an ordinary American citizen – easy enough to do for a plain and simple kinda guy.

It always boiled down to one thing. Change was not easy and people don't like hearing they have to change for the good of all. That bordered on being admonished to do better or try harder. What he knew most about himself, was if he were handed an opportunity to help his family, he would jump at the chance to do so, if it agreed with his personal values.

He had folded up his notes and stuffed them in his pants pocket back at the hotel before leaving, thinking that they probably wouldn't be all relevant in this setting. Seeing the stage set in the middle of the arena, with elevated walkways leading from portals used to enter and exit the arena, he felt a bit apprehensive. He would be surrounded by the audience, standing center stage without a lectern or anything to hide behind. He laughed at himself for being self-conscious about being exposed and feeling naked.

A technician fitted him with a wireless mic and earpiece, just as the band finished their first set. The lead singer announced that they'd invited these two candidates to speak, because of what their policies would mean for the inner city school district. And when he said Harold's name there was silence, perhaps because they'd heard about the shooting in Clayton. And that was the way Regina and he were introduced, walking the hundred feet to center stage to the deafening silence in the arena.

Regina gave him a nudge to begin. She wasn't going to say anything because the crowd was waiting to hear from him about his wife. "Ah, thank you," and he didn't remember the man's name, standing there naked in the silence. "My name is Harold Robertson and I guess I need to tell you that my wife, Abbey, who was shot two days ago, will recover, and you will meet her after the election, as the new First Lady."

The cheers erupted and the people rose to their feet in a thunderous applause that went on and on. Regina's hand was covering her mouth when glanced at her.

He would never get the chance to introduce her or say anything else, because the lead singer started singing the song, America The Beautiful. And then his lead guitarists came out to accompany, and something special happened that evening, which didn't require any exposition on his part.

Tonight was about family, and how precious and fragile life can be. Abbey had stirred their love for family and country, and shown both him and Regina, the true nature of Americans. Everyone in the arena that night sang the song which stirs the heart, about the love of country and life, but most of all, about the love of family.

The rest of the band had filtered in quickly, hearing what was going on with the people. And when it was finished, the lead singer stepped between them and raised their hands with his to thank the people for hearing their message, and then walked them off the stage and down the walkway, and gave them a farewell hug before they were out of view.

What happened that night would probably never happen again in his lifetime, and it was seared into his heart and mind, that this is the America he knew and wanted to help emerge more. Through all the cheers and the music starting back up, he didn't say a word to Regina until they reached their SUV. Even then, few words were spoken. They hugged, each knowing what they'd experienced was special, and would be seen throughout the country in the coming days.

****

Regina and he spoke about that night several times during the next few days on the final campaign circuit, always bringing home the point that what had happened would never happen again; different, yes, but the same, no, because it was created by those present in the moment. Harold had felt similar things in the classroom when his students all became of one mind; points of recognition shared by all when the lights go on inside their minds. It was always a marvelous experience.

They were in New York City for their final stop of and were both ready to call it quits and go home and rest. Abbey was still in a coma and he ached to return and be by her side. What he and Regina had experienced together in the four days they were on the road, would be long remembered, and respected by them both. The first night in LA had brought them into a mindset, which would serve them both well, even if they didn't win the election four days from now. When they parted ways that evening after three campaign gatherings in the Bronx, Brooklyn, and at the Javits Center in Manhattan, he was going to see Abbey at Chicago Memorial, and Regina was going home to her family in Springfield. They would meet at their election headquarters in Regina's hometown, Springfield, Illinois the night of the election.

Chapter 48

GOING HOME
November 5th

Harold got the text from Pete at 5 a.m., waking him from a deep sleep. His phone was vibrating on the nightstand when he reached for it and knocked it to the floor.

"Waking up. Come home."

It took a minute for the message to register. He would not be there when Abbey woke. His flight didn't leave until 10 a.m. And that was how his morning began.

As he pushed open the door into the ICU at 11 a.m., he prepared himself for whatever condition Abbey would be in. He stopped at the desk and inquired about her, as his phone had died at the airport shortly before he boarded. So, he knew nothing.

"Oh, Mr. Robertson, she was moved a half hour ago to a private room. Here it is, room 1245 on the twelfth floor. You can use the elevator down the hall."

He asked her to write it down for him and thanked her. Stepping out of the elevator on the twelfth floor, he wished that he'd remembered to get some flowers from the shop in the lobby. It was just one more forgotten thing in his drowsy head. Her room was the last one at the end of the hallway and had music playing softly as he entered. Pete and Sharon were sitting by the bed and Abbey was sitting up with a tray of food to one side.

"Look who's here," Pete said.

Abbey turned her head, a smile appearing as she did like she already knew it was Harold. He gathered her free hand into his and raised it up, kissing it and rubbing it against his cheek. His heart was racing.

"Good to see you," she said.

Her faint smile vanished as her eyes flooded, and she frowned in concentration. "How do you feel?" he asked, as his own emotional freight train approached.

"I'm okay," she said reaching out with her arms.

Harold bent over the raised safety bar and kissed her gently on the cheek. He pressed his cheek to hers and fought back his emotions.

"I was so worried," he whispered in her ear. He forced the memory of cradling her in his arms in the dark hallway from his mind, not ever wanting to see that image again.

"Doc said you'd be okay, just needed to rest before waking up," he said softly.

"I'm going to be alright," she said stroking his cheek. "All I really have are few memory glitches and a big fat headache. The doctor said I was lucky that the bullet fragmented hitting the RV wall, with only a small piece of it finding my head. Daddy's been quizzing me about the important stuff, you know, like we're married – stuff like that. I'm tired though, and thirsty. My water is on the tray."

He handed her the plastic mug with a straw and watched as she sipped slowly. The ripple effect of days of stress was cascading through him, finally being able to let some of it go, now that she was awake and out of danger.

"So, how long you been awake?" Harold asked, taking back the mug and moving the tray closer to her. Abbey looked at her father to answer.

"What was it, 4 a.m.?" Pete said to his daughter. "She called out to me, waking me from a dream. Said she was thirsty."

"Has the doc been in to see you yet?"

"Not till 2 p.m. the nurse told us. A physical therapist was in earlier, and took her for a walk down the hall." Pete said. "She did okay."

"Glad to hear it," he bent down and kissed her. "You anxious to get out of here?" He said next to her ear. She nodded. "I'm going to speak with the head nurse for a minute." He said turning to leave. "Anything I can get either of you?"

"Strawberry ice cream please," Abbey said.

Harold raised an eyebrow at her. "See what I can do." He said from the doorway.

Strawberry ice cream was a code phrase to his campaign manager during his run for Governor, for I need to get away from this group or this person because they're inundating me with questions, criticism, or the like. He'd started using it right after a journalist had criticized his policies in the House, in a not so kind way. The guy had cornered him in a park next to an ice cream vendor and Harold had bought him a cone of strawberry ice cream and then bumped into him as he left, knocking the cone into his face as he took a bite. Abbey had told him that she wanted out of here, asap.

He checked his phone for messages, while he waited for the nurse to get off the phone. He had six from Rodger and one from Gene, asking him to come to DHS headquarters in DC after the election, to fill out a complete report of the incident, so that an accurate press release could be provided. "Humf," he mumbled, wondering what more the press could need.

"May I help you," the nurse said.

He pocketed his phone. "Yes, about Abbey Robertson in 1245. What's it going to take to get her released? I think she really would rather go home to recuperate if that works with her doctor." He smiled pleasantly at her.

"And you are?"

"Oh, sorry. I'm her husband."

"Well, Mr. Robertson, it's really up to her doctor, but usually in a couple of days is the norm with similar cases. You'll have to speak with her doctor."

"Thank you."

He went to the cafeteria and got her strawberry ice cream, as requested, and donuts and coffee for himself and Pete. Abbey wolfed down the tiny container of ice cream and ate his donut, and asked for a sip of his coffee when the doctor came in early.

"Well I see you're feeling much better," the doctor said examining her chart and checking the monitor readouts with his tablet. The nurse said you asked about going home?"

Abbey nodded.

"I don't see why not. Everything looks goods, and you can finish healing at home. I'll put the paperwork in and tomorrow morning you'll be on your way."

"Thank you for everything, Dr. Harlow." Abbey smiled at him.

****

Abbey had refused to go back to the farm, wanting to stay at Harold's home, saying something about not wanting to look at the crime scene. It was fine with him; he wasn't too big on the idea either. Besides, the RV was off limits and part of the investigation and the farmhouse would be overcrowded with seven people in two bedrooms and a living room sofa. At least at his place in town, there was a small guest room above the detached garage, three bedrooms and two baths in the house. The only hard part was all of Ruth's stuff, which still was in every room.

Clayton was a small town of seven thousand, west of Chicago about sixty miles with homes dating from the early nineteenth century. Some of the old building in town had been preserved in part, through the years, and still had their original raised boardwalks, creaky wood floors, and fourteen-foot tin ceilings. The dry goods store still used the floor to ceiling shelves behind the solid wood counter and had a rolling ladder to access them. The descendants of the family still ran it, along with a meat market and hardware store, all attached to each other, with wide passageways between them. Harold's grandparents and parents had shopped at these stores, and so did he. He took home enough groceries for three days of dinners and breakfasts.

After dinner, Abbey helped him pack a few of Ruth's things from the bedroom and living room, making him keep things Ruth liked out on display, at least for now. They both retired early.

One of the things he needed to do before the chaos of Election Day arrived, was go to the Clayton Cemetery and talk with Ruth and his brother Alex. He tried to talk Abbey out of going, but she'd insisted, wanting to know his family better, and not wanting to be left behind with an agent who had replaced West, who had died hours after the shooting, in the wee hours of the morning at the Regional Hospital.

They drove to the family plots together and sat in the car for a long time before getting out. Harold had never visited his brother with anyone else, always preferring to be alone. Abbey respected his wishes and stayed in the car, watching from a short distance away.

Harold brought a small bouquet of artificial flowers for each of his family members buried there. It meant that he had a box full of thirty-three bouquets, gathering up the old ones and replacing them with new. Clayton cemetery's oldest resident dated from eighteen thirty-nine, a baby of six months, firstborn of the Moore family, who had settled in Clayton. The Moore and Robertson families were two of the oldest in the area and their family plots were next to each other.

Harold knelt beside Alex's headstone, which was next to his mother and father's, and told them all the news in his life, from the Rushmore incident to the shooting at the Nelson farm, which had ended the madness in his life. And then he spoke to Alex and said all the same things he'd said over the past forty-eight years, telling him how much he missed his company but knew he was together with Mom and Dad now.

"You know, I got married this year to that young squirt of a girl out on the Nelson farm, you know, where Jimmy lived – go figure. I'm crazy in love with her and I'm sixty-four. She told me she had a crush on me ever since she was nine years old. Wow. We got married in the old courthouse in town and old Judge Simmons presided. The town gathered outside while we were in there so that when we came out it was to a cheering crowd. God, I missed this place when I had to live in DC."

"Oh, speaking of DC, I'm running for President. Tomorrow I'll go vote and then later in the night, I'll know if we'll be moving to DC to live for four years. What do you think about that, huh? A President from Clayton. The town will go wild on Election night. Well, Abbey is in the car waiting for me, so I'll come back in a few days and let you know how it all turned out."

He went back for her and they walked the short distance to Ruth's grave, the closest to the road in his family area. Abbey said she wanted to say a few words, her being the mother of his children and all.

"You probably don't remember me," she said, "because I was nine years younger and lived outside of town. I hope you don't mind me saying these things, but it seems we loved the same man all of our lives. I'll do my best to take good care of him. I know he'll always love you and that doesn't bother me at all, as a matter of fact, I wouldn't have it any other way. Anyway, I'll come every year with our Harold to visit and tell you how we're doing."

Harold wiped a tear away and squeezed her hand, swallowing the growing lump in his throat. "I married this farm girl from out at the Nelson place. I fell in love with her in South Dakota of all places. She saved me from myself, twice now. You know what I mean, the same thing you did countless times. I still love you, my dear Ruth, always will, but Abbey helped me out of my grieving, and got me back on my feet. You'd really like her because she's strong, stubborn, and forgiving of all my faults. But, I guess you two have already met."

A feeling of resolution seemed to approach from afar, remembering his dream of Ruth and Abbey talking together, as if this was always the plan. Harold was not one for strange explanations, but this was a feeling which was growing within him, and it felt right. He felt the peace which it was bringing, a simple, quiet peace, the kind found only rarely in life. He looked into Abbey's eyes and saw that same serenity. He drew her hand up into his and kissed it, knowing that it was going to be alright.

"Your hand is cold," he said rubbing some warmth into it. "Perhaps we should be going."

He turned and hugged Abbey and led her back to the car. It wouldn't be until much later that evening that they talked about their feelings.

Chapter 49

ELECTION DAY

November 8th

Harold lay in bed next to Abbey, thinking about the day ahead, and what it would mean to the two of them if the American people saw fit to elect him as their President. Their lives would be turned upside down from what they were both accustomed to. It would be difficult and exciting to finally have the chance to try out his lifelong dream of serving the American people as President. He was terrified and hopeful at the same time. Abbey was recovering quickly and her hair had begun the long road of growing to its former glory. She was wearing a wig to cover her shaved head, not something she was too wild about. He turned his head, pecked her cheek, and rolled out of bed.

"Ready for coffee?" he said pulling his pants on. She mumbled something, which he took as a yes. He found Russell and Jeff in the kitchen huddled around their mugs of coffee at the table. "Morning," he said. "You mind?" He pointed to the pot.

"Not at all, Mr. Robertson," Russell said. "We'll make more."

He put cream and sugar in Abbey's and left them to their discussion. "Coffee?" he asked touching her on the shoulder. "Two of our house guests made coffee for us."

"That's nice," she stretched and yawned. "My head itches and I'm bald as a baby's butt." She scratched everywhere around the small bandaged area. "Prickly though."

"You're beautiful hon. Want your mop top?" He was trying hard not to laugh as he plunked the wig on crooked but lost it in the end. She smacked his thigh and got sat up, straightening the wig.

"Coffee please," she held her hand out.

He placed the mug in her hand and kept his mouth shut, at least for the moment. He sipped his coffee, wrinkling his nose at the half hour old, and now bitter coffee. He should have doctored his mug like hers. "They're making another pot," he said setting his mug on the nightstand. "I'd like us to spend some time in town at the polls talking with people when they come out. Rodger wants us in Springfield by two o'clock, so we'll have to leave by eleven. It's after eight now."

"Okay. Mind if I finish a second cup?" She held it out to him.

It was getting close to ten o'clock by the time they'd voted and had taken two chairs outside of courthouse to sit and talk with their friends and neighbors. They were going to be late. He was certain of that. Everyone wanted to chat. Some even brought donuts and coffee to entice a longer chat session.

They didn't leave until noon, putting them in Springfield at 3 p.m. to the cheers of hundreds outside of the campaign headquarters, located in an older six-story red brick building. They occupied the first two floors, those being the only ones that had been renovated by the owner. He was thankful they'd found them and also that the owner allowed them to store boxes and such on the third floor in a locked area where he kept building supplies. The front office was jammed with campaign workers on phones to other offices around the country. He found Regina in her office on the second floor with Rodger, their feet up on opposite sides of her desk.

"Harold, you made it," Regina stood and walked around Rodger to hug him. "Hi, Abbey. You're looking well." Regina gave Abbey a gentle hug. "I'm so glad you're alright. Pull up a chair."

"Glad you could make it," Rodger said in a teasing tone.

"How's it going, Rodger?" Abbey said taking his overstuffed chair for herself.

Now he did laugh because if they won, Rodger would wind up in his cabinet as press secretary, and Abbey would take it upon herself to tell him how to do his job. The whole picture in his head amused him to no end because Abbey was better at managing people than Rodger.

"So, what am I supposed to be doing today?" Harold joked with them.

"Press is camped out at the capitol, waiting for you to get there." Regina sat down in a folding chair next to Abbey.

"Okay. I'm ready." Harold smoothed back his windblown hair. "What time do we move to the war room?" He called the Prairie Capitol Convention Center the war room because it would be packed with over seven thousand, banner waving, slogan chanting, and cheering supporters. This would be the place where he'd announce at the magic hour, around one o'clock in the morning, that the other camp had conceded, or God forbid, that he'd concede the win to the other camp, and thank them for their support. Their press conference was in the lobby, which would be packed with over a thousand people.

Their parade of three black SUVs arrived out front of the Center and was greeted by a throng of cameras, microphones, and hungry journalists, newscasters, and spectators. "Well, here we go," Harold said bailing from the back seat and turning around to help Abbey out of the SUV. The din of the endless questions just behind him came to life, surging with each new voice. He made sure that Abbey's wig didn't get bumped and put his arm around her waist, smiling to the cameras, and waving with his other hand. "You feeling okay," he said close to her ear. She nodded, putting on her best smile, even though he knew she had issues with headaches.

"Shall we go inside ladies and gentlemen." He spoke into the mics. That was the go sign for his Secret Service detachment to move forward, parting the turbulent waters of the media. He waved and smiled to the spectators, pausing several times to shake hands with children and their parents. To him, they were the heart of the matter, not the media, which was there to solely to pass on the events of the day to the American people and the world.

Once inside the expansive lobby, they moved slowly through the packed room towards the podium and bank of microphones set up for the interview. Russell walked beside Abbey shielding her from any contact with the crowd. Harold had asked him to because he worried that she would be bumped inadvertently in the packed lobby. Regina took the mic first, to quiet the crowd and set the tone.

"Ladies and gentlemen of the media, if I may have your attention," Regina said loudly into the mic. "Quiet please," echoed off of the three-story open air part of the lobby. "Thank you all for being so patient. I will remind you that Abbey Robertson is just out of the hospital after having surgery for her gunshot wounds eight days ago, and she is still healing, so we will keep the tone respectful."

Abbey gave them a wave and a smile from his side. He gave her a kiss and stepped to the microphones with Regina, taking her hand and raising it with his. "To four years of progress for our nation. We will keep our promises to the American people." He shook Regina's hand and gave her a hug. She stepped back and to his right while he addressed the media, before answering their questions.

"Let me begin by saying how thankful I am that Abbey and I survived the relentless pursuit of a terrorist. I am humbled by the strength of her character and resolve to see her way through whatever adversity befalls her. Ladies and gentlemen, my wife Abbey Robertson, soon to be First Lady of our great nation."

"Atta girl Abbey," a man's voice yelled from the far side of the lobby.

"Would someone kindly point this person out for us." The voice was familiar to Harold, so that when someone yelled. "Here he is," and he saw that it was Travis, Abbey's old boss, he wasn't surprised in the least. "Hey, Travis. Everybody, this is Travis London, Abbey's old boss from WKIRK in Rapid City, SD." There was some laughter traveling around the lobby with that comment. "As I was saying, Regina and I will keep those campaign promises we made with the help of the American people. Our country needs strong leadership, and Regina and I gave our word to deliver just that to your doorstep. Sometimes it won't be easy, change never is. But we promise you, that at the end of four years, America will have: unified the people of our nation under the Constitutional Rights guaranteed us by the Founding Fathers of our nation that 'all men [sic] are created equal;' grown the economy so that the tag on the things we buy says, made in the USA more often than anywhere else; and secured our borders and enforced the existing immigration laws. This is our mission in the first four years and will be front and center in our daily agenda, along with, of course, everything else that arises on the world stage. We will work hard for you because that is what we promised." He motioned Regina to step up beside him. "I believe the Vice President has a few words to say as well." Harold moved back half a step to give her the lead.

"I will make this promise to all the women of our nation, that the 'glass ceiling' will be dismantled, removed, and otherwise shattered in the coming years. That is my mission, to give the more than 157 million women in our great nation equal standing in the workplace, with equal pay. A tall order, but with the help of the 157 million women, how can we fail."

He returned to Regina's side and raised her hand with his, to the cheers of all the women in the lobby, which was well more than half of those present. "We will take your questions now."

The next thirty minutes swept him deep into the world of politics on the open market, with the good, the bad and the ugly all coming to the forefront. Both he and Regina took it all in stride because that's what they did for a living in the US House and Senate. Supporters of Oliver Plunkett were still bitter about his defeat at the RNC in July, but that's the nature of politics. They left the lobby of the Prairie Capitol Center at 5:30 p.m. for an American Diner close to campaign headquarters, and then it was back to his office at headquarters to monitor the election results coming in until later that evening close to midnight. When the nail-biting was over, he'd return to the Convention Center to address his supporters.

"Harold, you might want to wake up for this." Abbey's voice filled the office.

"Hm?" He opened his eyes in a rush of anticipation, having fallen asleep a half hour ago. He took a long drink of water from the bottle on his desk, clearing his throat. "I must have been tired."

"Come in the other room, Mr. President. Your opponent has just conceded the election to you." Abbey hugged him and pushed him into what they called the situation room, with lounge chairs, a big screen TV, a dozen or so workstations with computers, phones, and stacks of papers. Regina was waiting for him with their team gathered in front of the TV. Senator Victoria Hemstead was speaking to her supporters at her campaign headquarters in Miami, thanking them for their dedication and loyalty. Harold's pants pocket was vibrating, as he watched Victoria holding her phone to her head. He pulled his out and answered. "Good evening, this is Harold," he said, trying to calm his growing anticipation of her words to him and the American public. "Yes, I just woke from a nap, and I'm standing in front of a TV."

"Harold Robertson, it has been my pleasure to run against you for the Office of the Presidency, you are a true patriot. I know you will serve our nation's people well. I am calling to inform you that the American people have spoken, and have elected you as the next President. All our hopes and dreams go with you, President-elect Robertson. It will be a pleasure to work with you in the coming years, as I will return to the Senate and finish my term." Victoria ended the call.

The room erupted in cheers for one brief moment before they hustled to the Convention Center to make the announcement to their supporters. Harold Robertson swallowed his nervousness as he stepped onto the stage with Regina, to the thunderous chants of seven thousand wildly happy supporters. He turned his head offstage and motioned Abbey and his daughter and family to come out, wiping a tear from the corner of his eye. His dream as a youthful idealist was about to begin and all he could think about was waking up tomorrow morning next to Abbey.

EPILOGUE
January 20th, 2017

Abbey held the bible on this blustery winter's day, Inauguration Day, the first day of a most challenging and difficult reality for him. He was the leader of the Free World and would be held responsible for his nation's actions in the world. He tried to focus only on the Oath of Office, not wanting to fumble on his first day at work, which also meant no tripping on their walk down Pennsylvania Ave. A warm and bright glow filled him as he took the Oath.

"I, Harold Robertson,
do solemnly swear
that I will faithfully execute
the Office of President of the United States,
and will to the best of my ability,
preserve, protect and defend
the Constitution of the United States.
So help me God."

Chief Justice Franklin Peters was solemn and all business until the final words. They both broke out into huge smiles and Justice Peters clasped his hand and congratulated him, holding his shoulder with his other hand. Harold was struck by the applause, which was spreading out into the 1.7 million people seated in front of the Capitol, and standing room only in the National Mall. He waved to the masses and turned to hug the First Lady, the lady of his dreams. The band played, Hail to the Chief, and it was done.

John C Morgan

Photo by Kim E. Morgan

About the author

John was born in Evanston, Illinois and raised in the rural community of Glenview during the 1950's, a time when patriotism was strong after WWII. These are the roots of On The Way Home, forged by family values, and love of country. John lives with his wife, Kim, in Coeur d' Alene, Idaho.